Oxford School Shakespeare

JOHN K ③

Hamlet

Edited by
Roma Gill, OBE
M.A. *Cantab.*, B.Litt. *Oxon.*

Oxford University Press

OXFORD

UNIVERSITY PRESS

Great Clarendon Street, Oxford OX2 6DP

Oxford University Press is a department of the University of Oxford.
It furthers the University's objective of excellence in research, scholarship,
and education by publishing worldwide in

Oxford New York

Athens Auckland Bangkok Bogotá Buenos Aires Calcutta
Cape Town Chennai Dar es Salaam Delhi Florence Hong Kong Istanbul
Karachi Kuala Lumpur Madrid Melbourne Mexico City Mumbai
Nairobi Paris São Paulo Singapore Taipei Tokyo Toronto Warsaw

with associated companies in Berlin Ibadan

Oxford is a registered trade mark of Oxford University Press
in the UK and in certain other countries

© Oxford University Press 1992
First published 1992
Reprinted 1993, 1994, 1995 (twice), 1997 (twice), 1998, 1999 (twice), 2000, 2001
Trade edition first published 1994
Reprinted 1996 (twice), 1998, 1999, 2000, 2001

ISBN: 0 19 831960 6 (School edition)
ISBN: 0 19 831985 1 (Trade edition)

Typeset by Gem Publishing Company, Brightwell, Wallingford, Oxon
Printed in the United Kingdom by the Alden Group, Oxford

For Matthew

Oxford School Shakespeare
edited by Roma Gill

A Midsummer Night's Dream
Romeo and Juliet
As You Like It
Macbeth
Julius Caesar
The Merchant of Venice
Twelfth Night
Henry IV Part I

The Taming of the Shrew
Othello
Hamlet
King Lear
Henry V
The Winter's Tale
Antony and Cleopatra
The Tempest

Illustrations: Alexy Pendle
Cover photograph by Donald Cooper (Photostage) shows Sophie
Thompson as Ophelia, and Kenneth Branagh as Hamlet, in the
Renaissance Theatre Company's 1988 production of *Hamlet*.

Contents

Revenge!

or

Getting Your Own Back

It's only natural—you hit me, I hit you back! It doesn't matter whether we are children quarrelling in the playground, or mighty nations fighting global warfare. The impulse to retaliate, to give tit for tat, is strong, and primitive, and human.

Most societies make rules to control this natural urge. In the Bible, we can read how the Jews of the Old Testament were instructed under the law of Moses to exact strict penalties for injuries: an eye for an eye, a tooth for a tooth, and a life for a life (Exodus, chapter 26). In the New Testament, however, Jesus taught Christians to love their enemies, and to 'turn the other cheek' to their assailants (St Luke, chapter 6).

For the well-being of any community, hidden injuries must be revealed, and wrongs must be punished. And there is in all of us, surely, a desire to see that justice is done, and that everyone gets what they deserve? In real life, of course, this does not always happen; but sometimes in the imaginary world of fiction we can have the satisfaction of seeing the crime disclosed, the criminal unmasked, and the forces of good triumphing over evil. Even if the victims cannot always be recompensed—the murdered cannot be restored to life—at least their suffering is avenged.

Such fiction, sometimes based on fact, has always been popular: today there is no shortage of 'whodunnit' detective novels and television plays. In times past, the theatre was the place to find this kind of entertainment.

Revenge drama has a very long history, going back at least as far as the time of Aeschylus (*c.* 500 BC) and his great Oresteian trilogy. About five centuries later, the Greek plays were adapted for Roman audiences by the dramatist Seneca—and in the sixteenth century Seneca's plays, translated from Latin into English, became the model for the English playwrights.

The most famous of early English revenge plays is *The Spanish Tragedy* (*c.* 1588), written by Thomas Kyd. Other notable plays are Shakespeare's own *Titus Andronicus* (*c.* 1590), *Antonio's Revenge* (*c.* 1599), by John Marston, *The Revenger's Tragedy* (*c.* 1607), attributed to Cyril Tourneur, and John Webster's *Duchess of Malfi* (*c.* 1614).

Hamlet is the finest of all the plays in the English revenge tradition. It is the most serious, because it asks so many questions; and it is also the most understandable. Shakespeare's characters are like real people—people of today—even though the action of the play belongs to a remote past. Later writers tried to follow Shakespeare's example, copying his ideas and theatrical devices just as he had copied those of his predecessors. But no one—even today—could imitate the character of Shakespeare's Prince. Hamlet is unique.

Leading characters in Shakespeare's play

Hamlet
： The Prince of Denmark, son of Gertrude and nephew of Claudius. He is presented with a terrible problem when the Ghost of his dead father accuses Claudius of murder and demands revenge. Doubt makes him indecisive, and for a time he pretends to be mad. But when he knows the truth he is resolute and fearless.

Two Brothers

King Hamlet
： Father of the Prince. He is now dead, and we see only his Ghost. But other characters, and especially Prince Hamlet, speak of his courage and virtues.

Claudius
： Brother to the dead King, and now King of Denmark. He is newly married to Gertrude, his dead brother's wife. At first he seems to be courteous and efficient, but the play reveals him as a 'smiling, damned villain'.

Victims of the disaster

Gertrude
： Hamlet's mother, and the Queen of Denmark. She married Claudius as soon as her first husband was dead, and now acquiesces in all his plans.

Ophelia
： The daughter of Polonius and sister of Laertes. She loves Hamlet, and is distressed by his treatment of her.

Polonius
： The King's trusted councillor, whose interference triggers off the action of the play. He is the father of Laertes and Ophelia, and takes himself very seriously.

Laertes
： Son to Polonius, and brother of Ophelia. He is passionate in defence of the family honour, and (unlike Hamlet) does not scruple to avenge his injuries.

Rosencrantz and Guildenstern
： Said to be schoolfriends of Hamlet. They are summoned to court by the King (Claudius), and used as his instruments.

The Survivors

Fortinbras
Prince of Norway. Headstrong and (as his name—French *fort* = strong—suggests) physically active. He is the complete opposite of Hamlet, although their situations are alike: Fortinbras's uncle has also succeeded to his brother's throne.

Horatio
Hamlet's friend. He is a model of friendship and can always be trusted to give sensible advice and an honest opinion. Sometimes he is not so much a *character* as a choric figure, giving necessary information to the audience.

The Action

Act 1

Scene 1   'Who's there?'—The play opens with a challenge. The scene is set on the gun-platform outside the castle of Elsinore, and the soldiers on guard-duty must be professionally suspicious. Tonight they are more than usually tense, because they have been frightened by something which they dare not even name—a 'thing', 'a dreaded sight', an 'apparition'.

They are joined by a civilian, Horatio, who makes light of their fears, just as a father might comfort a nervous child: 'Tush, tush, 'twill not appear'. Sitting in a huddle on the ground, they listen as Barnardo begins his ghost story. And we, the play's audience, listen too, sharing in the suspense.

The Ghost startles us all when it suddenly appears, and then vanishes in an instant. It makes no sound, although (as we learn in Scene 2) it is clad in full armour. The frightened soldiers discuss what we have *all* witnessed, turning to Horatio to confirm the Ghost's identity: 'Is it not like the King?' Horatio was once sceptical, and dismissed the soldiers' fears as 'fantasy'. But now he has seen the Ghost himself, and he must believe 'the sensible and true avouch' of his own eyes.

Because Horatio is convinced of the Ghost's reality, we—Shakespeare's audience—are also persuaded to believe in it, no matter what we may think of ghosts. Like Horatio, though, we may question its nature and the reason for its appearance at this time.

There was a very old superstition that ghosts would return from the dead in order to give some kind of warning to the living. This is Horatio's first thought, especially now that the whole country of Denmark is getting ready for war and expecting trouble from Young Fortinbras of Norway. All this is explained (like a lesson in modern history) to the soldiers—but really for the benefit of the audience! And Horatio recalls a historic precedent for such supernatural manifestations: he describes the ghosts that were seen in ancient Rome when Julius Caesar was murdered.

At the climax of his speech the Ghost returns, and Horatio challenges it boldly. But he gets no response. The cock crows, and the Ghost disappears. Dawn breaks, life returns to normal, and Horatio takes Barnardo and Marcellus in search of Young Hamlet. Perhaps the Ghost will speak to *him*.

Scene 2   After the eerie silence of the guards' midnight watch and its mysterious happenings, we are taken into the daytime activity of the royal court. The sound of trumpets heralds the entry of Claudius, the new King of Denmark, with his Queen and all the members of his Council. Prince Hamlet follows, at the end of the royal procession.

From the tone of his address, it sounds as though Claudius is making his first public appearance as the king; he delivers a well-prepared speech, calculated to make a good impression. He speaks of grief for his brother's death, and pleasure at his own marriage—sorrow has been mixed with joy, there has been 'mirth in funeral' and 'dirge in marriage'. He thanks the counsellors, who have guided him with their 'better wisdoms'. And then he moves on to talk of less embarrassing matters, demonstrating his efficiency in handling the Norwegian threat, and dispatching ambassadors with his official letter to the King of Norway.

He turns now to Laertes, speaking more naturally and showing some affection to the young man, the son of his most valued counsellor: 'What wouldst thou have, Laertes?' Laertes asks permission to leave Denmark and go back to Paris. His wish is granted. But no such graciousness is extended to Hamlet, whose request to go back to his university is flatly refused: 'It is most retrograde to our desires'.

The Prince is marked off from the rest of the courtiers by the 'nighted colour' of his clothes—his 'inky cloak' and 'suits of solemn black'. Hamlet is still in mourning for his father, and he refuses to accept the trite words of consolation offered by Claudius and the Queen. In public, Hamlet's grief and bitterness are controlled, hidden behind the sardonic wit when he tells Claudius that he is 'A little more than kin, and less than kind'. In private, however, his anger bursts out in passionate reproaches—and we now learn that his mother's hasty re-marriage has almost broken Hamlet's heart.

Sorrow has a moment's respite when Hamlet recognizes Horatio, and finds a much-needed friend. Horatio comes, with Marcellus and Barnardo, to recount the experience of the previous night; Hamlet is convinced that they have indeed seen his father's spirit—and he too suspects the worst. He is impatient—'Would night were come'.

Scene 3   But we must allow for a little time to pass. The suspense is slackened as the mood and pace of the play change once again. The scene is now domestic, showing an intimate glimpse of a loving and close-knit family. The brother, Laertes, is going away to Paris, but he does not want to lose touch with his sister—'let me hear from you'. He worries about her boyfriend—perhaps Prince Hamlet *says* he loves her—and perhaps he does love her *now*—but she must remember that a prince is not like ordinary men, who are free to choose wives for themselves. Ophelia must be careful to protect her good name—and her virginity.

    Their father adds some of his store of worldly wisdom, first counselling Laertes about his behaviour in Paris—the sort of friends he should make, how he should dress, and how to handle his money. When his son has left, Polonius turns his attention to his daughter, lecturing Ophelia about her friendship with Prince Hamlet. He scoffs at the idea of love, because he is afraid that Hamlet will seduce his daughter, and he orders Ophelia to end their friendship.

Scene 4   Midnight has come at last, and Hamlet waits with the guards on the gun-platform outside the palace. From the banqueting hall within, they can hear the sound of revelry. Guns are fired in celebration when the King drinks a toast. With some disgust, Hamlet describes how the heavy drinking of the Danes lowers their reputation in the eyes of other nations.

    His moralizing breaks off when the Ghost appears, startling Hamlet so that he invokes divine protection: 'Angels and ministers of grace defend us'. He is determined to speak to this apparition, regardless of whether it is a good spirit or an evil one, because he recognizes its likeness to his father. The tone of his demands becomes almost hysterical, but the Ghost speaks no word—only indicating that Hamlet should follow where it leads. His companions try to restrain Hamlet, fearing that an evil spirit might be trying to lead him into suicidal madness. But Hamlet's grim wit threatens to 'make a ghost' of anyone who holds him back.

Scene 5   Alone with Hamlet, the Ghost speaks. It has come from some terrifying purgatory, where it is being punished for the sins of a lifetime. But the Ghost does not ask pity—it demands revenge! Hamlet's father claims to have been betrayed by his 'most seeming-virtuous queen' and murdered by 'that adulterate beast', his brother Claudius. The Ghost's language is violent with hatred, and Hamlet is faint with disgust and horror. The signs of dawn appear, which means that the Ghost must depart. Hamlet has sworn to avenge his father, and will keep his word.

Now Horatio and Marcellus come on the scene, searching for Hamlet. They find him in a very odd mood, and his words do not make sense: they are 'wild and whirling'. He makes them swear never to reveal what they have seen, and they take their oath on the cross-piece of Hamlet's sword. A ghostly voice speaks from under the ground each time Hamlet—with a strange joke—repeats the oath. He speaks of a madness—an 'antic disposition'—that he means to pretend, and which they are sworn not to disclose. His final words are cryptic: 'The time is out of joint. O cursed spite, That ever I was born to set it right'. Hamlet seems to have found a vocation, a purpose for his life.

His friends must be bewildered. They have all seen the Ghost, *but only Hamlet*—and the audience—*knows what the Ghost has said.*

Act 2

Scene 1   Some time has passed. Laertes is now in Paris, and his father—always suspicious—is sending Reynaldo to spy on him. Although Reynaldo accepts the job, he does not like what he has to do. Ophelia comes to find her father. She has been badly frightened by Prince Hamlet, and she describes how he came into her private room, only half-dressed—his doublet was not buttoned, and his stockings hung loose around his ankles. He did not say anything, but he was obviously upset.

Polonius decides at once that Hamlet is mad with love for Ophelia, and he is even more sure of his diagnosis when he hears that Ophelia (as he had ordered in *Act 1*, Scene 3) has been refusing either to see the Prince, or to receive his letters. Full of his own importance, Polonius hurries his daughter off to see the King.

Scene 2   We find Claudius interviewing Rosencrantz and Guildenstern. He had commanded the two young men to come to the court, and now he tells them of the distressing change in Hamlet's behaviour; perhaps these two boys, being of Hamlet's own age ('so neighbour'd to his youth'), will be able to find out what is wrong with him. In fact, Rosencrantz and Guildenstern are being set to spy on Hamlet, just as Reynaldo was told to spy on Laertes.

xii The Action

Dismissing them, the King listens to the report of the ambassadors who have returned from their successful mission to Norway. They tell Claudius how 'old Norway' has rebuked his nephew, sending him to fight against the Poles (which means, incidentally, that he will need to pass, peaceably, through Denmark). Then at last it is Polonius's turn to speak.

At first, his pompous formality irritates the Queen, but Polonius carries on to tell everything he knows about Hamlet's love for Ophelia. He has found one of the Prince's love-letters, which he reads aloud. He is quick to point out that he has not encouraged this affair, and that he has told his daughter that 'Lord Hamlet is a prince out of thy star'. But, he concludes, Ophelia's rejection of his love must have driven Hamlet out of his mind. The King seems unconvinced, and asks for some proof of what Polonius says. The two men decide that they will hide where they can listen to a meeting (which will be arranged by Polonius) between Hamlet and Ophelia.

The Prince comes in just as they are making their plans. When Polonius tries to talk to him, Hamlet replies with answers that make no sense to Polonius, who seems to accept that it is only another fit of madness. But the audience may suspect that Hamlet is assuming his 'antic disposition' (as he promised in *Act 1*, Scene 5) in order to insult Polonius. This suspicion is confirmed by Hamlet himself after Polonius has left the stage; he drops his disguise with an exasperated comment, 'These tedious old fools'.

Hamlet's manner changes when he meets his old friends Rosencrantz and Guildenstern. He laughs with them—but it is no joke when he tells them 'Denmark's a prison'! He soon becomes suspicious of them, and starts to ask questions. They have to admit that they have come to Elsinore because they were 'sent for'. Hamlet tells them only what he wants them to know—that he is depressed and nothing seems to satisfy him. But news of some travelling players diverts him for a while.

He recognizes the actors, and recalls a particular production that he has seen. The leading actor (flattered, no doubt, by the royal attention) declaims the whole of the speech that Hamlet remembers. And this gives Hamlet an idea! He chooses the programme for the evening's entertainment, asking for a performance of *The Murder of Gonzago*—with an additional speech which he will write himself. The players go off to get ready, Rosencrantz and Guildenstern are dismissed, and Hamlet is left alone to ponder on what he has seen.

The audience is taken into his confidence as he thinks aloud. The pretended grief of the actor has sharpened Hamlet's sense of his own grief, and spurred him to take some action. He wonders *why* he cannot get anything done—after all, he has never been frightened of defending himself, and he has a very good cause to fight for now . . . Only at the end of the speech do we find out what is really worrying Hamlet: can he trust the Ghost? It could be an *evil* spirit, which will lead him to damnation. But if the actors could perform 'something like the murder of my father', perhaps Claudius will show his guilt by his reaction. And that would be better proof than the word of a ghost!

Act 3

Scene 1 Rosencrantz and Guildenstern report to Claudius. They have nothing much to tell him, since Hamlet, 'with a crafty madness', refuses to confide in them. They are dismissed, and Claudius explains his next stratagem to Gertrude—whose concern for Hamlet seems to be genuine. Ophelia is set in position by her father, then Polonius takes the King aside—but not before Claudius has mumbled a few words (overheard only by the audience) about his 'heavy burden' of guilt.

Hamlet, meditating on the problems of living and dying, is surprised when he comes upon Ophelia—especially when she hands back to him the little presents ('remembrances') that he had given to her in the past. Angered by this, he lets loose on Ophelia all the bitterness he has been feeling since his mother's marriage to Claudius. He begins to suspect Ophelia too, and seems conscious that there are unseen listeners to this conversation. In his apparent madness, he drops a veiled threat (which Claudius *must* hear): 'I say we will have no mo marriage. Those that are married already—*all but one*—shall live'.

His departure—with a final insult—leaves Ophelia terribly upset and quite convinced of his madness. Claudius is not so sure about this—he is certain, however, that the cause of Hamlet's strange behaviour is not love. He says he will send his nephew to England, to collect an unpaid debt; perhaps the change of air will do him good!

Polonius prefers his love-sickness theory, and suggests that the Queen should have a word with her son—and he, Polonius, will be there to listen; he will hide behind the 'arras'—the great tapestry that hangs in Gertrude's room.

Scene 2 Hamlet is lecturing to the actors on the theory of drama ('to hold as 'twere the mirror up to nature') and the art of acting. The professional actors listen meekly to the royal amateur until they are sent away to get ready for their performance. After a speech in praise of Horatio's friendship, Hamlet explains what he is planning. Apparently Horatio has already been told about the Ghost's accusation, and now he too is to watch the King 'the whilst this play is playing', and look for any tell-tale signs of guilt. Afterwards, they can compare notes.

The idle chatter of an assembling audience (on stage) becomes heavy with insult and irony—from Hamlet—which is only interrupted by the dumb-show. The mime prepares *us*—Shakespeare's audience—for what is to come in the play's main action. Then, like Horatio, we shall probably be watching Claudius.

The Murder of Gonzago is written in an obviously 'old-fashioned' style; its heavily regular verse sounds artificial, and contrasts with the language spoken by the 'real' people of Shakespeare's play. Its plot, however, is very relevant to the situation in Elsinore. A king, feeling that death is near, recalls his happy marriage and wonders whether his wife will ever marry again. She insists that she will never think of a second husband. At the end of the first little scene, Hamlet asks his mother for her opinion. Gertrude is evidently uneasy, and Claudius is beginning to feel uncomfortable.

The second scene has hardly started—the murderer has just poisoned his victim—when Claudius brings it to a sudden end. He leaves the hall, and his courtiers follow. The actors disappear. Only Hamlet and Horatio are left behind. Hamlet is triumphant—his plot has worked, and Claudius has convicted himself.

Rosencrantz and Guildenstern come to summon Hamlet: the Queen wishes to speak to her son. But Hamlet must first show his former friends that he understands what they are doing; and he warns them that they will fail: 'though you fret me, you cannot play upon me'. Polonius comes to call Hamlet: the Queen is waiting. Hamlet will come—but before he leaves the stage, he lets the audience see something of his new-found resolution.

Scene 3   Claudius is now sure that his secret is known, and he proceeds with his plan to send Hamlet to England, guarded by Rosencrantz and Guildenstern. Hamlet's former friends appreciate the importance of their job to the national security. They go to pack for the journey. Polonius drops in for a moment—he is on his way to hide behind the arras in the Queen's room

For the very first time, we see Claudius alone and hear what *he* thinks about the whole business. He is a very unhappy man, trapped in a horrible dilemma—of his own making. He admits his guilt (to himself), but feels that he cannot pray, or repent, or ask for God's forgiveness, since he is still in possession of the rewards of his crime—his queen and his throne. But he tries to pray, forcing himself to kneel. In this position he is discovered by Hamlet, who draws his sword—but fails to act. Hamlet argues with himself that this would not be true revenge for his father's murder: the Ghost had told him of its sufferings in Purgatory, but Claudius would avoid these if he were to die just now, when he is in a state of grace. So Hamlet will wait, until he can find a more suitable occasion.

Ignorant of the danger he has just missed, Claudius gets to his feet. He has not been able to pray, after all.

Scene 4   Another trap is being set. Gertrude is prepared for the part that she is to play, and Polonius conceals himself behind the arras. The interview starts well enough—a mother scolding her son: 'Hamlet, thou hast thy father much offended'. But her son immediately takes control of the situation: 'Mother, you have my father much offended'. His passion alarms Gertrude, and her call for help is echoed by the unseen listener hidden behind the arras. Hamlet runs his sword through the tapestry, thinking that this must be the King. But he has killed Polonius.

His passion undiminished, Hamlet forces his mother to look at two portraits, 'the counterfeit presentment of two brothers'. He describes them to her—though his description tells us more about Hamlet himself than about the brothers. One is idealized, and given all the attributes of the Greek gods: 'Hyperion's curls, the front of Jove himself, An eye like Mars . . .' The other receives nothing but contempt: he is 'a mildew'd ear'—Hamlet's scorn lacks words!

His disgust speaks out, however, when he talks of his mother's relationship with Claudius. He loathes the very idea of her lust, and dwells on its physical aspects with horrified fascination as he contemplates Gertrude and Claudius 'honeying and making love Over the nasty sty'. The Queen pleads with him to stop, but Hamlet has got carried away by his own emotion, and he will not hear her. He stops only when he sees the Ghost which seems to have come (as Hamlet understands it) to urge Hamlet on to some action. Gertrude sees and hears nothing but her son's strange behaviour, and she worries even more about his sanity. After the Ghost has left them, Hamlet speaks once more to his mother. He is calmer now, but he continues to exhort her to repent of her marriage to Claudius, and to put an end to their sexual relationship.

Hamlet turns to the body of Polonius, which has been lying on stage throughout this scene. His death was regrettable, and Hamlet repents of the murder. But by this deed, Hamlet himself has become a murderer—and will now become the object of another revenge plot.

Before he parts from his mother, Hamlet refers to the King's decision to send him to England. All preparations have been made, and Hamlet is ready to go.

Act 4

Scene 1   The King comes to Gertrude's room to find out about her interview with Hamlet. He is accompanied by Rosencrantz and Guildenstern, but these are quickly dismissed by the Queen. She confirms that her son is completely mad, and tells of the murder of Polonius. Claudius is quick to realize that *he* was the intended victim: 'It had been so with us had we been there'. He says that Hamlet's madness is a threat to *everyone*, and it must be dealt with immediately: Hamlet must be sent to England, and Claudius himself must devise some kind of cover-up story. Rosencrantz and Guildenstern are sent off to find the Prince, and to get the body of Polonius.

From this point the action of the play moves quickly; the conventional—and useful—division into 'scenes' can seem an interruption.

Scene 2   Rosencrantz and Guildenstern encounter Hamlet. He evades their questions—but he lets them know that he understands their roles as the King's informers.

Scene 3   Claudius is now very frightened. Hamlet answers his questions with a grim playfulness—but Claudius knows that there is a deadly seriousness behind all that Hamlet says. The letters for England are 'seal'd and done', ready for Rosencrantz and Guildenstern to carry them. When everyone has gone, Claudius reveals that his letter 'imports . . . The present death of Hamlet'—he has told the King of England to have Hamlet murdered.

Scene 4   Young Fortinbras leads his army across the stage. He is going to fight in Poland and needs to cross Denmark. A Captain is dispatched to the Danish court to remind the King—*and the audience*—that this has all been pre-arranged (in *Act 2*, Scene 2).

Ing The Captain meets Hamlet and his escort, who are on their way to the port, to take ship for England. Questions are asked, and Hamlet learns that Young Fortinbras and his army will be fighting only 'to gain a little patch of ground That hath in it no profit but the name'. The Captain is not enthusiastic, but Hamlet is filled with admiration for the enterprise. The example of Young Fortinbras, engaging in such a battle over a matter of honour, serves as a reproach to Hamlet for his own inactivity, and strengthens his resolve to act.

Scene 5   Hamlet has left Elsinore to go to England, and Horatio is attending on the Queen. A Gentleman brings news of Ophelia, and almost immediately, the girl herself comes in. She is literally mad with grief. Her father is dead, murdered by the man she loves! Everyone understands her anguish—even Claudius, who also witnesses the scene.

   When Ophelia has left the room, Claudius tells Gertrude of a new danger—Laertes has returned from France and, hearing rumours of the suspicious circumstances of his father's death, is threatening rebellion. The threat becomes real when Laertes bursts into the room. The King takes control of the situation, calming Laertes' anger for a moment. But then the appearance of Ophelia, crazily singing of love and death, gives her brother more cause for passion. Claudius seizes his opportunity, and takes Laertes aside to explain his plot.

Scene 6   There is news from sea. Horatio learns that pirates have captured Hamlet—and rescued him from Rosencrantz and Guildenstern. He is now back in Denmark.

Scene 7   Claudius has given *his* account of the events which have taken place while Laertes has been away from Denmark, and is now explaining why he has not been able to do anything about the situation. He seems to have a plan, however, and he is just about to divulge it when Hamlet's letters are brought in.

   Claudius thinks quickly. He flatters Laertes with talk of fencing and of Hamlet's jealousy; then he returns to the subject of Polonius's death. A fencing match is arranged—Laertes will fight Hamlet—but one of the foils will be 'unbated': there will be nothing to protect its sharp point. Laertes has bought some poison, and he will put this on the point of the sword, so that the least scratch will prove fatal. In case this fails, the King will have prepared a cup of wine—and this too will be poisoned. Hamlet will not escape!

The Queen interrupts their scheming with news of fresh disaster. Ophelia is drowned. There is a lyrical beauty in Gertrude's description of Ophelia's death which forbids us to ask how the Queen knew all these details. Laertes weeps—but promises action.

Act 5

Scene 1   The pace of the play slows down, and there is even time for a kind of humour as we watch a Gravedigger going about his work, and we listen as he talks to another character (who is not identified). Gradually, we realize that it is Ophelia whose grave is being dug. Was her death accidental, or did she commit suicide? The two characters debate the issues until one goes off to fetch the beer and the other sings to himself as he digs.

Hamlet and Horatio come to the graveyard and watch the man at work. Hamlet speaks his thoughts on death, and starts up a conversation with the Gravedigger. A funeral procession interrupts them, and Hamlet recognizes the mourners. But the funeral is conducted with very little ceremony. A young man questions the priest about this—and Hamlet identifies Laertes, 'a very noble youth'. The priest will allow no further rites of burial, because there is some doubt about the cause of death.

In his agonized grief, Laertes refers to his 'sister' and this, together with Gertrude's tender farewell, reminds Hamlet that he had once loved Ophelia. He reveals himself to Laertes, who is so enraged that he attacks Hamlet. They start to fight by Ophelia's open grave. The other mourners separate them. With a strange threat, Hamlet leaves the scene.

Scene 2   Hamlet tells Horatio the full story of his adventures at sea. It is a story full of accidents, and Hamlet is now convinced that there is a divine power in control of everything that happens: 'There's a divinity that shapes our ends'.

Hamlet describes how, unable to sleep one night when he was on the ship sailing to England, he had discovered the letter that Rosencrantz and Guildenstern were carrying. From it, he learned that Claudius was plotting to have him killed. Hamlet substituted *another* letter, which he had just written, ordering the deaths of the two messengers. But Hamlet's own life was saved when the ship was attacked by pirates (as Horatio had learned from Hamlet's letter in *Act 4*, Scene 6). They took the Prince as their only prisoner, leaving Rosencrantz and Guildenstern behind—who have sailed to meet their deaths. Hamlet feels no remorse for this, although he regrets his behaviour to Laertes. He now has no doubt of the King's guilt, and Horatio too is convinced. But time is short.

A courtier, Osric, interrupts; he has come to inform Hamlet of the planned fencing bout with Laertes, and the King's wager on Hamlet's skill. Osric's affectation amuses and irritates Hamlet, but he replies in a similar style. He accepts the challenge, but Horatio warns him— 'You will lose this wager, my lord'. We in the audience must share his fatalism, because we have heard the talk about the 'shuffling' planned in *Act 4*, Scene 7: we know about the 'unbated' rapier with the poisoned tip, and the poison in the cup of wine.

The thought of death does not worry Hamlet: 'If it be now, 'tis not to come; if it is not come, it will be now'.

The entire court assembles to watch the duel. Hamlet begs pardon of Laertes, blaming his 'madness' for some of the things he has done. Laertes accepts the apology, but says that his 'terms of honour' demand the satisfaction of a duel. They choose their rapiers. Hamlet is easily pleased, but Laertes needs to make sure that he has got the deadly weapon. The wine is set on the table, and the King orders trumpets and guns to mark his toast—just as his drinking was celebrated in *Act 1*, Scene 4.

Hamlet and Laertes fight, and Hamlet makes the first hit. The King drinks to Hamlet—and drops the poison in the cup. Hamlet refuses to drink, and they fight again. Again Hamlet hits Laertes. The Queen drinks to Hamlet—and Claudius (in an 'aside') reveals that she has drunk from the poisoned cup.

In a further bout of fighting, Laertes wounds Hamlet; the rapiers are dropped and picked up—but this time Hamlet gets the poisoned one. There is a further bout of fighting, and Hamlet wounds Laertes. The Queen falls, and dies. Laertes confesses the poisoning of the weapon and the wine. He denounces Claudius: 'The King—the King's to blame'.

Hamlet, incensed, wounds the King with the poisoned rapier, and forces him to drink from the poisoned cup. Claudius dies. Laertes, having asked Hamlet's forgiveness, also dies—and Hamlet himself feels the approach of death. He orders Horatio (who is willing, himself, to drink from the poisoned cup) to 'Report me and my cause aright' to the world.

Before he dies, he hears the noise of marching soldiers. Fortinbras has returned from the war in Poland (to which he was going in *Act 4, Scene 4*), and now Hamlet elects him to the throne of Denmark. The Prince dies.

Fortinbras is accompanied by the English ambassadors, who have come to report the deaths of Rosencrantz and Guildenstern. Horatio shows them what has happened, and Fortinbras takes command.

Shakespeare's Verse

Shakespeare's plays are mainly written in 'blank verse', the form preferred by most dramatists in the sixteenth and early seventeenth centuries. It is a very flexible medium, which is capable—like the human speaking voice—of a wide range of tones. Basically the lines, which are unrhymed, are ten syllables long. The syllables have alternating stresses, just like normal English speech; and they divide into five 'feet'. The technical name for this is 'iambic pentameter'.

> **Horatio**
> Befóre my Gód, I míght not thís beliéve
> 60 Withoút the sénsible and trúe avoúch
> Of míne own eyés.
> > **Marcellus**   Is ít not líke the Kíng?
> **Horatio**
> As thóu art tó thysélf.
> Such wás the véry ármour hé had on
> When hé th'ambítious Nórway combattéd.
> 65 So frown'd he once, when in an angry parle
> He smóte the slédded Pólacks on the íce.
> 'Tis stránge.
> > **Marcellus**
> > Thus twíce befóre, and jump at thís dead hóur,
> > With mártial stálk hath hé gone bý our wátch.

1, I, 59–69

In this quotation, most of the lines are regular in length and normal in iambic stress pattern. But sometimes Shakespeare deviates from the norm, writing lines that are longer or shorter than ten syllables, and varying the stress patterns for unusual emphasis. In lines 62 and 67, for instance, Horatio speaks only part of a pentameter; it is as though his bewilderment can only be expressed in silence. When two speakers share a pentameter (as in line 61), Shakespeare can show the closeness of their thoughts, and the quickness of their reactions to each other.

The verse line sometimes contains the grammatical unit of meaning—'When he th'ambitious Norway combatted'—thus allowing for a pause at the end of the line, before a new idea is started; at other times, the sense runs on from one line to the next—'the sensible and true avouch Of mine own eyes'. This makes for the natural fluidity of speech, avoiding monotony but still maintaining the iambic rhythm. Occasionally, for the sake of the rhythm, words are elided or otherwise abbreviated ('th'ambitious Norway')—but this is also a feature of normal spoken English.

Source

Once upon a time there was a real Prince Amleth whose father, the king of Jutland, was murdered by King Fengo, his brother . . . The story was told in the thirteenth century by a Danish historian, Saxo Grammaticus. It was retold in the sixteenth century, with additions, by Belleforest, a Frenchman. His version, translated into English, was probably the source for Shakespeare's tragedy.

There was an earlier play, perhaps written by Thomas Kyd, which might have linked Shakespeare's *Hamlet* with Belleforest's *Histoire Tragique* of Hamblet. But this link is now missing—the play was never published.

Date and text

Shakespeare's play was known in England at the end of the sixteenth century, but the version we have today cannot have been written before 1601. This date is fixed by two topical references in the play itself. The boy actors described in *Act 2*, Scene 2 had a very successful season at the Blackfriars playhouse in 1601; and the 'innovation' spoken of in *2*, 2, 330–331 could have been the rebellion which was led by the Earl of Essex in February of that year.

Hamlet was first published in a quarto volume (Q1) in 1603. A second edition (Q2) appeared the following year, giving a rather different version of the play. Yet another text, different from both the others, was published in 1623 in the collection of all Shakespeare's plays, which is known as the First Folio (F).

Throughout the twentieth century there has been much scholarly argument about the respective merits of these editions. Recently, however, a masterly study was published by Professor Harold Jenkins in his Arden edition of the play (1982), and this is the text now followed in this *Oxford School Shakespeare* edition. Professor Jenkins believes that Q2 is the most reliable of the three texts, and probably based directly on Shakespeare's own manuscript. But even Q2 is obscure in some places, and a modern edition must seek help from Q1 and F to clarify the difficulties.

Characters in the play

Ghost	*of Hamlet King of Denmark, recently deceased*
Gertrude	*his wife, now married to Claudius*
Claudius	*his brother, now King of Denmark*
Hamlet	*Prince of Denmark, son to the late King Hamlet and his wife, Gertrude*
Horatio	*friend to Prince Hamlet*
Rosencrantz **Guildenstern**	*former schoolfriends of Prince Hamlet*
Polonius	*the King's councillor*
Laertes	*his son*
Ophelia	*his daughter*
Reynaldo	*his servant*
Fortinbras	*Prince of Norway*
A Norwegian Captain	

At the King's Court in Elsinore

Voltemand **Cornelius**	*Danish ambassadors sent to Norway*
Osric	*a foppish courtier*
A Lord	
A Gentleman	
Francisco **Barnardo** **Marcellus**	*soldiers of the King's guard*
A Gravedigger	
Another	*the Gravedigger's companion*
A Priest	

Players Visiting the Court in Elsinore

First Player	*acting the part of the king*
Second Player	*acting the part of the queen*
Third Player	*acting the part of the king's nephew*
Fourth Player	*speaking the Prologue*

English Ambassadors, Messengers,
Lords, Attendants, Guards, Players,
Soldiers, Sailors

SCENE: Elsinore — in the royal castle and its environs

Act I

Act I   Scene I

It is cold; and it is midnight. In a country
preparing for war the sentries who guard the
castle are nervous. They have been frightened by
something extraordinary, and tonight they have
asked Horatio, whose opinion they value, to
accompany their watch. The Ghost appears, then
vanishes; and the awe-struck men discuss what
they have witnessed. The Ghost returns, and
Horatio tries to make contact — but it will not
hear him, and disappears again. They must tell
Hamlet.

2   *answer me*: It is the sentry on duty who has
    the right to challenge.
    unfold: reveal.
3   Barnardo's response — perhaps an
    accepted password — shows him to be a
    friend.
6   *carefully*: promptly.

9   *I am . . . heart*: I've had enough.

14   *rivals*: partners.

Scene I

Enter Barnardo *and* Francisco, *two
Sentinels.*

Barnardo
Who's there?

Francisco
Nay, answer me. Stand and unfold yourself.

Barnardo
Long live the King!

Francisco
Barnardo?

Barnardo
5   He.

Francisco
You come most carefully upon your hour.

Barnardo
'Tis now struck twelve. Get thee to bed, Francisco.

Francisco
For this relief much thanks. 'Tis bitter cold,
And I am sick at heart.

Barnardo
10   Have you had quiet guard?

Francisco
Not a mouse stirring.

Barnardo
Well, good night.
If you do meet Horatio and Marcellus,
The rivals of my watch, bid them make haste.

Francisco
15   I think I hear them.

Enter Horatio *and* Marcellus.

Stand, ho! Who is there?

68   *jump*: exactly.
70   'I don't really know what to think of it.'
71   *in the gross and scope*: in general.
72   *bodes*: threatens. Horatio tries to find a
       meaning in the apparition.
       strange eruption: violent disturbance.
73   *Good now*: please.
       he that: if anyone.
74-81 Marcellus describes the activity of a
       nation preparing for war — the forging of
       armaments by night as well as by day, seven
       days a week; and the international trade in
       weapons.
74   *watch*: wakefulness.
75   *the subject of the land*: all the king's subjects.
77   *mart*: trading.
78   *impress*: conscription.
80   *What . . . toward*: what is going on.
82   *That can I*: Horatio has to serve a number
       of functions in the play. At this point his
       role is to let *the audience* know what has
       happened before the action started; his
       description of events also illuminates the
       character of the dead king, and the power
       of the country under his rule.
83   *whisper*: rumour.
84   *even but*: only just.
86   *prick'd*: urged.
       emulate: competitive.
87   *Dar'd*: challenged.
       Hamlet: the family name, to which Prince
       Hamlet is heir.
88   *this side of our known world*: our western
       world.
89   *seal'd compact*: certified (bearing official
       seals) agreement. The stress is on the
       second syllable of 'compact'.
90   *heraldry*: the code of chivalry.
92   *seiz'd of*: in possession of. Horatio explains
       that the rival monarchs had wagered lands
       which they personally possessed (*not* their
       kingdoms) in this fight to the death.
93   *moiety competent*: sufficient portion. Hamlet
       did not need to wager all his possessions to
       equal those of Fortinbras.
94   *gaged*: wagered.
       had return'd: would have gone to.
96   *same cov'nant*: the 'compact' of line 89.
97   'In accordance with the clause referred to.'
98   *His*: i.e. the land of Fortinbras; Horatio in
       these lines has been speaking the language
       of lawyers.

Marcellus
Thus twice before, and jump at this dead hour,
With martial stalk hath he gone by our watch.
     Horatio
70 In what particular thought to work I know not,
But in the gross and scope of my opinion,
This bodes some strange eruption to our state.
     Marcellus
Good now, sit down, and tell me, he that knows,
Why this same strict and most observant watch
75 So nightly toils the subject of the land,
And why such daily cast of brazen cannon
And foreign mart for implements of war,
Why such impress of shipwrights, whose sore task
Does not divide the Sunday from the week.
80 What might be toward that this sweaty haste
Doth make the night joint-labourer with the day,
Who is't that can inform me?
     Horatio   That can I.
At least the whisper goes so: our last King,
Whose image even but now appear'd to us,
85 Was as you know by Fortinbras of Norway,
Thereto prick'd on by a most emulate pride,
Dar'd to the combat; in which our valiant Hamlet
(For so this side of our known world esteem'd him)
Did slay this Fortinbras, who by a seal'd compact
90 Well ratified by law and heraldry
Did forfeit, with his life, all those his lands
Which he stood seiz'd of to the conqueror;
Against the which a moiety competent
Was gaged by our King, which had return'd
95 To the inheritance of Fortinbras,
Had he been vanquisher; as, by the same cov'nant
And carriage of the article design'd,
His fell to Hamlet. Now, sir, young Fortinbras,

99 *unimproved mettle*: undisciplined energy.
    full: vigorous.
100 *skirts*: remote parts.
101 *Shark'd up*: got together.
    list of lawless resolutes: band of determined outlaws.
102 The 'enterprise' which Fortinbras is plotting needs such 'lawless resolutes' just as a stomach needs food.
104 *doth well appear*: looks very much like it.
    state: government.
105 *of*: from.
    strong hand: force.
106 *terms compulsatory*: compulsion.
109 *chief head*: fountain-head.
110 *post-haste*: furious activity.
    rummage: turmoil.
111 *but e'en so*: just as it is.
112 *Well may it sort*: it is appropriate.
    portentous: ominous.
114 *question*: cause.
115 The Ghost is not important in itself (a 'mote' is a speck of dust), but it reminds Horatio of something: the scholar gives a lesson in Roman history to the two soldiers. Shakespeare also describes these phenomena in his play *Julius Caesar* (*1*, *3* and *2*, *2*).
116 *palmy*: flourishing.
117 *the mightiest Julius*: Julius was the first and most powerful of all the Caesars.
118 *sheeted dead*: bodies in their shrouds.
119 *squeak and gibber*: wail in high-pitched voices.
120 *As*: The awkwardness of the syntax here suggests that something has been lost from the text.
    stars . . . fire: comets with fiery tails.
    dews of blood: red dews (which are actually caused by insects, not by comets).
121 *Disasters*: portents (Shakespeare uses an astrological term).
121–3 *moist . . . eclipse*: there was almost total eclipse of the moon. The planet is 'moist' because it was thought to draw up water from the sea; and it was known to have influence on the tides ('Neptune's empire'). St Matthew prophesies that on the Day of Judgement ('doomsday') 'the moon shall not give her light' (24:29).
124–8 'The same sort of thing has happened in our country, and always been a warning of some coming crisis.'
124 *precurse*: forerunner.

Of unimproved mettle, hot and full,
100 Hath in the skirts of Norway here and there
Shark'd up a list of lawless resolutes
For food and diet to some enterprise
That hath a stomach in't, which is no other,
As it doth well appear unto our state,
105 But to recover of us by strong hand
And terms compulsatory those foresaid lands
So by his father lost. And this, I take it,
Is the main motive of our preparations,
The source of this our watch, and the chief head
110 Of this post-haste and rummage in the land.
        Barnardo
I think it be no other but e'en so.
Well may it sort that this portentous figure
Comes armed through our watch so like the King
That was and is the question of these wars.
        Horatio
115 A mote it is to trouble the mind's eye.
In the most high and palmy state of Rome,
A little ere the mightiest Julius fell,
The graves stood tenantless and the sheeted dead
Did squeak and gibber in the Roman streets;
120 As stars with trains of fire and dews of blood,
Disasters in the sun; and the moist star,
Upon whose influence Neptune's empire stands,
Was sick almost to doomsday with eclipse.
And even the like precurse of fear'd events,

125 *harbingers*: heralds.
   still: always.
   fates: calamities; *and* the powers that ordain
   them.
126 *omen*: disaster.
128 *climatures*: regions of the earth.

129 *soft*: hush.
130 *cross it*: i.e. cross its path (and so expose
   himself to a dangerous influence).
   blast: damn.

132 *Speak to me*: Horatio interrogates the Ghost
   with an almost ritual incantation,
   suggesting some of the usual reasons for
   which ghosts were thought to appear — to
   demand something; to deliver a warning; or
   to haunt the site of buried treasure.
134 *to thee . . . to me*: Perhaps the body has not
   been properly laid to rest; and to bury it
   would be accounted as a credit to Horatio.
136 *privy to*: secretly aware of.
137 *happily*: perhaps (also 'fortunately').
140 *Extorted*: ill-gotten.
141 *your*: these.
143 *partisan*: pike.

148 *being*: since it is.
149 *show*: The violence can be only in
   appearance.
150 'Because the Ghost is incorporeal, and
   therefore cannot be harmed.'
151 *vain*: useless.
   malicious mockery: only the pretence of
   hurting.

125 As harbingers preceding still the fates
   And prologue to the omen coming on,
   Have heaven and earth together demonstrated
   Unto our climatures and countrymen.

Enter Ghost

   But soft, behold. Lo, where it comes again.
130 I'll cross it though it blast me.

Ghost spreads its arms.

                              Stay, illusion:
   If thou hast any sound or use of voice,
   Speak to me.
   If there be any good thing to be done
   That may to thee do ease, and grace to me,
135 Speak to me;
   If thou art privy to thy country's fate,
   Which, happily, foreknowing may avoid,
   O speak;
   Or if thou hast uphoarded in thy life
140 Extorted treasure in the womb of earth,
   For which they say your spirits oft walk in death,
   Speak of it, stay and speak.

The cock crows

                    Stop it, Marcellus.
   Marcellus
   Shall I strike at it with my partisan?
   Horatio
   Do if it will not stand.
   Barnardo
145 'Tis here.
   Horatio
   'Tis here.   [*Exit* Ghost
   Marcellus
   'Tis gone.
   We do it wrong, being so majestical,
   To offer it the show of violence,
150 For it is as the air, invulnerable,
   And our vain blows malicious mockery.

Barnardo
It was about to speak when the cock crew.
   Horatio
And then it started like a guilty thing
Upon a fearful summons. I have heard
155 The cock, that is the trumpet to the morn,
Doth with his lofty and shrill-sounding throat
Awake the god of day, and at his warning,
Whether in sea or fire, in earth or air,
Th'extravagant and erring spirit hies
160 To his confine; and of the truth herein
This present object made probation.
   Marcellus
It faded on the crowing of the cock.
Some say that ever 'gainst that season comes
Wherein our Saviour's birth is celebrated,
165 This bird of dawning singeth all night long;
And then, they say, no spirit dare stir abroad,
The nights are wholesome, then no planets strike,
No fairy takes, nor witch hath power to charm,
So hallow'd and so gracious is that time.
   Horatio
170 So have I heard and do in part believe it.
But look, the morn in russet mantle clad
Walks o'er the dew of yon high eastward hill.
Break we our watch up, and by my advice
Let us impart what we have seen tonight
175 Unto young Hamlet; for upon my life
This spirit, dumb to us, will speak to him.
Do you consent we shall acquaint him with it
As needful in our loves, fitting our duty?
   Marcellus
Let's do't, I pray, and I this morning know
180 Where we shall find him most convenient.   [*Exeunt*

154 *I have heard*: Horatio's early scepticism is waning.
155 *trumpet*: trumpeter. The farmyard cock crows just before daybreak.
156 *lofty*: outstretched.
157 *god of day*: Phoebus Apollo, the classical sun-god. In the Christian tradition the cock, as herald of light, is also the harbinger of Christ.
158–60 *Whether . . . confine*: any spirit who is straying beyond its limits ('extravagant and erring') returns quickly ('hies') to its prison ('his confine') in one of the four elements.
160 *herein*: in this matter.
161 *made probation*: proved.
163–9 This Christmas story seems to have no other authority; but now the mood of the scene switches to one of hope and comfort with the coming of light.
163 *'gainst*: in preparation for.
164 *our Saviour*: Christ.
166 *stir abroad*: wander from its confines.
167 *strike*: exert an evil influence.
168 *takes*: casts a spell.
169 *hallow'd*: sanctified.
   gracious: filled with heavenly grace.
170 *in part*: Horatio's scepticism has not entirely disappeared.
171–2 A literary description of the reddish ('russet') sky at daybreak.
173 *watch*: guard.
175 *young Hamlet*: This is the play's first reference to the Prince of Denmark.
178 *needful in our loves*: necessary because we all love him.

Act 1   Scene 2

Inside the castle the new King addresses his
assembled court, speaking of the old King's
death, and of his own marriage. He tells them of
the Norwegian threat. Laertes requests that he
may return to Paris, and Hamlet asks permission
to go back to his university. The Prince appears
sullen and withdrawn, so both the King and the
Queen try to console him for the death of his
father. When he is left alone on the stage,
however, Hamlet reveals the cause of his sorrow
— not his father's death, but his mother's re-
marriage. Horatio greets Hamlet, and tells him of
the Ghost's appearance. They arrange to meet on
the gun-platform with the guards.

s.d.   *Flourish*: The trumpet heralds the formal
approach of the royal party, led by the
King; Hamlet, at the end, seems to be
separated from the rest.

1   *Hamlet our dear brother*: In an elective
monarchy such as Denmark was, Claudius
could have come legitimately to the throne
of his brother; but his situation, like his
speech, is full of ambiguities — and the
unctuousness of his style cannot totally
conceal the unease of his position.

2   *green*: fresh.
that it us befitted: although it would have
been more suitable for us. The King
cleverly merges the royal use with the
ordinary plural, identifying himself with
his audience.

4   *contracted*: knit together.

5–7   'We have had to be sensible about our
natural emotions, and grieve for him, but
also remember our own position.'

8   *sometime sister*: Gertrude was formerly his
sister-in-law; the Church of England
forbade such marriages, regarding them as
incestuous.

9   *jointress*: woman who shares property with
her husband; Claudius implies that
Gertrude has some part in the kingdom, so
that his marriage has somehow safeguarded
his claim to the throne.

10   *defeated*: subdued (by sorrow).

11   'With one eye smiling and the other
shedding tears.'

12   *dirge*: lamentation.

13   *In equal scale weighing*: with an equal
measure of.
dole: sorrow.

14   *Taken to wife*: married.
barr'd: acted without.

Scene 2

Flourish. Enter Claudius, King of
Denmark, Gertrude the Queen, Council,
including Voltemand, Cornelius, Polonius
and his son Laertes, Hamlet *dressed in black*,
with Others

   King
Though yet of Hamlet our dear brother's death
The memory be green, and that it us befitted
To bear our hearts in grief, and our whole kingdom
To be contracted in one brow of woe,
5   Yet so far hath discretion fought with nature
That we with wisest sorrow think on him
Together with remembrance of ourselves.
Therefore our sometime sister, now our queen,
Th'imperial jointress to this warlike state,
10   Have we, as 'twere with a defeated joy,
With an auspicious and a dropping eye,
With mirth in funeral and with dirge in marriage,
In equal scale weighing delight and dole,
Taken to wife. Nor have we herein barr'd
15   Your better wisdoms, which have freely gone
With this affair along. For all, our thanks.
Now follows that you know young Fortinbras,
Holding a weak supposal of our worth,
Or thinking by our late dear brother's death
20   Our state to be disjoint and out of frame,
Colleagued with this dream of his advantage,
He hath not fail'd to pester us with message
Importing the surrender of those lands
Lost by his father, with all bonds of law,
25   To our most valiant brother. So much for him.

15 *better*: i.e. better than those of ordinary men.

15–16 *freely . . . along*: willingly agreed to the marriage.

17 *Now follows . . . know*: The next thing I have to tell you. Claudius declares the details of what Fortinbras demands; the courtiers probably know already, but the audience needs to be informed – and introduced to the comparison between Fortinbras and Hamlet.

18 *weak supposal*: poor opinion.

20 *disjoint*: disturbed.
   frame: order.

21 *Colleagued*: allied. He believes Denmark to be vulnerable and has big ideas for himself.

22 *with message*: by sending demands.

26 *for . . . meeting*: the reason for our meeting at this time.

28 *Norway . . . Fortinbras*: the King of Norway. The Norwegian situation is parallel to Denmark's in that the elder Fortinbras has been succeeded by his brother and not by his son.

29 *impotent*: powerless.

30–31 *suppress . . . herein*: stop him going any further in this business.

31 *in that*: because.

32 *lists*: enrolment.
   full proportions: supporting force.

33 *subject*: subjects.

37 *To business*: to do business, to negotiate.

38 *dilated*: detailed.

39 *let . . . duty*: show your obedience by the speed with which you obey.

42 *Laertes*: With these caressing repetitions, Claudius shows his graciousness to the son of Polonius — and Shakespeare introduces the character who is to be the main foil for Hamlet.

43 *suit*: request.

45 *lose*: waste.
   thou: Claudius adopts an intimate form of address.

46 'That I won't give you before you ask for it.'

47 *native*: closely related. The commonplace parallel between the human body and the body politic of the state gives added force to this assertion.

49 *the throne*: the entire monarchy — not merely Claudius himself.

53 *show my duty*: i.e. by taking an oath of allegiance to the new king.

55 *bend*: turn.

Now for ourself, and for this time of meeting,
Thus much the business is: we have here writ
To Norway, uncle of young Fortinbras—
Who, impotent and bedrid, scarcely hears
30 Of this his nephew's purpose—to suppress
His further gait herein, in that the levies,
The lists, and full proportions are all made
Out of his subject; and we here dispatch
You, good Cornelius, and you, Voltemand,
35 For bearers of this greeting to old Norway,
Giving to you no further personal power
To business with the King more than the scope
Of these dilated articles allow.
Farewell, and let your haste commend your duty.
   Cornelius and **Voltemand**
40 In that, and all things, will we show our duty.
   King
We doubt it nothing. Heartily farewell.
         [*Exeunt* Voltemand *and* Cornelius
And now, Laertes, what's the news with you?
You told us of some suit: what is't, Laertes?
You cannot speak of reason to the Dane
45 And lose your voice. What wouldst thou beg, Laertes,
That shall not be my offer, not thy asking?
The head is not more native to the heart,
The hand more instrumental to the mouth,
Than is the throne of Denmark to thy father.
50 What wouldst thou have, Laertes?
   Laertes   My dread lord,
Your leave and favour to return to France,
From whence though willingly I came to Denmark
To show my duty in your coronation,
Yet now I must confess, that duty done,
55 My thoughts and wishes bend again toward France
And bow them to your gracious leave and pardon.
   King
Have you your father's leave? What says Polonius?
   Polonius
He hath, my lord, wrung from me my slow leave
By laboursome petition, and at last
60 Upon his will I seal'd my hard consent.
I do beseech you give him leave to go.

56 *pardon*: indulgence.
58 *wrung . . . leave*: got my permission at last.
60 'I reluctantly agreed that he could have what he wanted.' Polonius plays on two senses of 'will', and uses the image of fixing the seals that give authority to a legal document.
62 *Take thy fair hour*: enjoy yourself whilst you are young.
    time be thine: take as long as you like.
63 'You can do whatever you want with your skills' ('graces' = attractive qualities, accomplishments).
64 *cousin*: This was used for any kinsman other than a brother.
65 'Rather more than kinsmen in our relationship, but not very well-disposed ('kind') to one another'; *and* 'not part of the same family ('kind').' Hamlet puns on different senses of 'kind'.
67 *sun*: Hamlet puns on 'sun/son', perhaps implying his resentment at being still a king's son and not the king himself.
68 *nighted*: dark (see lines 77–8).
69 *Denmark*: Gertrude could mean either 'the King of Denmark' (i.e. Claudius), or the kingdom.
70 *vailed lids*: downcast eyes.
72 *'tis common*: it happens to everyone.
75 *particular with thee*: any different for you.
76 *Seems*: Hamlet snatches Gertrude's word to introduce his meditation on the appearance of grief and the reality of his own sorrow.
77 *not alone*: not only; Hamlet implies that Gertrude's mourning may be only a matter of dress.
78 *customary*: conventional; *and* habitual.
79 *windy . . . breath*: uncontrollable sighing.
81 *haviour*: expression.
82 *moods*: modes.
    shapes: appearances.
83 *denote*: portray (as an actor's appearance portrays the role he is acting).
84 *play*: perform (like an actor).
85 *passes show*: cannot be expressed in outward appearances.
90 *bound*: was bound.
92 *To . . . sorrow*: to perform the proper funeral rites.
    persever: The stress (normal in the early 17th century) is on the second syllable.
93 *condolement*: grieving.

95 *incorrect*: disobedient.

King
Take thy fair hour, Laertes, time be thine,
And thy best graces spend it at thy will.
But now, my cousin Hamlet, and my son—
       Hamlet
65 A little more than kin, and less than kind.
       King
How is it that the clouds still hang on you?
       Hamlet
Not so, my lord, I am too much in the sun.
       Queen
Good Hamlet, cast thy nighted colour off,
And let thine eye look like a friend on Denmark.
70 Do not for ever with thy vailed lids
Seek for thy noble father in the dust.
Thou know'st 'tis common: all that lives must die,
Passing through nature to eternity.
       Hamlet
Ay, madam, it is common.
       Queen   If it be,
75 Why seems it so particular with thee?
       Hamlet
Seems, madam? Nay, it is. I know not 'seems'.
'Tis not alone my inky cloak, good mother,
Nor customary suits of solemn black,
Nor windy suspiration of forc'd breath,
80 No, nor the fruitful river in the eye,
Nor the dejected haviour of the visage,
Together with all forms, moods, shapes of grief,
That can denote me truly. These indeed seem,
For they are actions that a man might play;
85 But I have that within which passes show,
These but the trappings and the suits of woe.
       King
'Tis sweet and commendable in your nature, Hamlet,
To give these mourning duties to your father,
But you must know your father lost a father,
90 That father lost, lost his—and the survivor bound
In filial obligation for some term
To do obsequious sorrow. But to persever
In obstinate condolement is a course
Of impious stubbornness, 'tis unmanly grief,
95 It shows a will most incorrect to heaven,

96 *unfortified*: not strengthened by religious discipline.
impatient: lacking the virtue of patience.
97 *simple*: untaught.
98–101 'Why should we be so obstinate as to be distressed by something which we know to be inevitable and which we can see is more common than anything else.'
100 *peevish*: perverse.
101 *fault to heaven*: a sin against God.
102 *a fault to nature*: an offence against the natural order of things.
103 *whose common theme*: regular subject matter.
104 *still*: always.
105 *the first corse*: The first body was that of Abel, who was killed by his brother Cain (see Genesis, 4:8).
he: him.
106 *throw to earth*: overcome (as a wrestler throws his opponent).
107 *unprevailing*: unavailing.
109 *most immediate*: next in succession. Hamlet is a popular prince (see Ophelia's praise of him, *3*, 1, 151–5; and Claudius's acknowledgement that he is loved by the people, *4*, 3, 4 and *4*, 7, 18). But the present admission strengthens Hamlet's position.
110 *nobility*: A father's love for his son was regarded as a very noble emotion.
112 *impart toward*: deal generously with.
For: as for.
113 *school in Wittenberg*: Wittenberg was famous as Luther's university — and (for theatre audiences) as the university of the eponymous hero in Marlowe's *Dr Faustus*.
114 *retrograde*: contrary.
115 *bend you*: submit yourself.
116 *eye*: presence.
119 *stay with us*: Gertrude aligns herself with her husband.
120 *all my best*: to the best of my ability.
obey you: Hamlet ignores the King's remarks.
123 *unforc'd accord*: willing agreement.
124 *Sits . . . heart*: gives my heart much pleasure.
grace: thanksgiving.
125 *Denmark*: the King of Denmark, i.e. himself. The King seems to find every occasion for a drink.

A heart unfortified, a mind impatient,
An understanding simple and unschool'd;
For what we know must be, and is as common
As any the most vulgar thing to sense—
100 Why should we in our peevish opposition
Take it to heart? Fie, 'tis a fault to heaven,
A fault against the dead, a fault to nature,
To reason most absurd, whose common theme
Is death of fathers, and who still hath cried
105 From the first corse till he that died today,
'This must be so'. We pray you throw to earth
This unprevailing woe, and think of us
As of a father; for let the world take note
You are the most immediate to our throne,
110 And with no less nobility of love
Than that which dearest father bears his son
Do I impart toward you. For your intent
In going back to school in Wittenberg,
It is most retrograde to our desire,
115 And we beseech you bend you to remain
Here in the cheer and comfort of our eye,
Our chiefest courtier, cousin, and our son.
      Queen
Let not thy mother lose her prayers, Hamlet.
I pray thee stay with us, go not to Wittenberg.
      Hamlet
120 I shall in all my best obey you, madam.
      King
Why, 'tis a loving and a fair reply.
Be as ourself in Denmark. Madam, come.
This gentle and unforc'd accord of Hamlet
Sits smiling to my heart; in grace whereof
125 No jocund health that Denmark drinks today

126 *great cannon . . . tell*: See *1, 4, 6*.
127 *rouse*: carousal.
    bruit again: re-echo the noise of the cannon.

129 *sullied*: contaminated. Hamlet's flesh is
    impure because it is human, and liable to
    sin; it is also the flesh he shares with his
    mother. Q2 and Q1 both have 'sallied' (an
    Elizabethan form of the word), and the
    Folio text has 'solid', which may well have
    had the same sound in the 17th century.
130 *resolve itself*: dissolve.
132 *canon 'gainst self-slaughter*: A 'canon' is a
    religious law; and the sixth commandment,
    'Thou shalt not kill' (Exodus, 20:13), was
    generally interpreted as a prohibition of
    suicide.
134 *all the uses*: the whole business.
136 *rank . . . nature*: weeds, which grow
    strongly and spread wildly.
137 *merely*: entirely.
138 *But*: only.
140 *Hyperion to a satyr*: a god compared with a
    beast. Hyperion was the glorious sun-god
    of classical mythology; a satyr was a
    creature half man and half goat.
141 *beteem*: permit. The majesty of the love that
    seemed to control even the winds, is
    contrasted with the sensuality — the
    'appetite' — of the Queen's affection.
147 *or ere*: before.
149 *Niobe*: The type of sorrowing womanhood:
    in Greek mythology Niobe, who mourned
    the deaths of all her children, wept until she
    was turned to a stone fountain.
150 *wants discourse of reason*: is incapable of
    rational thought processes.
153 *Hercules*: The superman of classical
    mythology. Hamlet is already conscious of
    inadequacy, although he is as yet ignorant
    of his task.
154 *unrighteous*: insincere — because her tears
    are betrayed by her conduct.
155 'Had ceased to make her eyes red and sore.'
157 *dexterity*: skill.
    incestuous: See note to line 8.
159 *break . . . tongue*: Unspoken griefs were
    said to break the heart.

But the great cannon to the clouds shall tell,
And the King's rouse the heaven shall bruit again,
Re-speaking earthly thunder. Come away.
                    [*Flourish. Exeunt all but* Hamlet
                Hamlet
O that this too too sullied flesh would melt,
130 Thaw and resolve itself into a dew,
Or that the Everlasting had not fix'd
His canon 'gainst self-slaughter. O God! God!
How weary, stale, flat, and unprofitable
Seem to me all the uses of this world!
135 Fie on't, ah fie, 'tis an unweeded garden
That grows to seed; things rank and gross in nature
Possess it merely. That it should come to this!
But two months dead—nay, not so much, not two—
So excellent a king, that was to this
140 Hyperion to a satyr, so loving to my mother
That he might not beteem the winds of heaven
Visit her face too roughly. Heaven and earth,
Must I remember? Why, she would hang on him
As if increase of appetite had grown
145 By what it fed on; and yet within a month—
Let me not think on't—Frailty, thy name is woman—
A little month, or ere those shoes were old
With which she follow'd my poor father's body,
Like Niobe, all tears—why, she—
150 O God, a beast that wants discourse of reason
Would have mourn'd longer—married with my uncle,
My father's brother—but no more like my father
Than I to Hercules. Within a month,
Ere yet the salt of most unrighteous tears
155 Had left the flushing in her galled eyes,
She married—O most wicked speed! To post
With such dexterity to incestuous sheets!
It is not, nor it cannot come to good.
But break, my heart, for I must hold my tongue.

        Enter Horatio, Marcellus, *and* Barnardo
            Horatio
160 Hail to your lordship.
            Hamlet   I am glad to see you well.
Horatio, or I do forget myself.

163 *change that name with you*: Hamlet seems to be using the words of Jesus (as reported in St John, 15:15): 'Henceforth I call you not servants, for the servant knoweth not what his Lord doeth: but I have called you friends.'

164 *what make you*: what are you doing. *from*: away from.

166 *good even*: A normal greeting any time after noon.

170 *say so*: say that of you.

174 *Elsinore*: The Danish name was well-known to the Elizabethans; some of Shakespeare's company on tour had performed there.

175 *deep*: well. Hamlet speaks ironically of the Danish drinking habits.

180–81 'The food cooked for the funeral was served up cold at the wedding.'

182 *Would*: I wish. *dearest foe*: worst enemy.

183 *Or ever*: before.

185 *mind's eye*: imagination.

186 *once*: This seems inconsistent with Horatio's apparent familiarity with the dead king at *1, 1*, 62–66 and later in this scene.

187 *'A was a man*: He was the ideal of manhood. *all in all*: perfect in every way.

Horatio
The same, my lord, and your poor servant ever.
  Hamlet
Sir, my good friend, I'll change that name with you.
And what make you from Wittenberg, Horatio?—

165 Marcellus.
  Marcellus
My good lord.
  Hamlet
I am very glad to see you.—[*To* Barnardo] Good even, sir.—
But what in faith make you from Wittenberg?
  Horatio
A truant disposition, good my lord.
  Hamlet

170 I would not hear your enemy say so,
Nor shall you do my ear that violence
To make it truster of your own report
Against yourself. I know you are no truant.
But what is your affair in Elsinore?

175 We'll teach you to drink deep ere you depart.
  Horatio
My lord, I came to see your father's funeral.
  Hamlet
I prithee do not mock me, fellow-student.
I think it was to see my mother's wedding.
  Horatio
Indeed, my lord, it follow'd hard upon.
  Hamlet

180 Thrift, thrift, Horatio. The funeral bak'd meats
Did coldly furnish forth the marriage tables.
Would I had met my dearest foe in heaven
Or ever I had seen that day, Horatio.
My father—methinks I see my father—
  Horatio

185 Where, my lord?
  Hamlet   In my mind's eye, Horatio.
  Horatio
I saw him once; 'a was a goodly king.
  Hamlet
'A was a man, take him for all in all:
I shall not look upon his like again.
  Horatio
My lord, I think I saw him yesternight.

Hamlet

190 Saw? Who?

    Horatio My lord, the king your father.

    Hamlet

The king my father?

    Horatio

Season your admiration for a while

With an attent ear till I may deliver

Upon the witness of these gentlemen

195 This marvel to you.

    Hamlet   For God's love let me hear!

    Horatio

Two nights together had these gentlemen,

Marcellus and Barnardo, on their watch

In the dead waste and middle of the night

Been thus encounter'd: a figure like your father

200 Armed at point exactly, cap-à-pie,

Appears before them, and with solemn march

Goes slow and stately by them; thrice he walk'd

By their oppress'd and fear-surprised eyes

Within his truncheon's length, whilst they, distill'd

205 Almost to jelly with the act of fear,

Stand dumb and speak not to him. This to me

In dreadful secrecy impart they did,

And I with them the third night kept the watch,

Where, as they had deliver'd, both in time,

210 Form of the thing, each word made true and good,

The apparition comes. I knew your father;

These hands are not more like.

    Hamlet   But where was this?

    Marcellus

My lord, upon the platform where we watch.

    Hamlet

Did you not speak to it?

    Horatio   My lord, I did,

215 But answer made it none. Yet once methought

It lifted up it head and did address

Itself to motion like as it would speak.

But even then the morning cock crew loud,

And at the sound it shrunk in haste away

220 And vanish'd from our sight.

    Hamlet   'Tis very strange.

---

192 *Season your admiration*: control your wonderment.

193 *attent*: attentive.
deliver: report. Horatio's speech has been called (by S.T. Coleridge) 'a perfect model of dramatic narration and dramatic style, the purest poetry and the most natural style'.

194 *Upon the witness of*: witnessed by.

198 *dead waste*: most desolate part.

200 *at point*: correctly in every detail.
cap-à-pie: from head to foot (the phrase is French).

203 *oppress'd*: troubled.

204 *truncheon*: military baton.
distill'd: dissolved, melted.

205 *act*: action, effect.

207 *dreadful*: Marcellus and Barnardo were full of fear.

208–9 *in time, Form*: in time and form.

211 *knew*: was acquainted with.

212 *These . . . like*: The Ghost was as like Hamlet's father as Horatio's hands are like each other.

213 *platform*: terrace of a fort, where the guns are mounted.
watch: keep guard.

216 *it*: its.

216–7 *address . . . speak*: begin to move as though it were going to speak.

218 *even then*: at that very moment.

Horatio
As I do live, my honour'd lord, 'tis true;
And we did think it writ down in our duty
To let you know of it.
Hamlet
Indeed, sirs; but this troubles me.

224–43 The lines here have the rhythm of verse,
although they are not always strict
pentameter lines.

225 Hold you the watch tonight?
All   We do, my lord.
Hamlet
Arm'd, say you?
All   Arm'd, my lord.
Hamlet
From top to toe?
All   My lord, from head to foot.
Hamlet
Then saw you not his face?
Horatio

229 *beaver*: face-guard of a helmet.

O yes, my lord, he wore his beaver up.
Hamlet

230 *What*: how.
frowningly: i.e. as a warrior ought to look.

230 What look'd he, frowningly?
Horatio
A countenance more in sorrow than in anger.
Hamlet
Pale, or red?
Horatio
Nay, very pale.
Hamlet   And fix'd his eyes upon you?
Horatio
Most constantly.

234 *I would*: I wish.

Hamlet   I would I had been there.
Horatio

235 *amaz'd*: bewildered.

235 It would have much amaz'd you.
Hamlet   Very like.
Stay'd it long?
Horatio

237 *tell*: count.

While one with moderate haste might tell a hundred.
Marcellus and **Barnardo**
Longer, longer.
Horatio
Not when I saw't.
Hamlet

240 *grizzled*: grey.

240 His beard was grizzled, no?

Horatio
It was as I have seen it in his life,
A sable silver'd.   **Hamlet**   I will watch tonight.
Perchance 'twill walk again.
     Horatio   I war'nt it will.
     Hamlet
245 If it assume my noble father's person,
I'll speak to it though hell itself should gape
And bid me hold my peace. I pray you all,
If you have hitherto conceal'd this sight,
Let it be tenable in your silence still;
And whatsomever else shall hap tonight,
250 Give it an understanding but no tongue.
I will requite your loves. So fare you well.
Upon the platform 'twixt eleven and twelve
I'll visit you.
     All   Our duty to your honour.
     Hamlet
Your loves, as mine to you. Farewell.
          [*Exeunt* Horatio, Marcellus, *and*
          Barnardo
255 My father's spirit—in arms! All is not well.
I doubt some foul play. Would the night were come.
Till then sit still, my soul. Foul deeds will rise,
Though all the earth o'erwhelm them, to men's eyes.
               [*Exit*

242 *sable silver'd*: black with silver hairs.

243 *Perchance*: perhaps.
war'nt: warrant.

244 *assume . . . person*: has the appearance of my father (spirits, both good and bad, could manifest themselves in the likeness of human beings).

245 *hell . . . gape*: The gaping hell-mouth (open to receive those who communicated with evil spirits) was a common property on the Elizabethan stage.

249 *whatsomever*: whatever.
hap: happen.

251 *requite*: reward.
loves: friendship. Hamlet emends the formal respect of the guards' 'duty'.

255 *My father's spirit*: The belief that ghosts were spirits of the dead dates back to classical times, and was reinforced for Christians by the Roman Catholic doctrine of purgatory.

256 *doubt*: suspect. Hamlet is quick to suggest another reason (not mentioned by Horatio in the first scene) for a ghost's appearance: it wishes to reveal a crime that has been committed.

Act 1   Scene 3

After the chill of the battlements, and the cold formality of the royal court, we are shown an intimate family scene in which a brother parts from his sister. Laertes warns Ophelia not to put too much trust in Prince Hamlet, and his warnings are echoed by their father, Polonius, who comes to say goodbye to his son — and to give Laertes some words of worldly wisdom.

1 *necessaries*: luggage.
2 *as . . . benefit*: when the winds are favourable. Shakespeare thinks that communication with France must be by sea.
3 *convoy is assistant*: i.e. there is a ship available.

Scene 3

Enter Laertes *and* Ophelia, *his sister*

     Laertes
My necessaries are embark'd. Farewell.
And sister, as the winds give benefit
And convoy is assistant, do not sleep,
But let me hear from you.
     Ophelia   Do you doubt that?
     Laertes
5 For Hamlet, and the trifling of his favour,
Hold it a fashion and a toy in blood,

5 *trifling*: Both Laertes and Polonius assume that Hamlet is only trifling with Ophelia's affections.

6 *Hold it a fashion*: think it just a passing fancy.
   toy in blood: youthful sport.

7 *primy nature*: springtime of youth. Later in the play (5, 1, 139–57) Hamlet is said to be much older.

8–9 Hamlet's affection is compared to a violet, which flowers in early spring and smells very sweet, but does not live long.

8 *Forward*: early-flowering.

9 *suppliance*: pastime.

10 *No more but so*: nothing else. Ophelia questions her brother's judgement of Hamlet's love.

11 *crescent*: as it grows.

12 *thews and bulk*: muscles and size.
    this temple: i.e. the body, which in Christian teaching is called the temple of the Holy Ghost (see 1 Corinthians, 3:16).

14 *Grows wide withal*: increases too. Laertes suggests that Hamlet will have more to think about than his love for Ophelia.

15 *soil*: stain.
    cautel: deceit.

16 *the virtue of his will*: the honourableness of his intentions. 'Will' is capable of a wide range of meanings, and in this line the sexual overtones are strong.

17 *greatness*: high position.
    weigh'd: taken into consideration.

18 *birth*: rank (just as the citizens are subject to their king).

19 *unvalu'd persons*: ordinary people (who have no obligations in such matters to society or the state).

20 *Carve for himself*: choose for himself (the expression is proverbial).

21 *sanity*: well-being.

23 *voice*: approval.
    yielding: consent.
    that body: i.e. the body politic, the state. Laertes assumes here that Hamlet must eventually inherit his father's throne.

26 *in . . . place*: in his position.

27 *give . . . deed*: do what he says.

28 *main voice*: general approval.
    goes withal: agrees to.

29 *weigh*: consider.
    honour: reputation.

30 *credent*: credulous.
    list his songs: listen to his charms.

A violet in the youth of primy nature,
Forward, not permanent, sweet, not lasting,
The perfume and suppliance of a minute,
10 No more.
      Ophelia No more but so?
      Laertes   Think it no more.
For nature crescent does not grow alone
In thews and bulk, but as this temple waxes,
The inward service of the mind and soul
Grows wide withal. Perhaps he loves you now,
15 And now no soil nor cautel doth besmirch
The virtue of his will; but you must fear,
His greatness weigh'd, his will is not his own.
For he himself is subject to his birth:
He may not, as unvalu'd persons do,
20 Carve for himself, for on his choice depends
The sanity and health of this whole state;
And therefore must his choice be circumscrib'd
Unto the voice and yielding of that body
Whereof he is the head. Then if he says he loves you,
25 It fits your wisdom so far to believe it
As he in his particular act and place
May give his saying deed; which is no further
Than the main voice of Denmark goes withal.
Then weigh what loss your honour may sustain
30 If with too credent ear you list his songs,

31 *chaste treasure*: virginity.
32 *unmaster'd importunity*: uncontrolled demands.
34 *keep . . . affection*: hold back in your desires. Laertes' metaphor is military, insisting that Ophelia should keep herself from being hurt.
36 'It is quite enough for a modest ('chary') girl to reveal her beauty to the moonlight.'
38 *scapes*: escapes. Laertes is uttering Elizabethan commonplaces.
39 *canker*: canker-worm.
    galls: injures.
    infants of the spring: young spring flowers.
40 *buttons be disclos'd*: buds have opened.
41 *liquid*: bright.
42 *Contagious blastments*: infections. The dawn — of day and of youth — is a time of brightest promise and greatest danger.
43 *fear*: i.e. of danger.
44 *to itself*: by itself.
    none: i.e. no other temptation.
45 *effect*: substance.
47 *ungracious pastors*: ungodly shepherds (contrasted with the good shepherd — the type of Christ — who leads his flock in the way that he himself has trodden).
49 *puff'd*: proud.
50 *primrose path*: easy way.
    dalliance: wanton amusement.
51 *recks . . . rede*: his own advice.
54 *Occasion smiles*: it is a happy opportunity.
    leave: leave-taking.

56 *sits . . . sail*: i.e. is favourable.
57 *you are stay'd for*: they are waiting for you.
    There: Polonius lays his hand on the head of the kneeling Laertes.
58 *precepts*: The matters on which Polonius advises Laertes were common topics for a father's parting words to his son.
59 *character*: engrave.
60 *unproportion'd*: reckless.
    his act: its deed.
61 'Be friendly enough, but don't make yourself cheap.'
62 *their adoption tried*: when you have tested their friendship.
63 *hoops*: bonds.
64–5 'Don't shake hands (in friendship) with every fresh young man.'
66 *entrance to*: beginning.
67 *Bear't*: conduct yourself in such a way.

Or lose your heart, or your chaste treasure open
To his unmaster'd importunity.
Fear it, Ophelia, fear it, my dear sister,
And keep you in the rear of your affection
35 Out of the shot and danger of desire.
The chariest maid is prodigal enough
If she unmask her beauty to the moon.
Virtue itself scapes not calumnious strokes.
The canker galls the infants of the spring
40 Too oft before their buttons be disclos'd,
And in the morn and liquid dew of youth
Contagious blastments are most imminent.
Be wary then: best safety lies in fear.
Youth to itself rebels, though none else near.

Ophelia
45 I shall th'effect of this good lesson keep
As watchman to my heart. But good my brother,
Do not as some ungracious pastors do,
Show me the steep and thorny way to heaven,
Whiles like a puff'd and reckless libertine
50 Himself the primrose path of dalliance treads,
And recks not his own rede.

Laertes   O fear me not.
I stay too long.

Enter Polonius

                    But here my father comes.
A double blessing is a double grace:
Occasion smiles upon a second leave.

Polonius
55 Yet here, Laertes? Aboard, aboard for shame.
The wind sits in the shoulder of your sail,
And you are stay'd for. There, my blessing with thee.
And these few precepts in thy memory
Look thou character. Give thy thoughts no tongue,
60 Nor any unproportion'd thought his act.
Be thou familiar, but by no means vulgar;
Those friends thou hast, and their adoption tried,
Grapple them unto thy soul with hoops of steel,
But do not dull thy palm with entertainment
65 Of each new-hatch'd, unfledg'd courage. Beware
Of entrance to a quarrel, but being in,
Bear't that th'opposed may beware of thee.

69 *censure*: opinion.

70 *habit*: dress.

71 *express'd in fancy*: with fancy trimmings.

73-4 'French noblemen are particularly renowned for having the height of good taste in clothes.'

77 *husbandry*: thrift.

81 *season*: ripen. His father's blessing will enrich these 'few precepts'.

83 *invests*: urges.
tend: attend.

86 *keep the key*: i.e. no one else can open the lock.

89 *touching*: relating to.

90 *Marry*: by the Virgin Mary (a mild oath).
bethought: remembered.

93 'Have willingly paid a lot of attention to him.'

94 *'tis put on me*: I am given to understand.

95 *in way of caution*: as a warning.

97 *it behoves*: it is fitting for.

98 *Give me up*: tell me.

99 *tenders*: declarations, offers. Polonius picks up the word's commercial usages.

Give every man thy ear, but few thy voice;
Take each man's censure, but reserve thy judgment.
70 Costly thy habit as thy purse can buy,
But not express'd in fancy; rich, not gaudy;
For the apparel oft proclaims the man,
And they in France of the best rank and station
Are of a most select and generous chief in that.
75 Neither a borrower nor a lender be,
For loan oft loses both itself and friend,
And borrowing dulls the edge of husbandry.
This above all: to thine own self be true,
And it must follow as the night the day
80 Thou canst not then be false to any man.
Farewell, my blessing season this in thee.
    Laertes
Most humbly do I take my leave, my lord.
    Polonius
The time invests you; go, your servants tend.
    Laertes
Farewell, Ophelia, and remember well
85 What I have said to you.
    Ophelia   'Tis in my memory lock'd,
And you yourself shall keep the key of it.
    Laertes
Farewell.   [*Exit*
    Polonius
What is't, Ophelia, he hath said to you?
    Ophelia
So please you, something touching the Lord Hamlet.
    Polonius
90 Marry, well bethought.
'Tis told me he hath very oft of late
Given private time to you, and you yourself
Have of your audience been most free and bounteous.
If it be so—as so 'tis put on me,
95 And that in way of caution—I must tell you
You do not understand yourself so clearly
As it behoves my daughter and your honour.
What is between you? Give me up the truth.
    Ophelia
He hath, my lord, of late made many tenders
100 Of his affection to me.

101 *green*: inexperienced.
102 *Unsifted*: untried.

107 *sterling*: real money.
Tender . . . dearly: take more care of yourself.
108–9 'Not to overwork the metaphor (as excessive work breaks a horse's wind).'
109 *you'll . . . fool*: give me a fool for a daughter.
111 *fashion*: manner. Polonius again twists the sense of the word.
112 *Go to*: An exclamation of impatience.
113 *countenance to*: confirmation of.
115 *springes to catch woodcocks*: A proverbial expression; woodcocks were thought to be foolish birds, easily caught in snares ('springes').
116 *blood*: sexual passion.
prodigal: with careless generosity.
117 *blazes*: flaring passions.
118 *extinct in both*: both light and heat are extinguished.
119 *it*: the promise.
121 *somewhat scanter of*: rather less generous with.
122–23 'Don't enter into negotiations with him just because he asks you to.' The presentation of courtship in terms of military strategy is traditional.
125 *larger tether*: longer rope — i.e. less restriction.
126 *few*: short.
127 *brokers*: traders, go-betweens.
128 *Not of that dye*: of a different colour.
investments: clothing. This word leads to the pun on 'suits' in the next line.
129 *implorators*: solicitors.
unholy suits: i.e. not the 'holy vows' which Ophelia described in line 114.
130 *Breathing*: persuading.
sanctified and pious: i.e. apparently genuine and sincere.
131 *beguile*: deceive.
for all: all I have to say.
132 *slander . . . leisure*: misuse any of your free time.
135 *Come your ways*: come along now.

Polonius
Affection? Pooh, you speak like a green girl,
Unsifted in such perilous circumstance.
Do you believe his tenders, as you call them?
Ophelia
I do not know, my lord, what I should think.
Polonius
105 Marry, I will teach you. Think yourself a baby
That you have ta'en these tenders for true pay
Which are not sterling. Tender yourself more dearly
Or—not to crack the wind of the poor phrase,
Running it thus—you'll tender me a fool.
Ophelia
110 My lord, he hath importun'd me with love
In honourable fashion.
Polonius
Ay, fashion you may call it. Go to, go to.
Ophelia
And hath given countenance to his speech, my lord,
With almost all the holy vows of heaven.
Polonius
115 Ay, springes to catch woodcocks. I do know,
When the blood burns, how prodigal the soul
Lends the tongue vows. These blazes, daughter,
Giving more light than heat, extinct in both
Even in their promise as it is a-making,
120 You must not take for fire. From this time
Be something scanter of your maiden presence,
Set your entreatments at a higher rate
Than a command to parley. For Lord Hamlet,
Believe so much in him that he is young,
125 And with a larger tether may he walk
Than may be given you. In few, Ophelia,
Do not believe his vows; for they are brokers
Not of that dye which their investments show,
But mere implorators of unholy suits,
130 Breathing like sanctified and pious bawds
The better to beguile. This is for all.
I would not, in plain terms, from this time forth
Have you so slander any moment leisure
As to give words or talk with the Lord Hamlet.
135 Look to't, I charge you. Come your ways.
Ophelia
I shall obey, my lord.   [*Exeunt*

Hamlet and Horatio join Marcellus on the
midnight watch, whilst the King and courtiers
enjoy a drunken revel within the castle. The
Ghost walks again; and Hamlet, recognizing the
likeness of his father, obeys the beckoning
command.

1   *shrewdly*: sharply.
3   *lacks of*: not quite.
6   *held . . . walk*: usually walked.
6s.d. *pieces*: i.e. the cannon commanded at *1,
2, 126*.
8   *wake*: stay up late.
    takes his rouse: carouses.
9   *Keeps wassail*: drinks healths.
    upspring: This seems to have been some
    kind of riotous ('swaggering') dance which
    the King performs ('reels') in his drunken
    revelry.
10 *Rhenish*: Rhine wine.
11 *kettle-drum and trumpet*: These give signals
    to the cannon (see *5, 2, 272–5*). The dance,
    the wine, and the instruments all give a
    'Danish' air to the play.
12 *triumph*: celebration.
    pledge: toast.
    Is it a custom: Horatio asks for the benefit of
    the audience.
15 *to the manner born*: inheriting this tradition.
    Hamlet's disapproval of this national
    custom serves to emphasize his alienation.
16 *in the breach*: by breaking it.
    observance: performance.
17–38 The whole of this passage is omitted in
    both the Q1 and F texts.
17–18 'These drunken orgies give us a bad
    reputation in other countries both to the
    east and to the west.'
18 *traduc'd*: censured.
    tax'd of: criticised by.

Scene 4

Enter Hamlet, Horatio, *and* Marcellus

Hamlet
The air bites shrewdly, it is very cold.
Horatio
It is a nipping and an eager air.
Hamlet
What hour now?
Horatio   I think it lacks of twelve.
Marcellus
No, it is struck.
Horatio   Indeed? I heard it not.
5 It then draws near the season
Wherein the spirit held his wont to walk.

*A flourish of trumpets, and
two pieces of ordnance go off*

What does this mean, my lord?
Hamlet
The King doth wake tonight and takes his rouse;
Keeps wassail, and the swagg'ring upspring reels;
10 And as he drains his draughts of Rhenish down,
The kettle-drum and trumpet thus bray out
The triumph of his pledge.
Horatio   Is it a custom?
Hamlet
Ay marry is't,
But to my mind, though I am native here
15 And to the manner born, it is a custom
More honour'd in the breach than the observance.
This heavy-headed revel east and west
Makes us traduc'd and tax'd of other nations—

19 *clepe*: call.
    with swinish phrase: calling us pigs.
20 *Soil*: blacken.
    addition: additional name given to describe or distinguish a person (or race).
20–22 *it takes . . . attribute*: This drunkenness (the 'heavy-headed revel') causes our achievements, although the greatest performed, to lose the best part ('pith and marrow') of the estimation they deserve.
22 *our attribute*: reputation, the character attributed to us.
23–38 *So . . . scandal*: Hamlet's meditation serves to slow the action, preparing for the Ghost's entrance.
23 *in particular men*: with individuals.
24 *for*: on account of.
    mole: defect.
25 *As*: for instance. Hamlet gives examples of defects in human beings.
26 *his*: its.
27 'By being temperamentally unbalanced.'
28 *pales*: fences.
29 *habit*: acquired practice.
    too much o'erleavens: has too strong an effect.
30 *form of plausive manners*: decent behaviour.
    that these men: Hamlet returns to the 'particular men' of line 23.
32 *Nature's livery or Fortune's star*: something they are born with, or something that their fate leads them to.
33 *His virtues else*: whatever the other virtues of such a man.
34 *undergo*: support.
35 *general censure*: the opinion of everyone.
35–6 *take corruption From*: be ruined by. If a man of many virtues has just a single fault, that fault will ruin his reputation — his 'public image'.
36 *dram*: very small amount.
37 *dout*: efface.
38 *his*: its.
    scandal: shame.
39 *ministers of grace*: guardian angels. Hamlet calls for divine protection.
40 *Be thou . . . damn'd*: whether you are angel or devil. Hamlet voices the doubts which the audience should be feeling.
42 *Be thy intents*: whether your intentions are.
43 *questionable shape*: appearance which invites questioning — i.e. the bodily form of Hamlet's father. When he calls the Ghost by name, Hamlet sheds some of his doubts about its nature.

They clepe us drunkards, and with swinish phrase
20 Soil our addition; and indeed it takes
From our achievements, though perform'd at height,
The pith and marrow of our attribute.
So, oft it chances in particular men
That for some vicious mole of nature in them,
25 As in their birth, wherein they are not guilty
(Since nature cannot choose his origin),
By their o'ergrowth of some complexion,
Oft breaking down the pales and forts of reason,
Or by some habit, that too much o'erleavens
30 The form of plausive manners—that these men,
Carrying, I say, the stamp of one defect,
Being Nature's livery or Fortune's star,
His virtues else, be they as pure as grace,
As infinite as man may undergo,
35 Shall in the general censure take corruption
From that particular fault. The dram of evil
Doth all the noble substance often dout
To his own scandal.

Enter Ghost

Horatio   Look, my lord, it comes.
Hamlet
Angels and ministers of grace defend us!
40 Be thou a spirit of health or goblin damn'd,
Bring with thee airs from heaven or blasts from hell,
Be thy intents wicked or charitable,
Thou com'st in such a questionable shape
That I will speak to thee. I'll call thee Hamlet,
45 King, father, royal Dane. O answer me.
Let me not burst in ignorance, but tell
Why thy canoniz'd bones, hearsed in death,
Have burst their cerements, why the sepulchre
Wherein we saw thee quietly inurn'd
50 Hath op'd his ponderous and marble jaws
To cast thee up again. What may this mean,
That thou, dead corse, again in complete steel
Revisits thus the glimpses of the moon,
Making night hideous and we fools of nature
55 So horridly to shake our disposition
With thoughts beyond the reaches of our souls?
Say why is this? Wherefore? What should we do?

Ghost beckons

45 *royal Dane*: King of Denmark.
47 *canoniz'd bones*: The body was properly buried, according to the orthodox rules — 'canons' — of the Christian Church.
hearsed: coffined.
48 *cerements*: grave-clothes. The body was shrouded when last seen.
49 *quietly inurn'd*: placed respectfully (as in a funeral urn).
52 *complete steel*: full armour (the stress is on the first syllable of 'complete').
53 *glimpses of the moon*: fitful moonlight.
54 *hideous*: frightening.
54–5 The Ghost causes the men, who are at the mercy of their human nature, to distress their minds ('our disposition').
57 *do*: Hamlet (like Horatio at *1*, 1, 133ff.) assumes that the Ghost requires some kind of action.
59 *some impartment did desire*: wanted to tell you something.
61 *more removed*: further away.
65 'My life is not worth a pin.'
69–74 Horatio fears that the Ghost may be an evil spirit tempting Hamlet to a suicidal madness.
69 *flood*: sea.
71 *beetles*: overhangs.
73 *deprive . . . reason*: take away the reason which rules over you.
75 *toys of desperation*: foolish thoughts of suicide.

82 *artire*: artery. The Elizabethans (not knowing the circulation of the blood) thought that the arteries conducted vital spirits to the brain.
83 *Nemean lion*: In Greek mythology, the slaying of this lion was the first labour of Hercules.
nerve: sinew.
84 *Unhand me*: take your hands off.
85 *lets*: hinders.

Horatio
It beckons you to go away with it,
As if it some impartment did desire
60 To you alone.
          Marcellus Look with what courteous action
It waves you to a more removed ground.
But do not go with it.
          Horatio   No, by no means.
          Hamlet
It will not speak. Then I will follow it.
          Horatio
Do not, my lord.
          Hamlet   Why, what should be the fear?
65 I do not set my life at a pin's fee,
And for my soul, what can it do to that,
Being a thing immortal as itself?
It waves me forth again. I'll follow it.
          Horatio
What if it tempt you toward the flood, my lord,
70 Or to the dreadful summit of the cliff
That beetles o'er his base into the sea,
And there assume some other horrible form
Which might deprive your sovereignty of reason
And draw you into madness? Think of it.
75 The very place puts toys of desperation,
Without more motive, into every brain
That looks so many fathoms to the sea
And hears it roar beneath.
          Hamlet   It waves me still.
Go on, I'll follow thee.
          Marcellus
80 You shall not go, my lord.
          Hamlet   Hold off your hands.
          Horatio
Be rul'd; you shall not go.
          Hamlet   My fate cries out
And makes each petty artire in this body
As hardy as the Nemean lion's nerve.
Still am I call'd. Unhand me, gentlemen.
85 By heaven, I'll make a ghost of him that lets me.
I say away.—Go on, I'll follow thee.
          [*Exeunt* Ghost *and* Hamlet

87   *waxes*: grows increasingly.

88   *thus*: i.e. when Hamlet is in this state.

89   *Have after*: let us follow him.

91   *Nay*: i.e. let's not leave it to Heaven. Marcellus checks Horatio's momentary wavering.

Horatio
He waxes desperate with imagination.
Marcellus
Let's follow. 'Tis not fit thus to obey him.
Horatio
Have after. To what issue will this come?
Marcellus
90   Something is rotten in the state of Denmark.
Horatio
Heaven will direct it.
Marcellus   Nay, let's follow him.   [*Exeunt*

Act 1   Scene 5

Hamlet follows the Ghost until it speaks, and tells him a tale of horror. There has been murder and adultery; and the Ghost demands revenge for his wrongs. Hamlet makes a promise before the Ghost leaves. When he is joined by Horatio and Marcellus, Hamlet swears them to secrecy.

2   *My hour*: i.e. daybreak. This Ghost, speaking for the first time now, alone with Hamlet, is not the creature of popular melodrama — although the words are horrific enough.

3   *tormenting flames*: the purgatorial fires.

6   *bound*: i.e. by his filial duty, and by his unavoidable destiny (see *1*, *4*, *81*).

9–91   The firm rhythms and linguistic high style give an air of authority to the Ghost's speech.

11   *to fast*: The pains of spirits, although they have no bodies, can only be expressed in physical terms.

12   *in . . . nature*: while I was alive. The 'crimes' are the human sins — not necessarily serious offences.

16   *harrow up*: rack.

Scene 5

Enter Ghost *and* Hamlet

Hamlet
Whither wilt thou lead me? Speak, I'll go no further.
Ghost
Mark me.
Hamlet   I will.
Ghost   My hour is almost come
When I to sulph'rous and tormenting flames
Must render up myself.
Hamlet   Alas, poor ghost.
Ghost
5   Pity me not, but lend thy serious hearing
To what I shall unfold.
Hamlet   Speak, I am bound to hear.
Ghost
So art thou to revenge when thou shalt hear.
Hamlet
What?
Ghost
I am thy father's spirit,
10   Doom'd for a certain term to walk the night,
And for the day confin'd to fast in fires,
Till the foul crimes done in my days of nature
Are burnt and purg'd away. But that I am forbid
To tell the secrets of my prison-house,
15   I could a tale unfold whose lightest word
Would harrow up thy soul, freeze thy young blood,

17 *start from*: fall out of.
    spheres: i.e. sockets (see *4, 7, 15*).
18 *knotted and combined locks*: whole head of hair.
20 *porpentine*: porcupine.
21 *eternal blazon*: description ('blazon' is a term from heraldry) of eternity. The vagueness adds to the terror.
22 *List*: listen. The incantatory repetitions compel attention.

27 *in the best*: at best.
28 *strange and unnatural*: i.e. because it is a violation of the natural bond of kinship.

30 *meditation*: thought.

32 *duller*: more lethargic.
    fat weed: overgrown plant. Perhaps the asphodel — which grew in the fields of the Greek underworld — is intended.
33 *roots*: The F text has 'rots', which gives a more precise meaning.
    Lethe wharf: In classical mythology, the spirits of the dead congregated on the bank of the river Lethe, to drink its waters (which made them forget the things of earth) before being transported to Hades, the Greek underworld.
35 *orchard*: garden.
36 *the whole ear*: everyone who hears.
37 *forged process*: false account.
41 *prophetic soul*: Hamlet realized that something was wrong, but he did not, until this moment, guess at the nature of the offence.
42 *adulterate*: adulterous.

48 *dignity*: worthiness.

50 *decline*: descend to the level of.
51 *natural gifts*: The Ghost compares his own qualities with the 'traitorous gifts' which seduced the Queen.

Make thy two eyes like stars start from their spheres,
Thy knotted and combined locks to part,
And each particular hair to stand an end
20 Like quills upon the fretful porpentine.
But this eternal blazon must not be
To ears of flesh and blood. List, list, O list!
If thou didst ever thy dear father love—
        Hamlet
O God!
        Ghost
25 Revenge his foul and most unnatural murder.
        Hamlet
Murder!
        Ghost
Murder most foul, as in the best it is,
But this most foul, strange and unnatural.
        Hamlet
Haste me to know't, that I with wings as swift
30 As meditation or the thoughts of love
May sweep to my revenge.
        Ghost   I find thee apt.
And duller shouldst thou be than the fat weed
That roots itself in ease on Lethe wharf,
Wouldst thou not stir in this. Now, Hamlet, hear.
35 'Tis given out that, sleeping in my orchard,
A serpent stung me—so the whole ear of Denmark
Is by a forged process of my death
Rankly abus'd—but know, thou noble youth,
The serpent that did sting thy father's life
40 Now wears his crown.
        Hamlet
O my prophetic soul! My uncle!
        Ghost
Ay, that incestuous, that adulterate beast,
With witchcraft of his wit, with traitorous gifts—
O wicked wit, and gifts that have the power
45 So to seduce!—won to his shameful lust
The will of my most seeming-virtuous queen.
O Hamlet, what a falling off was there,
From me, whose love was of that dignity
That it went hand in hand even with the vow
50 I made to her in marriage, and to decline
Upon a wretch whose natural gifts were poor
To those of mine.

53 'Just as virtue will never be shaken.'

54 *in a shape of heaven*: in the appearance of an
    angel. The devil, it was said, could assume
    angelic likeness to tempt humans.

56 *sate itself . . . bed*: grow tired of the
    pleasures of lawful loving.

58 *scent the morning air*: When the Ghost senses
    the approach of day, he knows he must
    return to the imprisonment of purgatory.

61 *Upon my secure hour*: at a time when I was
    unsuspecting.

62 *hebenon*: a poison (which has never been
    identified, but which seems to be associated
    with henbane).

64 *leperous*: causing (like leprosy) an outbreak
    of scaly eruptions.

66 *courses*: rushes.

68 *posset And curd*: thicken and curdle.

69 *eager*: acid (which sours the milk).

71 'A scab, like the bark of a tree, spread
    immediately.'

72 *lazar-like*: like a leper.

75 *dispatch'd*: deprived.

76 *even . . . sin*: with all my sins.

77 *Unhousel'd*: without having received the
    sacrament ('housel').
    disappointed: unprepared (not having made
    confession of his sins and received
    absolution).
    unanel'd: not anointed with the oil of
    extreme unction. Hamlet's father was
    deprived of all rites of the Christian church
    — as Hamlet recalls at 3, 3, 80–81.

78 *reck'ning*: settling of his debt (his sins) with
    God.
    my account: give an account of myself at
    God's judgement seat.

79 'Taking all my guilt with me.'

81 *nature*: natural feeling.
    bear it not: do not condone it.

83 *luxury*: lustfulness.

84 'Whatever you do about this deed.'

85–6 'Do not have any bad thoughts or evil
    designs on your mother'. The Ghost wants
    only Claudius to be punished by Hamlet.

86 *to heaven*: i.e. to God's judgement.

87 *those thorns*: the prickings of her own guilty
    conscience.

89 *glow-worm*: a kind of beetle, whose
    abdomen produces a faint light which is
    visible only in darkness.
    matin: morning.

90 *gins*: begins.

But virtue, as it never will be mov'd,
Though lewdness court it in a shape of heaven,
55 So lust, though to a radiant angel link'd,
Will sate itself in a celestial bed
And prey on garbage.
But soft, methinks I scent the morning air:
Brief let me be. Sleeping within my orchard,
60 My custom always of the afternoon,
Upon my secure hour thy uncle stole
With juice of cursed hebenon in a vial,
And in the porches of my ears did pour
The leperous distilment, whose effect
65 Holds such an enmity with blood of man
That swift as quicksilver it courses through
The natural gates and alleys of the body,
And with a sudden vigour it doth posset
And curd, like eager droppings into milk,
70 The thin and wholesome blood. So did it mine,
And a most instant tetter bark'd about,
Most lazar-like, with vile and loathsome crust
All my smooth body.
Thus was I, sleeping, by a brother's hand
75 Of life, of crown, of queen at once dispatch'd,
Cut off even in the blossoms of my sin,
Unhousel'd, disappointed, unanel'd,
No reck'ning made, but sent to my account
With all my imperfections on my head.
80 O horrible! O horrible! most horrible!
If thou has nature in thee, bear it not,
Let not the royal bed of Denmark be
A couch for luxury and damned incest.
But howsomever thou pursuest this act,
85 Taint not thy mind nor let thy soul contrive
Against thy mother aught. Leave her to heaven,
And to those thorns that in her bosom lodge
To prick and sting her. Fare thee well at once:
The glow-worm shows the matin to be near
90 And gins to pale his uneffectual fire.
Adieu, adieu, adieu. Remember me.   [*Exit*

Hamlet

O all you host of heaven! O earth! What else?
And shall I couple hell? O fie! Hold, hold, my heart,
And you, my sinews, grow not instant old,

<table>
<tr><td>91s.d.</td><td>Exit: Critics suggest that the Ghost now vanishes through a trap-door in the stage — so that the actor can be ready for the following episode in the 'cellarage'.</td></tr>
<tr><td>93</td><td>shall I couple hell: Now that the Ghost has gone, Hamlet's doubts return, and he wonders whether to invoke hellish powers as well as those of heaven.</td></tr>
<tr><td>96</td><td>whiles: as long as.</td></tr>
<tr><td>97</td><td>distracted globe: bewildered head. Hamlet does not know what to think of the information he has just received.</td></tr>
<tr><td>98</td><td>table: tablet. The reference at first is to the monumental tablets bearing inscriptions, but Shakespeare extends it to include writing-tablets, or notebooks.</td></tr>
<tr><td>99</td><td>fond: foolish.
records: things to be remembered (accented on the second syllable).</td></tr>
<tr><td>100</td><td>saws of books: quotations from books.
forms: shapes, ideas.
pressures: impressions.</td></tr>
<tr><td>101</td><td>youth and observation: an observant young man. Hamlet seems to feel suddenly older as a result of what he has just learned.</td></tr>
<tr><td>105</td><td>Hamlet has already forgotten the warning of line 85; and this outburst is exactly the 'baser matter' that he has just forsworn.</td></tr>
<tr><td>107</td><td>tables: writing-tablets.</td></tr>
<tr><td>110</td><td>there you are: Hamlet refers to his writing.
to my word: motto. Hamlet perhaps inscribes this also on his 'tables'.</td></tr>
<tr><td>112s.d.</td><td>Horatio and Marcellus are searching for Hamlet in the darkness.</td></tr>
<tr><td>115</td><td>secure: protect.</td></tr>
<tr><td>116</td><td>Hamlet is very serious; it is as though he is saying 'amen' to Horatio's prayer.</td></tr>
<tr><td>117</td><td>Hillo: Marcellus calls like a falconer; and Hamlet responds in the same manner.</td></tr>
</table>

95 But bear me stiffly up. Remember thee?
Ay, thou poor ghost, whiles memory holds a seat
In this distracted globe. Remember thee?
Yea, from the table of my memory
I'll wipe away all trivial fond records,
100 All saws of books, all forms, all pressures past
That youth and observation copied there,
And thy commandment all alone shall live
Within the book and volume of my brain,
Unmix'd with baser matter. Yes, by heaven!
105 O most pernicious woman!
O villain, villain, smiling damned villain!
My tables. Meet it is I set it down
That one may smile, and smile, and be a villain—
At least I am sure it may be so in Denmark.   [*Writes*]
110 So, uncle, there you are. Now to my word.
It is 'Adieu, adieu, remember me.'
I have sworn't.

Enter Horatio *and* Marcellus [*calling*]

Horatio
My lord, my lord.
Marcellus
Lord Hamlet.
Horatio
115 Heavens secure him.
Hamlet
[*Aside*] So be it.
Marcellus
Hillo, ho, ho, my lord.
Hamlet
Hillo, ho, ho, boy. Come, bird, come.
Marcellus
How is't, my noble lord?
Horatio
120 What news, my lord?
Hamlet
O, wonderful!
Horatio
Good my lord, tell it.
Hamlet
No, you will reveal it.

Horatio

Not I, my lord, by heaven.

Marcellus

125   Nor I, my lord.

Hamlet

How say you then, would heart of man once think it—
But you'll be secret?

Horatio and **Marcellus**

Ay, by heaven.

Hamlet

There's never a villain dwelling in all Denmark
130   But he's an arrant knave.

Horatio

There needs no ghost, my lord, come from the grave
To tell us this.

Hamlet

          Why, right, you are in the right.
And so without more circumstance at all
I hold it fit that we shake hands and part,
135   You as your business and desire shall point you—
For every man hath business and desire,
Such as it is—and for my own poor part,
I will go pray.

Horatio

These are but wild and whirling words, my lord.

Hamlet

140   I am sorry they offend you, heartily—
Yes faith, heartily.

Horatio   There's no offence, my lord.

Hamlet

Yes by Saint Patrick but there is, Horatio,
And much offence too. Touching this vision here,
It is an honest ghost, that let me tell you.
145   For your desire to know what is between us,
O'ermaster't as you may. And now, good friends,
As you are friends, scholars, and soldiers,
Give me one poor request.

Horatio   What is't, my lord? We will.

Hamlet

Never make known what you have seen tonight.

Horatio and **Marcellus**

150   My lord, we will not.

Hamlet

Nay, but swear't.

---

130   *arrant knave*: utter rascal. As Hamlet is about to confide in his friends, he suddenly swerves into a jest.

131–2   'There is no need for a ghost to come from the grave and tell us this.' Horatio is mildly reproachful of Hamlet's levity.

133   *circumstance*: explanation.

135   *point*: direct.

139   *whirling*: excited.

140   *heartily*: with all my heart.

141   *faith*: in faith, sincerely.
no offence: no need to apologize.

142   *Saint Patrick*: Hamlet swears by the Irish saint, whom early Christian tradition associated with visions of purgatory.

143   *Touching*: regarding. Later in the play (*3, 2, 77*) it is clear that Hamlet has confided in Horatio.

144   *honest*: genuine (not a devil impersonating the dead king).

146   *as you may*: any way you can.

152 Horatio swears by his faith not to tell anything.

154 *Upon my sword*: The hilt of the sword formed a cross, which made the oath even more strongly binding.

157s.d. The 'underground' episode blends grim burlesque humour with a sense of eery strangeness in a moment of 'comic relief'.

158 *truepenny*: honest fellow.

159 *cellarage*: cellars, space underneath the Elizabethan platform stage.

164 *Hic et ubique*: here and everywhere. The Latin tag sounds like a description of the omnipresence of God.

171 *pioner*: miner.

173 *as a stranger . . . welcome*: Horatio must observe the Christian teaching that strangers should be welcomed (St Matthew, 25:35).

Horatio
In faith, my lord, not I.
Marcellus
Nor I, my lord, in faith.
Hamlet
Upon my sword.
Marcellus
155 We have sworn, my lord, already.
Hamlet
Indeed, upon my sword, indeed.
Ghost
[*Cries under the stage*] Swear.
Hamlet
Ah ha, boy, say'st thou so? Art thou there, truepenny?
Come on, you hear this fellow in the cellarage.
160 Consent to swear.
Horatio   Propose the oath, my lord.
Hamlet
Never to speak of this that you have seen.
Swear by my sword.
Ghost
Swear.

They swear

Hamlet
Hic et ubique? Then we'll shift our ground.
165 Come hither, gentlemen,
And lay your hands again upon my sword.
Swear by my sword
Never to speak of this that you have heard.
Ghost
Swear by his sword.

They swear

Hamlet
170 Well said, old mole. Canst work i'th' earth so fast?
A worthy pioner! Once more remove, good friends.
Horatio
O day and night, but this is wondrous strange.
Hamlet
And therefore as a stranger give it welcome.

175   *in your philosophy*: by any philosophers.

177   *so help you mercy*: as you hope that God may
      have mercy on you. The disordered syntax
      reflects Hamlet's state of excitement.
178   *some'er*: soever.
180   *antic disposition*: strange behaviour.

182   *encumber'd*: folded.
183   *doubtful*: ambiguous.
184   *and if*: if only.

185   *list*: wanted.
186   *giving out*: indication.
      note: suggest.
188   *at your most need*: i.e. at the Day of
      Judgement.

193   *friending*: friendship.

195   *still*: always.
196   *out of joint*: completely disordered.

There are more things in heaven and earth, Horatio,
175 Than are dreamt of in your philosophy.
     But come,
     Here, as before, never, so help you mercy,
     How strange or odd some'er I bear myself—
     As I perchance hereafter shall think meet
180 To put an antic disposition on—
     That you, at such time seeing me, never shall,
     With arms encumber'd thus, or this head-shake,
     Or by pronouncing of some doubtful phrase,
     As 'Well, we know', or 'We could and if we would',
185 Or 'If we list to speak', or 'There be and if they
          might',
     Or such ambiguous giving out, to note
     That you know aught of me—this do swear,
     So grace and mercy at your most need help you.
          Ghost
     Swear.

                    They swear

              Hamlet
190 Rest, rest, perturbed spirit. So, gentlemen,
     With all my love I do commend me to you;
     And what so poor a man as Hamlet is
     May do t'express his love and friending to you,
     God willing, shall not lack. Let us go in together.
195 And still your fingers on your lips, I pray.
     The time is out of joint. O cursed spite,
     That ever I was born to set it right.
     Nay, come, let's go together.   [*Exeunt*

Act 2

Act 2　Scene 1

Some time has passed since the events of *Act I*.
Laertes is now in Paris and his father, the
suspicious Polonius, is sending money to his
student son — and setting a spy to find out what
he is doing. Ophelia comes to her father in great
distress, and tells him of the strange behaviour of
Prince Hamlet. It may be that he has now
assumed an 'antic disposition', as he warned his
friends (*I*, 5, 180); or perhaps his strange
appearance is an indication of his state of mind.

Os.d.　*old*: This stage direction gives a
　suggestion of how Shakespeare thought of
　the character of Polonius.
1　*notes*: letters.
3　*shall . . . wisely*: it would be a very good
　thing.
4　*inquire*: inquiry.
7　*Inquire me*: This construction (with 'me' in
　the so-called 'ethic dative' case) is no longer
　used in English.
　Danskers: Danish nationals.
8　*what means*: how much money they have.
　keep: lodge.
10　*encompassment . . . question*: roundabout
　way of questioning.
11–12　*come you . . . it*: you will get closer than if
　you ask specific questions (about Laertes).
13　*Take you*: assume.

Scene 1

Enter old Polonius, *with his man* Reynaldo

Polonius
Give him this money and these notes, Reynaldo.
Reynaldo
I will, my lord.
Polonius
You shall do marvellous wisely, good Reynaldo,
Before you visit him, to make inquire
5　Of his behaviour.
Reynaldo　　My lord, I did intend it.
Polonius
Marry, well said, very well said. Look you, sir,
Inquire me first what Danskers are in Paris,
And how, and who, what means, and where they keep,
What company, at what expense; and finding
10　By this encompassment and drift of question
That they do know my son, come you more nearer
Than your particular demands will touch it.
Take you as 'twere some distant knowledge of him,
As thus, 'I know his father, and his friends,
15　And in part him'—do you mark this, Reynaldo?

Reynaldo
Ay, very well, my lord.
    Polonius
'And in part him. But', you may say, 'not well;
But if't be he I mean, he's very wild,
Addicted so and so'—and there put on him
20 What forgeries you please—marry, none so rank
As may dishonour him—take heed of that—
But, sir, such wanton, wild, and usual slips
As are companions noted and most known
To youth and liberty.
    Reynaldo
25 As gaming, my lord?
    Polonius   Ay, or drinking, fencing, swearing,
Quarrelling, drabbing—you may go so far.
    Reynaldo
My lord, that would dishonour him.
    Polonius
'Faith no, as you may season it in the charge.
You must not put another scandal on him,
30 That he is open to incontinency—
That's not my meaning; but breathe his faults so
    quaintly
That they may seem the taints of liberty,
The flash and outbreak of a fiery mind,
A savageness in unreclaimed blood,
35 Of general assault.
    Reynaldo
But my good lord—
    Polonius   Wherefore should you do this?
    Reynaldo
Ay, my lord, I would know that.

19 *put on him*: charge him with.
20 *forgeries*: false accusations.
    rank: disgraceful.
22 *usual slips*: common faults.
23 *noted and most known To*: well known and associated with.

26 *drabbing*: frequenting prostitutes.
28 *season*: moderate.
30 *incontinency*: sexual excesses.
31–6 *breathe . . . assault*: Reynaldo should imply that Laertes is behaving like any young man who has been given his freedom.
31 *quaintly*: cunningly.
34 *savageness . . . blood*: wildness of untamed youth.
35 *Of general assault*: which happens to most men.

38 *drift*: scheme.
39 *fetch of warrant*: legitimate device.
40 *sullies*: This is F's reading (= smears); Q2
    has an apparently alternative form, 'sallies'
    (see *1, 2, 129*).
41 *a little . . . working*: that got grubby while it
    was being made.
42 *Mark you*: listen to me.
43 *Your . . . converse*: the one you are talking
    to. The stress is on the second syllable of
    'converse'.
    would sound: want to question.
44 *prenominate*: already named.
46 *closes . . . consequence*: naturally agrees with
    you in the following terms.
48 *phrase or the addition*: manner of speaking
    or form of address.

50 *'a*: he.
58 *o'ertook in's rouse*: the worse for drink.
59 *tennis*: Royal (or real) tennis was a popular
    game in Paris.
61 *Videlicet*: that is to say.
63 *takes*: catches. A 'carp' is a freshwater fish,
    and there may also be a pun on 'carp' =
    talk.
64 *we . . . reach*: we wise and experienced
    men.
65 *windlasses*: roundabout courses.
    assays of bias: devious tests. In the game of
    bowls, a player must not aim directly, but
    must weigh his bowl's 'bias'.

66 'By indirect methods learn what is the right
    way.'
67 *lecture*: lesson.
68 *have me*: have understood me.
69 *buy*: be with.
70 *Good my lord*: Reynaldo humbly accepts the
    dismissal.
71 'Go along with what he wants to do.'

Polonius
Marry, sir, here's my drift,
And I believe it is a fetch of warrant.
40 You laying these slight sullies on my son,
As 'twere a thing a little soil'd i'th' working,
Mark you,
Your party in converse, him you would sound,
Having ever seen in the prenominate crimes
45 The youth you breathe of guilty, be assur'd
He closes with you in this consequence:
'Good sir', or so, or 'friend', or 'gentleman',
According to the phrase or the addition
Of man and country.
            Reynaldo   Very good, my lord.
Polonius
50 And then, sir, does 'a this—'a does—what was I about
to say? By the mass, I was about to say something.
Where did I leave?
            Reynaldo
At 'closes in the consequence'.
            Polonius
At 'closes in the consequence', ay, marry.
55 He closes thus: 'I know the gentleman,
I saw him yesterday', or 'th'other day',
Or then, or then, with such or such, 'and as you say,
There was a gaming', 'there o'ertook in's rouse',
'There falling out at tennis', or perchance
60 'I saw him enter such a house of sale'—
Videlicet a brothel, or so forth.
See you now,
Your bait of falsehood takes this carp of truth;
And thus do we of wisdom and of reach,
65 With windlasses and with assays of bias,
By indirections find directions out.
So by my former lecture and advice
Shall you my son. You have me, have you not?
            Reynaldo
My lord, I have.
            Polonius   God buy ye, fare ye well.
            Reynaldo
70 Good my lord.
            Polonius
Observe his inclination in yourself.

72   *ply his music*: get on with what he is doing
     (Polonius may be changing the subject, and
     referring to his son's education).
73   *Well*: Reynaldo expresses duty as he takes
     his leave.

77   *closet*: small private room.
78   *unbrac'd*: unfastened. The garment should
     properly be buttoned down the front.

79   *No hat*: In Elizabethan England, gentlemen
     wore hats at all times.
80   *down-gyved*: Hamlet's stockings hung
     around his ankles like prison fetters
     (gyves).
83   *loosed*: released.
88   *goes . . . arm*: backs away, holding me at
     arm's length.
90   *perusal*: careful scrutiny.
91   *As 'a would*: as though he wanted to.

95   *all his bulk*: his whole body.

100 *bended their light*: turned his gaze.

Reynaldo
I shall, my lord.
     Polonius   And let him ply his music.
Reynaldo
Well, my lord.   [*Exit*

          Enter Ophelia

     Polonius
Farewell. How now, Ophelia, what's the matter?
     Ophelia
75   O my lord, my lord, I have been so affrighted.
     Polonius
With what, i'th' name of God?
     Ophelia
My lord, as I was sewing in my closet,
Lord Hamlet, with his doublet all unbrac'd,
No hat upon his head, his stockings foul'd,
80   Ungarter'd and down-gyved to his ankle,
Pale as his shirt, his knees knocking each other,
And with a look so piteous in purport
As if he had been loosed out of hell
To speak of horrors, he comes before me.
     Polonius
85   Mad for thy love?
          Ophelia   My lord, I do not know,
But truly I do fear it.
          Polonius   What said he?
     Ophelia
He took me by the wrist and held me hard.
Then goes he to the length of all his arm,
And with his other hand thus o'er his brow
90   He falls to such perusal of my face
As 'a would draw it. Long stay'd he so.
At last, a little shaking of mine arm,
And thrice his head thus waving up and down,
He rais'd a sigh so piteous and profound
95   As it did seem to shatter all his bulk
And end his being. That done, he lets me go,
And with his head over his shoulder turn'd
He seem'd to find his way without his eyes,
For out o'doors he went without their helps,
100 And to the last bended their light on me.

102   *ecstasy*: madness.

103   *property*: nature.
       fordoes: destroys.

Polonius
Come, go with me, I will go seek the King.
This is the very ecstasy of love,
Whose violent property fordoes itself
And leads the will to desperate undertakings
105   As oft as any passion under heaven
That does afflict our natures. I am sorry—
What, have you given him any hard words of late?

108   *as you did command*: i.e. in *Act I*, scene 3.

109   *repel*: send back.

Ophelia
No, my good lord, but as you did command,
I did repel his letters and denied
110   His access to me.
       Polonius   That hath made him mad.
I am sorry that with better heed and judgment

111   *heed*: attention.

112   *quoted*: observed.

113   *wrack*: ruin.
       beshrew my jealousy: Polonius curses the
       suspicious fear which has prevented him
       (he thinks) from understanding Hamlet's
       behaviour.

114   *proper to our age*: normal for old men.

115   *cast . . . opinions*: get unreasonable ideas (in
       hunting, a hound is said to *cast* when it
       searches for a scent).

118   *close*: secret.

118–9 *being . . . love*: might cause more trouble
       if we keep quiet than anger if we talk
       about his love.

I had not quoted him. I fear'd he did but trifle
And meant to wrack thee. But beshrew my jealousy!
By heaven, it is as proper to our age
115   To cast beyond ourselves in our opinions
As it is common for the younger sort
To lack discretion. Come, go we to the King.
This must be known, which, being kept close, might move
More grief to hide than hate to utter love.
120   Come.   [*Exeunt*

Act 2   Scene 2

The King gives instructions to Rosencrantz and Guildenstern — who have been at university with Hamlet — and tells them how they are to watch the Prince. Polonius ushers in the ambassadors who were sent to Norway in *Act I*, scene 2. They have returned, and can describe the Norwegian King's treatment of his own headstrong nephew. Their business is quickly done, and when they leave the stage Polonius remains behind to tell Claudius and Gertrude what he has found out about Hamlet's love for Ophelia, and of his own plans to trap the Prince. When Hamlet comes on to the stage, Polonius engages him in conversation; but he can make no sense of the younger man's oblique insults, and so he departs. Hamlet is at first pleased to meet his old friends from the university, but he quickly becomes suspicious of Rosencrantz and Guildenstern. Polonius returns, bringing news of a company of actors, and Hamlet is glad to welcome these. They are his old friends, and after they have demonstrated something of their acting skills, Hamlet speaks of the play they are to perform. He indicates to the audience that this is to be, in some way, a trap for the King.

2   *Moreover that*: besides the fact that.
6   *Sith nor . . . nor*: since neither . . . nor.
12 *sith so neighbour'd to*: since then (their 'young days') you have been so closely acquainted with. The King's appeal sounds very reasonable — Hamlet's old friends ought to understand his ways ('haviour').
13 *vouchsafe your rest*: agree to stay.
16 *occasion*: any chance opportunity.
    glean: pick up.
18 *open'd*: revealed.
    lies . . . remedy: we can put right.
21 *adheres*: stays close to.
22 *gentry*: gentlemanliness, courtesy.
23 *expend*: spend.
24 *supply and profit of our hope*: hopefully we shall profit.
26 *fits*: is appropriate.
27–9 'You have the power to order rather than request us to do what you want.' Guildenstern seems to adopt the King's rather unwieldy language.
27 *of*: over.
28 *dread*: respected.
30 *in the full bent*: to the best of our abilities. The 'bent' in archery is the extreme to which the bow can be drawn.

Scene 2

Flourish. Enter King *and* Queen, Rosencrantz *and* Guildenstern, *with* Attendants

    King
Welcome, dear Rosencrantz and Guildenstern.
Moreover that we much did long to see you,
The need we have to use you did provoke
Our hasty sending. Something have you heard
5 Of Hamlet's transformation—so I call it,
Sith nor th'exterior nor the inward man
Resembles that it was. What it should be,
More than his father's death, that thus hath put him
So much from th'understanding of himself
10 I cannot dream of. I entreat you both
That, being of so young days brought up with him,
And sith so neighbour'd to his youth and haviour,
That you vouchsafe your rest here in our court
Some little time, so by your companies
15 To draw him on to pleasures and to gather,
So much as from occasion you may glean,
Whether aught to us unknown afflicts him thus
That, open'd, lies within our remedy.
    Queen
Good gentlemen, he hath much talk'd of you,
20 And sure I am, two men there is not living
To whom he more adheres. If it will please you
To show us so much gentry and good will
As to expend your time with us awhile
For the supply and profit of our hope,
25 Your visitation shall receive such thanks
As fits a king's remembrance.
    Rosencrantz   Both your Majesties
Might, by the sovereign power you have of us,
Put your dread pleasures more into command
Than to entreaty.
    Guildenstern   But we both obey,
30 And here give up ourselves in the full bent
To lay our service freely at your feet
To be commanded.
    King
Thanks, Rosencrantz and gentle Guildenstern.

Queen
Thanks, Guildenstern and gentle Rosencrantz.
35 And I beseech you instantly to visit
My too much changed son. Go, some of you,
And bring these gentlemen where Hamlet is.
    Guildenstern
Heavens make our presence and our practices
Pleasant and helpful to him.
    Queen   Ay, amen.

                    [*Exeunt* Rosencrantz *and*
                    Guildenstern *and an* Attendant

            Enter Polonius

    Polonius
40 Th'ambassadors from Norway, my good lord,
Are joyfully return'd.
        King
Thou still hast been the father of good news.
    Polonius
Have I, my lord? I assure my good liege
I hold my duty as I hold my soul,
45 Both to my God and to my gracious King;
And I do think—or else this brain of mine
Hunts not the trail of policy so sure
As it hath us'd to do—that I have found
The very cause of Hamlet's lunacy.
        King
50 O speak of that: that do I long to hear.
    Polonius
Give first admittance to th'ambassadors.
My news shall be the fruit to that great feast.
        King
Thyself do grace to them and bring them in.
                            [*Exit* Polonius
He tells me, my dear Gertrude, he hath found
55 The head and source of all your son's distemper.
        Queen
I doubt it is no other but the main,
His father's death and our o'er-hasty marriage.
        King
Well, we shall sift him.

36   *some*: some one of you. Gertrude speaks to
the Attendants.

38   *practices*: devices — *both* harmless enter-
tainments *and* deceits.

42   *still*: always.

44–5   For orthodox Elizabethan Christians,
duty to God and to the monarch were
interdependent.

47–8   *Hunts . . . do*: is not so good at sniffing
things out as it used to be; 'policy' (=
statecraft) often has undertones of 'subtle
cunning'.

52   *fruit*: dessert.

53   *grace*: honour. The King takes up the
banqueting metaphor.

55   *head*: fountainhead.
distemper: disorderly behaviour.

56   *doubt*: suspect.

58   *sift him*: interrogate Polonius.

Enter Polonius, Voltemand, *and* Cornelius

Welcome, my good friends.
Say, Voltemand, what from our brother Norway?

Voltemand

59 *brother Norway*: brother-king of Norway.

60 Most fair return of greetings and desires.
Upon our first, he sent out to suppress
His nephew's levies, which to him appear'd

61 *Upon our first*: as soon as we raised the
subject — as they had been instructed in
Act 1, scene 2.

To be a preparation 'gainst the Polack;
But better look'd into, he truly found

63 *preparation 'gainst*: army raised — levied —
to make war on.
the Polack: the King of Poland.

65 It was against your Highness; whereat griev'd
That so his sickness, age, and impotence

66 *impotence*: feebleness.

Was falsely borne in hand, sends out arrests

67 *borne in hand*: deceived.
arrests: prohibitions.

On Fortinbras; which he, in brief, obeys,
Receives rebuke from Norway, and, in fine,

69 *fine*: conclusion.

70 Makes vow before his uncle never more
To give th'assay of arms against your Majesty:

71 *give . . . against*: challenge.

Whereon old Norway, overcome with joy,
Gives him three thousand crowns in annual fee
And his commission to employ those soldiers

75 So levied, as before, against the Polack,
With an entreaty, herein further shown, [*Gives a paper*]
That it might please you to give quiet pass

77 *quiet pass*: safe passage. Shakespeare seems
to have thought that Denmark lay between
Norway and Poland.

Through your dominions for this enterprise
On such regards of safety and allowance

79 *regards . . . allowance*: terms relating to
safety and permission.

80 As therein are set down.

80 *likes*: pleases. Claudius uses the royal
plural.

King   It likes us well;
And at our more consider'd time we'll read,

81 *at . . . time*: when we have more time to
think about it.

Answer, and think upon this business.
Meantime, we thank you for your well-took labour.

83 *well-took*: well done, successful.

Go to your rest, at night we'll feast together.

85 Most welcome home.

[*Exeunt* Voltemand *and* Cornelius

Polonius

This business is well ended.

86 *expostulate*: inquire into.

My liege and madam, to expostulate

87 *What . . . duty is*: i.e. the nature of
kingship and the duty of a subject.

What majesty should be, what duty is,
Why day is day, night night, and time is time,
Were nothing but to waste night, day, and time.

90 *wit*: intelligence. Polonius utters a wise
maxim — but rarely follows his own advice.

90 Therefore, since brevity is the soul of wit,
And tediousness the limbs and outward flourishes,
I will be brief. Your noble son is mad.
Mad call I it, for to define true madness,

94 *What . . . mad*: it would be mad to try (to define true madness).

95 *let that go*: drop the subject. A satire by the Roman poet Horace argues that the true madness is that of the whole world, not just the deviant individual. Polonius is wise to let the topic 'go by'.
art: tricks of rhetoric.

98 *figure*: rhetorical figure of speech — Polonius proceeds to use more 'figures' in a speech which is tediously artful.

101–3 'Something has had the effect of making Hamlet mad, and madness is a weakness.'

104 'This is the way it is; and what we have now . . .' Polonius has himself lost the 'matter' in all the wordiness of his 'art'.

105 *Perpend*: take note of this.

106 *while she is mine*: i.e. until she is married.

108 *gather and surmise*: draw your own conclusions.

109s.d. *Reads*: Hamlet's letter to Ophelia is a parody of contemporary love-letters. It is necessary to the plot — a dramatic device which has little relevance to the character of the Prince.

110 *beautified*: made beautiful; it is 'a vile phrase' because it implies the use of cosmetics.

112 *these*: i.e. the lines — his letter.
in . . . &c: The letter ('&c' serves for a formal phrase of greeting) is to be kept next to her heart.

114 *be faithful*: tell you truly.

115 *Doubt*: suspect.

116 *move*: Ptolemaic astronomy taught that the sun moved round the earth.

119 *ill at these numbers*: bad at making poetry like this. English love-poets of the 1590s used such 'metaphysical' ideas in their verse.

120 *reckon*: give an account of.

122–3 *whilst . . . him*: so long as my body belongs to me. The Elizabethans were fond of the notion of the human body as a complex mechanism.

125 *more above*: in addition.

126 *fell out*: happened.

What is't but to be nothing else but mad?
95 But let that go.
   Queen   More matter with less art.
Polonius
Madam, I swear I use no art at all.
That he is mad 'tis true; 'tis true 'tis pity;
And pity 'tis 'tis true. A foolish figure—
But farewell it, for I will use no art.
100 Mad let us grant him then. And now remains
That we find out the cause of this effect,
Or rather say the cause of this defect,
For this effect defective comes by cause.
Thus it remains; and the remainder thus:
105 Perpend,
I have a daughter—have while she is mine—
Who in her duty and obedience, mark,
Hath given me this. Now gather and surmise.
[*Reads*]   *To the celestial and my soul's idol, the most*
110 *beautified Ophelia*—That's an ill phrase, a vile phrase,
'beautified' is a vile phrase. But you shall hear—
these; in her excellent white bosom, these, &c.
   Queen
Came this from Hamlet to her?
   Polonius
Good madam, stay awhile, I will be faithful.
115   *Doubt thou the stars are fire,*
   Doubt that the sun doth move,
   Doubt truth to be a liar,
   But never doubt I love.
O dear Ophelia, I am ill at these numbers. I have not art to
120 *reckon my groans. But that I love thee best, O most best,*
believe it. Adieu.
   Thine evermore, most dear lady, whilst this
      machine is to him, Hamlet.
This in obedience hath my daughter shown me,
125 And, more above, hath his solicitings,
As they fell out by time, by means, and place,
All given to mine ear.
   King
But how hath she receiv'd his love?
   Polonius
What do you think of me?

King

130 As of a man faithful and honourable.

Polonius

I would fain prove so. But what might you think,
When I had seen this hot love on the wing—
As I perceiv'd it, I must tell you that,
Before my daughter told me—what might you

135 Or my dear Majesty your queen here think,
If I had play'd the desk or table-book,
Or given my heart a winking mute and dumb,
Or look'd upon this love with idle sight—
What might you think? No, I went round to work,

140 And my young mistress thus I did bespeak:
'Lord Hamlet is a prince out of thy star.
This must not be.' And then I prescripts gave her,
That she should lock herself from his resort,
Admit no messengers, receive no tokens;

145 Which done, she took the fruits of my advice,
And he, repelled—a short tale to make—
Fell into a sadness, then into a fast,
Thence to a watch, thence into a weakness,
Thence to a lightness, and, by this declension,

150 Into the madness wherein now he raves
And all we mourn for.

King   Do you think 'tis this?

Queen

It may be; very like.

Polonius

Hath there been such a time—I would fain know that—
That I have positively said ''Tis so',

155 When it prov'd otherwise?

King   Not that I know.

Polonius

Take this from this if this be otherwise.

Points to his head and shoulder

If circumstances lead me, I will find
Where truth is hid, though it were hid indeed
Within the centre.

King   How may we try it further?

Polonius

160 You know sometimes he walks four hours together
Here in the lobby.

---

131   *would fain*: very much wish to.

136   *play'd . . . table-book*: i.e. been the means
       of communicating. A 'table-book' (see *1*, 5,
       107) was a notebook.
137   *winking*: closed my eyes.
138   *idle sight*: carelessly, uncomprehending.
139   *round*: directly.

141   *out of thy star*: of higher birth (the position
       of the stars was thought to determine social
       status; Polonius demonstrates his humility
       before the Queen).
142   *prescripts*: orders.
143   *resort*: visitation.

147–50 Polonius describes the classical
       symptoms of a melancholy caused by
       unrequited love: depression ('sadness')
       with loss of appetite ('fast') and insomnia
       ('watch'). These bring about general
       weakness and delirium ('lightness'), and
       lead in a downward course ('declension') to
       insanity.

156   Polonius is prepared to bet his life on his
       judgement.

159   *centre*: centre of the earth.
       try: test.

160   *four*: several (no precise number is
       intended).

162   *loose*: Polonius speaks like a farmer.

163   *arras*: tapestry wall-hanging (named after the town of Arras).

165   *thereon*: on account of that.

166   *assistant for a state*: minister of state.

168   *sadly*: seriously.

170   *board*: accost.
      presently: at once.
      give me leave: Polonius hastens the departure of Claudius and Gertrude.

171   *does*: is.

172   *God-a-mercy*: A polite response (= God have mercy on you) to the greeting of a social inferior.

174   *a fishmonger*: Hamlet's intention is undoubtedly offensive, although his meaning is obscure. There seems to be sexual innuendo in the lines, which may have some method in their madness — as Polonius suspects (line 205).

Queen   So he does indeed.
Polonius
At such a time I'll loose my daughter to him.
Be you and I behind an arras then,
Mark the encounter. If he love her not,
165 And be not from his reason fall'n thereon,
Let me be no assistant for a state,
But keep a farm and carters.
            King   We will try it.

Enter Hamlet, *reading on a book*

Queen
But look where sadly the poor wretch comes reading.
Polonius
Away, I do beseech you both, away.
170 I'll board him presently. O give me leave.

        [*Exeunt* King *and* Queen
        and Attendants

How does my good Lord Hamlet?
        Hamlet
Well, God-a-mercy.
        Polonius
Do you know me, my lord?
        Hamlet
Excellent well. You are a fishmonger.
        Polonius
175 Not I, my lord.
        Hamlet
Then I would you were so honest a man.

Polonius

Honest, my lord?

Hamlet

Ay sir. To be honest, as this world goes, is to be one man picked out of ten thousand.

Polonius

180 That's very true, my lord.

Hamlet

For if the sun breed maggots in a dead dog, being a good kissing carrion—Have you a daughter?

Polonius

I have, my lord.

Hamlet

Let her not walk i'th' sun. Conception is a blessing,

185 but as your daughter may conceive—friend, look to't.

Polonius

[Aside] How say you by that? Still harping on my daughter. Yet he knew me not at first; 'a said I was a fishmonger. 'A is far gone. And truly in my youth I

190 suffered much extremity for love, very near this. I'll speak to him again.—What do you read, my lord?

Hamlet

Words, words, words.

Polonius

What is the matter, my lord?

Hamlet

Between who?

Polonius

195 I mean the matter that you read, my lord.

Hamlet

Slanders, sir. For the satirical rogue says here that old men have gray beards, that their faces are wrinkled, their eyes purging thick amber and plum-tree gum, and that they have a plentiful lack of wit,

200 together with most weak hams—all which, sir, though I most powerfully and potently believe, yet I hold it not honesty to have it thus set down. For yourself, sir, shall grow old as I am—if like a crab you could go backward.

Polonius

205 [Aside] Though this be madness, yet there is method in't.—Will you walk out of the air, my lord?

---

181 *sun . . . dog*: Hamlet appears to be reading from his book (which scholars have been unable to identify).

182 *a good kissing carrion*: a carcass (like that of the dead dog) that is ripe for the sun to shine on.

184 *walk i'th'sun*: go about in public.

187 *How . . . by that*: what do you think of that. Polonius is triumphant in his exclamation. *Still*: always. *harping*: constantly sounding one note.

188 *'a said*: he said.

190 *near*: like.

193 *matter*: subject. Hamlet wilfully misunderstands.

196 *satirical rogue*: No particular writer has been identified; the sentiments are commonplace.

198 *purging*: exuding.

199 *gum*: sap (from the bark of the plum-tree).

200 *hams*: thighs.

202 *honesty*: decency. *set down*: written down.

203 *old as*: as old as.

205 *method*: some kind of sense.

206 *walk out of the air*: come inside. Polonius treats Hamlet like an invalid who should avoid cold air.

208 *pregnant*: meaningful. The image is
continued in 'delivered of'.

212 *suddenly*: immediately.

215 *will not*: Such a double negative (with
'cannot') was not uncommon in
Elizabethan usage.

227 'Like any ordinary men.'
229 *button*: The button at the top of a hat was
the highest point.

233 *favours*: i.e. sexual favours.

Hamlet
Into my grave?
Polonius
Indeed, that's out of the air.—[*Aside*] How pregnant
sometimes his replies are—a happiness that often
210 madness hits on, which reason and sanity could not
so prosperously be delivered of. I will leave him and
suddenly contrive the means of meeting between him
and my daughter.—My lord, I will take my leave
of you.
Hamlet
215 You cannot, sir, take from me anything that I will
not more willingly part withal—except my life,
except my life, except my life.
Polonius
Fare you well, my lord.
Hamlet
These tedious old fools.

Enter Rosencrantz *and* Guildenstern

Polonius
220 You go to seek the Lord Hamlet. There he is.
Rosencrantz
God save you, sir.   [*Exit* Polonius
Guildenstern
My honoured lord.
Rosencrantz
My most dear lord.
Hamlet
My excellent good friends. How dost thou,
225 Guildenstern? Ah, Rosencrantz. Good lads, how do
you both?
Rosencrantz
As the indifferent children of the earth.
Guildenstern
Happy in that we are not over-happy: on
Fortune's cap we are not the very button.
Hamlet
230 Nor the soles of her shoe?
Rosencrantz
Neither, my lord.
Hamlet
Then you live about her waist, or in the middle of
her favours?

234   *privates*: private parts (i.e. the sexual
        organs) of the body.

236   *strumpet*: It was commonplace to speak in
        such a way of the fickleness of Fortune.

238   *Then . . . near*: then the world must be
        coming to an end.

245   *confines*: places of confinement.
246   *wards*: cells.

254   *count*: consider.

257–9 *the very substance . . . dream*: all that an
        ambitious man achieves is no more than a
        shadow of what he dreamed of.

Guildenstern
Faith, her privates we.
Hamlet
235 In the secret parts of Fortune? O most true, she is a
strumpet. What news?
Rosencrantz
None, my lord, but the world's grown honest.
Hamlet
Then is doomsday near. But your news is not true.
Let me question more in particular. What have you,
240 my good friends, deserved at the hands of Fortune
that she sends you to prison hither?
Guildenstern
Prison, my lord?
Hamlet
Denmark's a prison.
Rosencrantz
Then is the world one.
Hamlet
245 A goodly one, in which there are many confines,
wards, and dungeons, Denmark being one o'th'
worst.
Rosencrantz
We think not so, my lord.
Hamlet
Why, then 'tis none to you; for there is nothing
250 either good or bad but thinking makes it so. To me
it is a prison.
Rosencrantz
Why, then your ambition makes it one: 'tis too narrow
for your mind.
Hamlet
O God, I could be bounded in a nutshell and count
255 myself a king of infinite space—were it not that I
have bad dreams.
Guildenstern
Which dreams indeed are ambition; for the very
substance of the ambitious is merely the shadow of a
dream.
Hamlet
260 A dream itself is but a shadow.
Rosencrantz
Truly, and I hold ambition of so airy and light a
quality that it is but a shadow's shadow.

263–4 Hamlet now pursues the argument to ridiculous lengths: if ambition is as insubstantial as Rosencrantz asserts, then the real people must be those without ambition ('beggars'), and the ambitious men ('monarchs' and 'heroes') must be shadows of these. The heroes are 'outstretched' because their ambition makes them stretch out beyond themselves.

265 *fay*: faith.
   reason: carry on this kind of argument.
266 *wait upon*: escort, attend.
267 *sort*: class.
268 *to . . . man*: to tell you the truth.
269 *the beaten way*: Hamlet abandons his verbal tricks and approaches more directly.
270 *make you*: are you doing.

274 *too dear*: not worth.
275 *inclining*: wish.
   free: voluntary.

278 *but*: Hamlet already suspects Rosencrantz and Guildenstern, and assumes that they will not give him a straight answer.
280 *colour*: disguise.

283 *conjure you*: ask you solemnly.
284 *rights of*: what is due to.
   consonancy: harmonious agreement.
286 *what more dear*: whatever there is that is more precious.
   a better proposer: one more skilled at framing oaths.
287 *even*: straightforward.

290 *have an eye of*: am watching.
291 *hold not off*: speak freely.

Hamlet
Then are our beggars bodies, and our monarchs
and outstretched heroes the beggars' shadows. Shall
265 we to th' court? For by my fay, I cannot reason.
Rosencrantz and **Guildenstern**
We'll wait upon you.
Hamlet
No such matter. I will not sort you with the rest of
my servants; for, to speak to you like an honest man,
I am most dreadfully attended. But in the beaten
270 way of friendship, what make you at Elsinore?
Rosencrantz
To visit you, my lord, no other occasion.
Hamlet
Beggar that I am, I am even poor in thanks, but I
thank you. And sure, dear friends, my thanks are too
dear a halfpenny. Were you not sent for? Is it your
275 own inclining? Is it a free visitation? Come, come,
deal justly with me. Come, come. Nay, speak.
Guildenstern
What should we say, my lord?
Hamlet
Anything but to th' purpose. You were sent for, and
there is a kind of confession in your looks, which your
280 modesties have not craft enough to colour. I know
the good King and Queen have sent for you.
Rosencrantz
To what end, my lord?
Hamlet
That, you must teach me. But let me conjure you,
by the rights of our fellowship, by the consonancy of
285 our youth, by the obligation of our ever-preserved
love, and by what more dear a better proposer
can charge you withal, be even and direct with me
whether you were sent for or no.
Rosencrantz
[*Aside to* Guildenstern] What say you?
Hamlet
290 Nay, then I have an eye of you. If you love me,
hold not off.
Guildenstern
My lord, we were sent for.

293-5 By anticipating their answer, Hamlet will forestall ('prevent') the revelation ('discovery'), and they will not need to break their promise of secrecy.

296 *forgone . . . exercises*: neglected my usual exercise.

297 *goes . . . disposition*: I am so depressed. Hamlet's description of his melancholy gathers together some classical commonplaces, and makes of them a new and uniquely powerful account of this state of mind.

298 *frame*: structure.

299 *a sterile promontory*: The image is of a barren outcrop of land jutting out into an unknown sea.

300 *brave*: splendid.

301 *fretted*: adorned. The term is especially used to describe ceilings with gilded decoration, and critics have suggested that in this speech Hamlet points to the Elizabethan theatre — perhaps Shakespeare's own Globe — as an emblem.
golden fire: Ceilings (and the canopy over the Elizabethan stage known as 'the heavens') were sometimes painted with the sun and stars in gold.

302 *pestilent . . . vapours*: It was a common belief that infectious diseases were carried on the air.

303 *piece of work*: masterpiece of craftsmanship.

305 *express*: direct. The adjective seems to apply to 'moving' rather than 'form'.

306 *apprehension*: power of understanding.

307 *paragon*: pattern of excellence.

308 *quintessence of dust*: dust in its finest form; the 'quintessence' is the fifth, most refined, form of the four elements — and in Genesis 3:19 the man is told that 'dust thou art, and unto dust shalt thou be turned again'.

315 *Lenten entertainment*: a poor reception. Lent is a time of fasting (and in the seventeenth century, London theatres were closed during Lent).

316 *coted*: overtook (the metaphor is from hound coursing).

Hamlet

I will tell you why; so shall my anticipation prevent
your discovery, and your secrecy to the King and
295 Queen moult no feather. I have of late, but wherefore
I know not, lost all my mirth, forgone all custom
of exercises; and indeed it goes so heavily with my
disposition that this goodly frame the earth seems to
me a sterile promontory, this most excellent canopy
300 the air, look you, this brave o'erhanging firmament,
this majestical roof fretted with golden fire, why, it
appeareth nothing to me but a foul and pestilent
congregation of vapours. What piece of work is a man,
how noble in reason, how infinite in faculties, in form
305 and moving how express and admirable, in action
how like an angel, in apprehension how like a god:
the beauty of the world, the paragon of animals—
and yet, to me, what is this quintessence of dust?
Man delights not me—nor woman neither, though
310 by your smiling you seem to say so.

Rosencrantz

My lord, there was no such stuff in my thoughts.

Hamlet

Why did ye laugh then, when I said man delights
not me?

Rosencrantz

To think, my lord, if you delight not in man, what
315 Lenten entertainment the players shall receive from
you. We coted them on the way, and hither are they
coming to offer you service.

319 *tribute on*: receive what is due to him. The
Prince proceeds to list some of the stock
characters in any acting company, and their
characteristic actions.

320 *target*: small shield.

321 *gratis*: for nothing.
humorous: passionate (it was thought that
passions arose from an imbalance of the
four temperamental humours).

323 *tickle a th' sear*: easily amused; the image
is of a gun whose trigger catch ('sear') is
very sensitive ('tickle').
say: speak. The stock female character was
evidently garrulous.

324 *blank verse*: iambic pentameters — the
regular form of dramatic verse (as used in
Hamlet).

326 *halt*: go lame, i.e. scan badly.

326 *wont*: accustomed.

327 *the tragedians of the city*: the London
company. Denmark is temporarily
forgotten, and Shakespeare seems to show a
personal interest in the fortunes of the
players.

328 *chances it*: does it happen.
travel: are on tour.
residence: permanent theatre.

330 *their inhibition*: they have been stopped
from acting.

331 *late innovation*: recent uprising
(Shakespeare seems to be alluding to the
rebellion led by the Earl of Essex in
February, 1601).

332 *estimation*: popularity.

333 *followed*: frequented.

336–58 These lines about the child actors and the
'War of the Theatres' (line 340) were
omitted in Q2 — perhaps because they
were no longer immediately topical. The
'children' were boys culled from the royal
chapel choirs, and given special training in
the art of elocution. They began
performing in London at the Blackfriars
Theatre towards the end of 1600.

336 *their . . . pace*: the standard of their work is
as high as ever it was.

337 *eyrie*: nestful.
little eyases: young hawks (which squawk
loudly).

338 *on the top of question*: louder than anyone
else.
tyrannically: excessively.

Hamlet

He that plays the king shall be welcome—his Majesty
shall have tribute on me, the adventurous knight
320 shall use his foil and target, the lover shall not sigh
gratis, the humorous man shall end his part in peace,
the clown shall make those laugh whose lungs are
tickle a th' sear, and the lady shall say her mind
freely—or the blank verse shall halt for't. What
325 players are they?

Rosencrantz

Even those you were wont to take such delight in,
the tragedians of the city.

Hamlet

How chances it they travel? Their residence, both
in reputation and profit, was better both ways.

Rosencrantz

330 I think their inhibition comes by the means of the
late innovation.

Hamlet

Do they hold the same estimation they did when I
was in the city? Are they so followed?

Rosencrantz

No, indeed are they not.

Hamlet

335 How comes it? Do they grow rusty?

Rosencrantz

Nay, their endeavour keeps in the wonted pace; but
there is, sir, an eyrie of children, little eyases, that
cry out on the top of question, and are most tyrannically clapped for't. These are now the fashion, and

340 *berattle*: abuse.
common stages: public theatres. The boy
actors performed in the private playhouses,
where admission was more expensive. Ben
Jonson first used the phrase 'common
stages' in a play, *Cynthia's Revels*, which
was performed by children in the winter of
1600; the play satirizes the regular theatres
— actors, dramatists, and audiences alike
— and initiated a period of rivalry between
'public' and 'private' playhouses which
earned the name 'War of the Theatres'.

341 *wearing rapiers . . . goose-quills*: gentlemen
wearing swords are afraid of being ridiculed
in the satires written for the children.
'Goose-quills' were the usual writing
instruments of the Elizabethans.

344 *escotted*: provided for.
quality: profession.

345 *no . . . sing*: after their voices break (when
they would be dismissed from the choirs).

347–8 *means are no better*: no better means of
earning a living.

349 *exclaim . . . succession*: insult the condition
they must come to.

350 *much . . . sides*: Shakespeare alludes to the
rivalry (led by the dramatists Jonson and
Dekker) between the child actors in private
playhouses and the adult companies in the
public theatres.

351 *the nation*: i.e. the audiences.
tar: incite. The word is used in dog-
fighting.

352–4 'For a time the only plays that made
money were those concerned with this
subject.'

353 *poet*: dramatist.
went to cuffs: came to (usually metaphorical)
blows.

356 *much . . . brains*: a great battle of wits.

357 *carry it away*: have any success.

358 *Hercules and his load*: This was the sign of
the Globe Theatre, where many of
Shakespeare's plays (including *Hamlet*)
were performed; the line seems to suggest
that the boys' success had affected even
Shakespeare's company. Hercules was the
superman of classical legend, who for a
time carried the whole world on his
shoulders; such mythical characters were
popular with the dramatists writing for the
children's companies.

360 *make mouths*: pull faces; Hamlet compares
the changed tastes of theatre audiences with
the swing in public affection for the new
king of Denmark.

340 so berattle the common stages—so they call them—
that many wearing rapiers are afraid of goose-quills
and dare scarce come thither.
  Hamlet
What, are they children? Who maintains 'em?
How are they escotted? Will they pursue the quality
345 no longer than they can sing? Will they not say
afterwards, if they should grow themselves to common
players—as it is most like, if their means are no
better—their writers do them wrong to make them
exclaim against their own succession?
  Rosencrantz
350 Faith, there has been much to do on both sides; and
the nation holds it no sin to tar them to controversy.
There was for a while no money bid for argument
unless the poet and the player went to cuffs in the
question.
  Hamlet
355 Is't possible?
  Guildenstern
O, there has been much throwing about of brains.
  Hamlet
Do the boys carry it away?
  Rosencrantz
Ay, that they do, my lord, Hercules and his load too.

  Hamlet
It is not very strange; for my uncle is King of Den-
360 mark, and those that would make mouths at him
while my father lived give twenty, forty, fifty, a
hundred ducats apiece for his picture in little.
'Sblood, there is something in this more than
natural, if philosophy could find it out.

A flourish of trumpets

  Guildenstern
365 There are the players.

362 *ducats*: gold coins.
   little: miniature.
363 *'Sblood*: by Christ's blood.
364 *philosophy*: science — natural philosophy.
364s.d. *A flourish of trumpets*: The actors' usual
   announcement of their arrival.
366–71 Hamlet insists on shaking hands with
   Rosencrantz and Guildenstern, so that his
   reception of them will show as warm as his
   welcome to the players; his real feelings are
   left in doubt.
367 *appurtenance*: proper accompaniment.
368 *fashion and ceremony*: conventional
   behaviour.
369 *garb*: manner.
   my extent: the welcome I extend.
371 *entertainment*: a friendly reception.
374 A madman's moods were thought to be
   affected by the weather; Hamlet is warning
   that he has not completely lost his senses.
375 *know*: can tell the difference between.
   handsaw: hernshaw (a kind of heron —
   another bird of prey).
377 *at each ear a hearer*: both of you listen.

380 *Happily*: perhaps.
381 *twice*: for the second time.

383–4 Hamlet pretends to be carrying on a
   conversation.

386 *Roscius*: The most famous of Roman actors.

389 *Buzz*: A contemptuous dismissal of stale
   news.

392–5 Polonius lists different kinds of drama;
   his catalogue starts seriously enough, but
   degenerates into self-parody. However
   Cymbeline, one of Shakespeare's last plays,
   can best be described as 'tragical-comical-
   historical-pastoral'.

Hamlet
Gentlemen, you are welcome to Elsinore. Your
hands, come then. Th'appurtenance of welcome is
fashion and ceremony. Let me comply with you in
this garb—lest my extent to the players, which I tell
370 you must show fairly outwards, should more appear
like entertainment than yours. You are welcome.
But my uncle-father and aunt-mother are deceived.
Guildenstern
In what, my dear lord?
Hamlet
I am but mad north-north-west. When the wind is
375 southerly, I know a hawk from a handsaw.

Enter Polonius

Polonius
Well be with you, gentlemen.
Hamlet
Hark you, Guildenstern, and you too—at each ear
a hearer. That great baby you see there is not yet out
of his swaddling-clouts.
Rosencrantz
380 Happily he is the second time come to them, for they
say an old man is twice a child.
Hamlet
I will prophesy he comes to tell me of the players.
Mark it.—You say right, sir, a Monday morning,
'twas then indeed.
Polonius
385 My lord, I have news to tell you.
Hamlet
My lord, I have news to tell you. When Roscius was
an actor in Rome—
Polonius
The actors are come hither, my lord.
Hamlet
Buzz, buzz.
Polonius
390 Upon my honour—
Hamlet
Then came each actor on his ass—
Polonius
The best actors in the world, either for tragedy,
comedy, history, pastoral, pastoral-comical, historical-

395 *scene . . . unlimited*: These categories are not known; perhaps Polonius is trying to make a distinction between works with a single location and those where the action moves from place to place.

396 *Seneca . . . Plautus*: Major Roman dramatists, who greatly influenced Shakespeare's own writing: his tragedies — from *Titus Andronicus* to *King Lear* — owe much to Seneca; and *The Comedy of Errors* is based on two plays by Plautus.

397 *the law . . . liberty*: This phrase has never been satisfactorily explained; Polonius seems to be commending the actors whether they follow the rules or play with more licence.
these: i.e. the actors.

399 *Jephthah, judge of Israel*: A ballad, dating from 1567, tells the story of Jephthah (see Judges, 11:30–40), who sacrificed his only daughter for political ends — just as Polonius will do. Hamlet quotes lines from this song.

404 *passing*: exceedingly.

405 *Still*: always.

409 *that follows not*: i.e. that Polonius should love his daughter as Jephthah did.

412–14 Hamlet continues to quote the ballad ('chanson') which is called 'pious' because of its biblical subject:
    And as by lot, God wot
    It came to pass most like it was
    Great wars there should be,
    And who should be the chief but he.

415 *row*: stanza.

416 *abridgement*: interruption — which cuts short Hamlet's speech *and* shortens the time with entertainment.

419 *valanced*: fringed (with a beard).

420 *beard*: confront.

421 *my young lady*: Hamlet greets the boy actor who will play the female roles.
By'r lady: Our Lady (the Virgin Mary).

422 *is nearer to heaven*: you have grown taller.

423 *chopine*: the high sole on a Venetian fashion shoe.

424–5 Hamlet's witticism makes play with several notions: (i) a sweet singing voice is called 'golden'; (ii) gold coins were often clipped ('cracked') for their gold, and if this extended inside the ring surrounding the monarch's head ('within the ring') they ceased to be legal tender ('uncurrent'); (iii) there were many jests comparing a woman's

---

pastoral, tragical-historical, tragical-comical-
historical-pastoral, scene individable, or poem
unlimited. Seneca cannot be too heavy, nor Plautus too
light. For the law of writ, and the liberty, these are
the only men.
        Hamlet
O Jephthah, judge of Israel, what a treasure hadst
thou!
        Polonius
What a treasure had he, my lord?
        Hamlet
Why,
    One fair daughter and no more,
    The which he loved passing well.
        Polonius
[*Aside*] Still on my daughter.
        Hamlet
Am I not i'th' right, old Jephthah?
        Polonius
If you call me Jephthah, my lord, I have a daughter
that I love passing well.
        Hamlet
Nay, that follows not.
        Polonius
What follows then, my lord?
        Hamlet
Why,
    As by lot God wot,
and then, you know,
    It came to pass, as most like it was.
The first row of the pious chanson will show you
more, for look where my abridgement comes.

        Enter the Players

You are welcome, masters. Welcome, all.—I am
glad to see thee well.—Welcome, good friends.—O,
old friend, why, thy face is valanced since I saw thee
last. Com'st thou to beard me in Denmark?—What,
my young lady and mistress! By'r lady, your ladyship
is nearer to heaven than when I saw you last by
the altitude of a chopine. Pray God your voice, like a
piece of uncurrent gold, be not cracked within the
ring.—Masters, you are all welcome. We'll e'en to't

lost virginity to a cracked coin; and (iv) if the boy's voice has broken, and so 'cracked' in its 'ring', it will be useless ('uncurrent') for the women's parts.

425 *e'en to't*: have a try at it.

426 *like . . . see*: In fact the French were expert at hunting with the falcon, a bird trained to take a specific quarry.

427 *straight*: at once.

428 *quality*: professional skill.

432 *play*: Hamlet's reference is imprecise, but a play similar to the one he describes was written for a children's company by Shakespeare's great rival, Christopher Marlowe; and the style of Marlowe's *Dido Queen of Carthage* is suggested in the speech begun by Hamlet and finished by the Player. Shakespeare neither parodies nor imitates Marlowe, but strives to give the sense of a play which Hamlet *might* have seen.

433 *caviare to the general*: Caviare was a new delicacy at this time, and regarded as a taste for the connoisseur, not for ordinary people.
    received: considered.

434–5 *whose . . . mine*: who knew more about these things than I do.

435 *digested*: organized.

436 *modesty*: restraint.
    cunning: skill.

437 *one*: someone.
    sallets: tasty bits — dirty jokes.

438 *matter in the phrase*: fancy language.

439 *affection*: affectation.

441 *more handsome than fine*: showing even more natural ability than acquired skill.

442 *Aeneas' tale*: The story of the sack of Troy is told in Book II of Virgil's *Aeneid*; the hero recounts his tale to Dido in Act 2 of Marlowe's play.

444 *Priam*: the Trojan king.

446 *Pyrrhus*: This was the son of the Greek hero Achilles, who led the final attack on Troy in revenge for the death of his father.
    th'Hyrcania beast: The tigers of Hyrcania (a province of Asia Minor, near the Caspian Sea) were famous in literature for their ferocity.

448 *sable arms*: black armour. The terms are from heraldry.

450 *couched . . . horse*: The Greeks entered Troy in a wooden horse which proved fateful ('ominous') to the city.

like French falconers, fly at anything we see. We'll have a speech straight. Come, give us a taste of your quality. Come, a passionate speech.

First Player
What speech, my good lord?
    Hamlet
430 I heard thee speak me a speech once, but it was never acted, or if it was, not above once—for the play, I remember, pleased not the million, 'twas caviare to the general. But it was, as I received it—and others, whose judgments in such matters cried in
435 the top of mine—an excellent play, well digested in the scenes, set down with as much modesty as cunning. I remember one said there were no sallets in the lines to make the matter savoury, nor no matter in the phrase that might indict the author of affection,
440 but called it an honest method, as wholesome as sweet, and by very much more handsome than fine. One speech in't I chiefly loved—'twas Aeneas' tale to Dido—and thereabout of it especially when he speaks of Priam's slaughter. If it live in your memory,
445 begin at this line—let me see, let me see—
    The rugged Pyrrhus, like th' Hyrcanian beast—
    'Tis not so. It begins with Pyrrhus—
    The rugged Pyrrhus, he whose sable arms,
    Black as his purpose, did the night resemble
450 *When he lay couched in the ominous horse,*

451 *complexion*: figure.
452 *dismal*: calamitous.
453 *total gules*: red all over.
   trick'd: spotted.

455–7 The blood has been baked into a crust by
   the hot air of the burning streets, whose
   flames shed a cruel light, like the fires of
   hell, to illumine the murder of their king.
458 *o'ersized*: smeared over (as with size).
459 *like carbuncles*: glowing fiery red.
   Carbuncles (precious stones) were thought
   to have their own light, and to shine in the
   dark.
460 *grandsire*: Priam was reputed to have
   fathered fifty sons.
461 *proceed you*: now you carry on.

464 *Anon*: soon afterwards.
465 *too short*: with blows that fell too short.
   antique sword: Priam, the old king, was
   trying to wield the sword he had fought
   with in his youth (see *Aeneid* ii. 509–11).
467 *Repugnant to command*: refusing to be
   commanded.
469 *fell*: cruel. Priam would have been
   unbalanced by the mighty broadsword.
470 *unnerved*: enfeebled.
   senseless: without human feelings.
   Ilium: the citadel of Troy.
471 *flaming top*: burning towers.
472 *his*: its.
473 *Takes . . . ear*: i.e. the noise makes Pyrrhus
   stop.
474 *declining*: descending.
   milky: white.
476 *painted*: in a picture.
477–8 Pyrrhus was momentarily impotent,
   unable to accomplish his desire — just as
   Hamlet will know himself to be.
479 *against*: just before.
480 *rack*: cloud-formation.
482 *hush*: silent.
483 *region*: skies.
484 'His desire for vengeance has re-awakened,
   and Pyrrhus sets to work afresh.'
485 *Cyclops' hammers*: In classical mythology,
   the Cyclops were giants who assisted the
   god Vulcan to make armour for the gods.
486 *Mars*: The classical god of war.
   for proof eterne: to be eternally resistant.
487 *remorse*: pity.
489 *strumpet Fortune*: see lines 235–6.
490 *synod*: assembly.

Hath now this dread and black complexion smear'd
With heraldry more dismal. Head to foot
Now is he total gules, horridly trick'd
With blood of fathers, mothers, daughters, sons,
455 *Bak'd and impasted with the parching streets,*
That lend a tyrannous and a damned light
To their lord's murder. Roasted in wrath and fire,
And thus o'ersized with coagulate gore,
With eyes like carbuncles, the hellish Pyrrhus
460 *Old grandsire Priam seeks.*
So proceed you.
       Polonius
'Fore God, my lord, well spoken, with good accent
and good discretion.
       First Player   *Anon he finds him,*
465 *Striking too short at Greeks. His antique sword,*
Rebellious to his arm, lies where it falls,
Repugnant to command. Unequal match'd,
Pyrrhus at Priam drives, in rage strikes wide;
But with the whiff and wind of his fell sword
470 *Th'unnerved father falls. Then senseless Ilium,*
Seeming to feel this blow, with flaming top
Stoops to his base, and with a hideous crash
Takes prisoner Pyrrhus' ear. For lo, his sword,
Which was declining on the milky head
475 *Of reverend Priam, seem'd i'th' air to stick;*
So, as a painted tyrant, Pyrrhus stood,
And like a neutral to his will and matter,
Did nothing.
But as we often see against some storm
480 *A silence in the heavens, the rack stand still,*
The bold winds speechless, and the orb below
As hush as death, anon the dreadful thunder
Doth rend the region; so after Pyrrhus' pause
Aroused vengeance sets him new awork,
485 *And never did the Cyclops' hammers fall*
On Mars's armour, forg'd for proof eterne,
With less remorse than Pyrrhus' bleeding sword
Now falls on Priam.
Out, out, thou strumpet Fortune! All you gods
490 *In general synod take away her power,*
Break all the spokes and fellies from her wheel,
And bowl the round nave down the hill of heaven
As low as to the fiends.

491 *her wheel*: The goddess Fortune is
traditionally represented with a wheel,
which constantly turns, as an emblem of
inconstancy; the 'fellies' are the curved
pieces which form the rim.

492 *nave*: hub.
495 *shall*: will have to go.
496 *a jig*: a comic turn, usually with song and
dance, which often followed a serious play
in the theatre.
497 *Hecuba*: The wife of King Priam, she
became the epitome of suffering
womanhood when she witnessed the deaths
of her husband and children at the
destruction of Troy.
498 *mobbled*: with face muffled. Even Hamlet
seems to question this obscure word.
502 *bisson rheum*: blinding tears.
clout: piece of old cloth.
503 *late*: recently.
504 *all o'erteemed*: thoroughly exhausted with
child-bearing.
506 *tongue . . . steep'd*: bitter words.
513–4 *made . . . gods*: drawn pity from the stars
like milk ('milch' = milk-giving), and
caused the gods to share sympathetically in
her sufferings — as they do in Ovid's
description of the scene (*Metamorphoses*,
XIII, 573).
515 *whe'er*: whether.
519 *bestowed*: accommodated.
used: treated.
520 *abstract*: summary.
521 *you were better*: it would be better for you.
523 *their desert*: what they deserve.
524 *God's bodkin*: by God's precious body.
525 *after*: according to.
scape: escape.
whipping: Travelling players like these
could be whipped as vagabonds unless they
were protected by some nobleman as his
'servants'.

Polonius
This is too long.
Hamlet
495 It shall to the barber's with your beard.—Prithee
say on. He's for a jig or a tale of bawdry, or he sleeps.
Say on, come to Hecuba.
First Player
But who—ah, woe!—had seen the mobbled queen—
Hamlet
'The mobbled queen'.
Polonius
500 That's good.
First Player
Run barefoot up and down, threat'ning the flames
With bisson rheum, a clout upon that head
Where late the diadem stood, and, for a robe,
About her lank and all o'erteemed loins
505 *A blanket, in th'alarm of fear caught up—*
Who this had seen, with tongue in venom steep'd,
'Gainst Fortune's state would treason have pronounc'd.
But if the gods themselves did see her then,
When she saw Pyrrhus make malicious sport
510 *In mincing with his sword her husband's limbs,*
The instant burst of clamour that she made,
Unless things mortal move them not at all,
Would have made milch the burning eyes of heaven
And passion in the gods.
Polonius
515 Look whe'er he has not turned his colour and has
tears in's eyes. Prithee no more.
Hamlet
'Tis well. I'll have thee speak out the rest of this
soon.—Good my lord, will you see the players well
bestowed? Do you hear, let them be well used, for
520 they are the abstract and brief chronicles of the time.
After your death you were better have a bad epitaph
than their ill report while you live.
Polonius
My lord, I will use them according to their desert.
Hamlet
God's bodkin, man, much better. Use every man
525 after his desert, and who shall scape whipping? Use
them after your own honour and dignity: the less

they deserve, the more merit is in your bounty. Take
them in.

Polonius

Come, sirs.

Hamlet

530 Follow him, friends. We'll hear a play tomorrow.
[*To* First Player] Dost thou hear me, old friend? Can
you play *The Murder of Gonzago*?

First Player

Ay, my lord.

Hamlet

We'll ha't tomorrow night. You could for a need

535 study a speech of some dozen or sixteen lines, which
I would set down and insert in't, could you not?

First Player

Ay, my lord.

Hamlet

Very well. [*To all the* Players] Follow that lord, and
look you mock him not.   [*Exeunt* Polonius *and* Players

540 [*To* Rosencrantz *and* Guildenstern] My good friends,
I'll leave you till night. You are welcome to Elsinore.

Rosencrantz

Good my lord.   [*Exeunt* Rosencrantz *and* Guildenstern

Hamlet

Ay, so, God buy to you. Now I am alone.
O what a rogue and peasant slave am I!

545 Is it not monstrous that this player here,
But in a fiction, in a dream of passion,
Could force his soul so to his own conceit
That from her working all his visage wann'd,
Tears in his eyes, distraction in his aspect,

550 A broken voice, and his whole function suiting
With forms to his conceit? And all for nothing!
For Hecuba!
What's Hecuba to him, or he to her,
That he should weep for her? What would he do

555 Had he the motive and the cue for passion
That I have? He would drown the stage with tears,
And cleave the general ear with horrid speech,
Make mad the guilty and appal the free,
Confound the ignorant, and amaze indeed

560 The very faculties of eyes and ears.

---

534   *for a need*: if necessary.

535   *study*: learn.

543   *God buy*: goodbye.

544   *peasant*: base.

546   *But*: merely.
        dream: pretence.

547–51 *force . . . conceit*: Hamlet praises the
        actor's skill, which controls his whole body
        and expresses his feigned emotion.

547   *conceit*: imagination.

548   *her*: i.e. the soul's.
        his visage wann'd: his face turned pale.

549   *aspect*: looks (the word is accented on the
        second syllable).

550   *function*: energy.

551   *forms*: gestures.

557   *cleave the general ear*: burst everyone's ears.
        horrid: horrifying.

558   *free*: innocent.

559   *amaze*: bewilder.

562 *muddy-mettled*: dull-spirited.
  peak: mope.
563 *John-a-dreams*: a dreamer.
  unpregnant of: not stirred to action by.
565 *property*: body (his proper person).
566 *defeat*: destruction.
567 *pate*: head.
568 *Plucks . . . beard*: To pull a man's beard
  was a great insult.
569–70 *gives . . . lungs*: calls me a downright liar,
  making me swallow the insult.
570 *me*: to me.
572 *'Swounds*: by God's wounds.
  take it: accept the insult.
573 *pigeon-liver'd . . . gall*: The pigeon was
  thought to secrete no gall in its liver; and
  gall was said to be the cause of bitterness
  and rancour.
574 *To . . . bitter*: which would make me resent
  such tyranny.
575 *region kites*: kites in the sky.
577 *Remorseless*: pitiless.
  kindless: unnatural (see *1, 2, 65*).
578 *brave*: admirable.
582 *drab*: prostitute.
583 *scullion*: kitchen servant. (The reading is
  from F and Q1; Q2 has 'stallion'.)
584 *About*: get to work.
586 *cunning of the scene*: art of the presentation.
587 *presently*: instantly.
592 *Before*: in front of. Hamlet seems to be
  guiding the audience's attention.
593 *tent*: probe — as with a surgical instrument.
  blench: flinch.

594–9 *The spirit . . . damn me*: Hamlet voices
  his own doubts about the Ghost he has
  seen: he fears this may have been the devil
  who, in likeness of the murdered King, was
  taking advantage of Hamlet's natural
  depression in order to lead him to eternal
  damnation.
598 *potent . . . spirits*: The devil (it was thought)
  could both intensify and exploit such
  moods as Hamlet has described.
600 *relative*: substantial, able to be
  communicated.
  this: the Ghost's words.

Yet I,
A dull and muddy-mettled rascal, peak
Like John-a-dreams, unpregnant of my cause,
And can say nothing—no, not for a king,
565 Upon whose property and most dear life
A damn'd defeat was made. Am I a coward?
Who calls me villain, breaks my pate across,
Plucks off my beard and blows it in my face,
Tweaks me by the nose, gives me the lie i'th' throat
570 As deep as to the lungs—who does me this?
Ha!
'Swounds, I should take it: for it cannot be
But I am pigeon-liver'd and lack gall
To make oppression bitter, or ere this
575 I should ha' fatted all the region kites
With this slave's offal. Bloody, bawdy villain!
Remorseless, treacherous, lecherous, kindless villain!
Why, what an ass am I! This is most brave,
That I, the son of a dear father murder'd,
580 Prompted to my revenge by heaven and hell,
Must like a whore unpack my heart with words
And fall a-cursing like a very drab,
A scullion! Fie upon't! Foh!
About, my brains. Hum—I have heard
585 That guilty creatures sitting at a play
Have, by the very cunning of the scene,
Been struck so to the soul that presently
They have proclaim'd their malefactions.
For murder, though it have no tongue, will speak
590 With most miraculous organ. I'll have these players
Play something like the murder of my father
Before mine uncle. I'll observe his looks;
I'll tent him to the quick. If 'a do blench,
I know my course. The spirit that I have seen
595 May be a devil, and the devil hath power
T'assume a pleasing shape, yea, and perhaps,
Out of my weakness and my melancholy,
As he is very potent with such spirits,
Abuses me to damn me. I'll have grounds
600 More relative than this. The play's the thing
Wherein I'll catch the conscience of the King.   [*Exit*

Act 3

Act 3   Scene 1

The King and Queen question Rosencrantz and
Guildenstern, but they get no satisfaction about
Hamlet's state of mind; so Claudius and Polonius
proceed with their plot to use Ophelia to spy on
the Prince. Hamlet enters in deep despair, voicing
his misery in the play's most famous soliloquy. He
encounters Ophelia, and quarrels with her — and
his angry words are overheard. The King unfolds
the next stage of his plot: he will send Hamlet to
England.

1   *by no . . . conference*: not in the course of
    conversation.
2   *puts on*: assumes. The King appears to
    suspect Hamlet's 'antic disposition'.
5   *distracted*: mentally confused.
7   *forward*: willing.
    sounded: questioned.
12 *disposition*: behaviour.
13 *Niggard*: reluctant. Rosencrantz seems to
    contradict the description given by
    Guildenstern in line 7.
14 *assay*: persuade.
16 *fell out*: happened.
17 *o'erraught*: overtook.

Scene 1

Enter King, Queen, Polonius, Ophelia,
Rosencrantz, Guildenstern

King
And can you by no drift of conference
Get from him why he puts on this confusion,
Grating so harshly all his days of quiet
With turbulent and dangerous lunacy?

Rosencrantz
5   He does confess he feels himself distracted,
But from what cause 'a will by no means speak.

Guildenstern
Nor do we find him forward to be sounded,
But with a crafty madness keeps aloof
When we would bring him on to some confession
10 Of his true state.   **Queen**   Did he receive you well?

Rosencrantz
Most like a gentleman.

Guildenstern
But with much forcing of his disposition.

Rosencrantz
Niggard of question, but of our demands
Most free in his reply.   **Queen**   Did you assay him
15 To any pastime?

Rosencrantz
Madam, it so fell out that certain players
We o'erraught on the way. Of these we told him,
And there did seem in him a kind of joy
To hear of it. They are here about the court,
20 And, as I think, they have already order
This night to play before him.

Polonius   'Tis most true,
And he beseech'd me to entreat your Majesties
To hear and see the matter.
     King
With all my heart; and it doth much content me
25 To hear him so inclin'd.
Good gentlemen, give him a further edge,
And drive his purpose into these delights.
     Rosencrantz
We shall, my lord.
        [*Exeunt* Rosencrantz *and* Guildenstern
     King   Sweet Gertrude, leave us too,
For we have closely sent for Hamlet hither
30 That he, as 'twere by accident, may here
Affront Ophelia.
Her father and myself, lawful espials,
We'll so bestow ourselves that, seeing unseen,
We may of their encounter frankly judge,
35 And gather by him, as he is behav'd,
If't be th'affliction of his love or no
That thus he suffers for.
     Queen   I shall obey you.
And for your part, Ophelia, I do wish
That your good beauties be the happy cause
40 Of Hamlet's wildness; so shall I hope your virtues
Will bring him to his wonted way again,
To both your honours.
     Ophelia   Madam, I wish it may.
        [*Exit* Queen
     Polonius
Ophelia, walk you here.—Gracious, so please you,
We will bestow ourselves.—Read on this book,
45 That show of such an exercise may colour
Your loneliness.—We are oft to blame in this,
'Tis too much prov'd, that with devotion's visage
And pious action we do sugar o'er
The devil himself.
     King [*Aside*]   O 'tis too true.
50 How smart a lash that speech doth give my
    conscience.
The harlot's cheek, beautied with plast'ring art,
Is not more ugly to the thing that helps it
Than is my deed to my most painted word.
O heavy burden!

26 *edge*: encouragement.
27 *drive his purpose*: stimulate his interest.

29 *closely*: privately.
31 *Affront*: come face to face with.
32 *espials*: spies (who are 'lawful' because their purpose is honourable).
33 *bestow*: hide.
35 'We can see from the way he acts.'
38 *for your part*: The extent of Ophelia's part in this deception is open to discussion. Gertrude perhaps hopes that his love for Ophelia is responsible for Hamlet's madness, rather than her own conduct (as she feared in 2, 2, 56–7).
40 *wildness*: disorder.
41 *wonted*: accustomed.
42 *both your honours*: the best for both of you. The Queen is in favour of the love between her son and Ophelia (see 5, 1, 236–8).
43 *Gracious*: Polonius addresses the King.
44 *this book*: Perhaps Polonius offers a prayerbook.
45 *exercise*: religious duty.
   colour: explain.
46 *loneliness*: being alone (without a chaperon).
   in this: for doing things like this.
47 *prov'd*: found.
   visage: outward appearance.
48 *action*: deeds.
50 *my conscience*: The audience can now be fairly sure that Claudius is guilty — although Hamlet's next appearance shows the Prince himself beginning to have doubts.
51 *plast'ring art*: the camouflage of cosmetics (hated by the Elizabethans, and associated with sexual prostitution and moral hypocrisy).
52 *the thing . . . it*: the paint. The sense here is unclear, but the loathing is evident.
53 *painted*: falsely coloured.

Polonius

55 I hear him coming. Let's withdraw, my lord.

[*Exeunt* King *and* Polonius

Enter Hamlet

Hamlet

To be, or not to be, that is the question:
Whether 'tis nobler in the mind to suffer
The slings and arrows of outrageous fortune,
Or to take arms against a sea of troubles
60 And by opposing end them. To die—to sleep,
No more; and by a sleep to say we end
The heart-ache and the thousand natural shocks
That flesh is heir to: 'tis a consummation
Devoutly to be wish'd. To die, to sleep;
65 To sleep, perchance to dream—ay, there's the rub:
For in that sleep of death what dreams may come,
When we have shuffled off this mortal coil,
Must give us pause—there's the respect
That makes calamity of so long life.
70 For who would bear the whips and scorns of time,
Th'oppressor's wrong, the proud man's contumely,
The pangs of dispriz'd love, the law's delay,
The insolence of office, and the spurns
That patient merit of th'unworthy takes,
75 When he himself might his quietus make
With a bare bodkin? Who would fardels bear,
To grunt and sweat under a weary life,
But that the dread of something after death,
The undiscover'd country, from whose bourn
80 No traveller returns, puzzles the will,
And makes us rather bear those ills we have
Than fly to others that we know not of?
Thus conscience does make cowards of us all,
And thus the native hue of resolution
85 Is sicklied o'er with the pale cast of thought,
And enterprises of great pitch and moment
With this regard their currents turn awry
And lose the name of action. Soft you now,
The fair Ophelia! Nymph, in thy orisons
90 Be all my sins remember'd.

Ophelia   Good my lord,
How does your honour for this many a day?

---

56 *To be*: to exist, to live.
     the question: Hamlet expands in the next four lines, debating with himself which is the more honourable course — patiently to endure earthly misfortunes, or boldly to oppose them.
58 *outrageous*: wilful.
59 *to take . . . troubles*: The metaphor (of fighting with human weapons against the superhuman force of the sea) is an apt expression of Hamlet's sense of futility.
60 *by opposing end them*: put an end to one's troubles by fighting against them (rather than stoically enduring them).
61 *No more*: that is all.
63 *consummation*: final ending.
65 *rub*: In the game of bowls, the 'rub' is anything that impedes the course of the bowl.
67 *shuffled off*: got free from.
     this mortal coil: this whole business of earthly living.
68 *give us pause*: make us stop to think.
68–9 'That's why misfortune goes on for so long.'
70 *time*: this (temporal) world.
72 *dispriz'd*: unvalued. (This is the F reading; Q2 has 'despised'.)
74 *merit*: the worthy one.
     of: from.
75 *his quietus make*: settle his final bill.
76 *bodkin*: short dagger.
     fardels: burdens.
79 *bourn*: frontier.
80 *puzzles*: perplexes.
81 *bear*: endure.
83 *conscience*: awareness, moral understanding.
     make cowards . . . all: cause us all to become cowards.
84–5 *the native . . . thought*: the natural colour of courage (which is blood-red) grows pale with too much thinking.
86 *pitch*: magnitude.
     moment: importance.
87 *regard*: consideration.
88 *Soft you now*: Hamlet silences himself as he observes Ophelia, apparently at her prayers ('orisons').
91 *for this many a day*: after all this time (i.e. since their last meeting).

Hamlet
I humbly thank you, well.
Ophelia
My lord, I have remembrances of yours
That I have longed long to redeliver.
95 I pray you now receive them.
Hamlet   No, not I.
I never gave you aught.
Ophelia
My honour'd lord, you know right well you did,
And with them words of so sweet breath compos'd
As made the things more rich. Their perfume lost,
100 Take these again; for to the noble mind
Rich gifts wax poor when givers prove unkind.
There, my lord.
Hamlet
Ha, ha! Are you honest?
Ophelia
My lord?
Hamlet
105 Are you fair?
Ophelia
What means your lordship?
Hamlet
That if you be honest and fair, your honesty should
admit no discourse to your beauty.
Ophelia
Could beauty, my lord, have better commerce than
110 with honesty?
Hamlet
Ay, truly, for the power of beauty will sooner trans-
form honesty from what it is to a bawd than the
force of honesty can translate beauty into his like-
ness. This was sometime a paradox, but now the
115 time gives it proof. I did love you once.
Ophelia
Indeed, my lord, you made me believe so.
Hamlet
You should not have believed me; for virtue cannot
so inoculate our old stock but we shall relish of it. I
loved you not.
Ophelia
120 I was the more deceived.

Notes:
92 *I humbly thank you*: Hamlet replies formally, as though to a stranger.
93 *remembrances*: keepsakes.
96 Hamlet is no longer the same man as the lover who gave presents to Ophelia.
100-1 The 'sentence' (Latin *sententia* = a pithy, wise saying) is a common feature of Elizabethan drama.
101 *prove unkind*: change into different people.
103 *Are you honest*: do you mean that. But 'honest' also means 'chaste', and Hamlet develops this sense just as he plays with different meanings of 'fair'.
107-8 *your honesty . . . beauty*: your chastity should allow no contact with your beauty. Ophelia appears to misunderstand — either from naive innocence or with a witty self-protection against Hamlet's rudeness.
109 *commerce*: business dealings.
113 *his*: its (i.e. the likeness of honesty).
114 *sometime*: once.
paradox: something contrary to reason.
115 *gives it proof*: proves it to be true. Hamlet seems to be alluding to his mother.
117-8 *virtue . . . stock*: virtue cannot be implanted like this into our human nature: 'inoculate' (= graft) is used horticulturally.
118 *relish of it*: taste of it — i.e. the original sin of human nature.

121 *nunnery*: where her chastity would be safe. The slang use of the word (= brothel) may add an extra tone to the line.
122 *indifferent*: moderately.

126 *at my beck*: waiting to be committed by me.

129 *We*: we men — see 'you' (= you women) at line 141; Hamlet ceases to think of either himself or Ophelia as individuals.

139 *wilt needs*: are determined to.
140 *monsters*: i.e. horned cuckolds (the implication is that all wives will sooner or later be unfaithful).

144 *paintings*: use of cosmetics.
146 *jig . . . lisp*: walk and talk affectedly. *nickname*: give new name to.
147–8 *make . . . ignorance*: pretend that these seductive wiles are done because you know no better.
149 *mo*: more.
150 *all but one*: Unknown to Hamlet, the hidden Claudius must hear and understand this threat.
152ff. The regular verse of the scene's final speeches restores a kind of normality after Hamlet's disjointed prose.
154 *expectancy*: Ophelia seems to regard Hamlet, whom she describes as the perfection of princes, as the heir to the royal throne — just as the 'rose' was, for the Elizabethans, the king of all flowers.
155 *glass*: looking-glass.

Hamlet
Get thee to a nunnery. Why, wouldst thou be a
breeder of sinners? I am myself indifferent honest,
but yet I could accuse me of such things that it were
better my mother had not borne me. I am very
125 proud, revengeful, ambitious, with more offences at
my beck than I have thoughts to put them in, imagination to give them shape, or time to act them in.
What should such fellows as I do crawling between
earth and heaven? We are arrant knaves all, believe
130 none of us. Go thy ways to a nunnery. Where's your
father?
Ophelia
At home, my lord.
Hamlet
Let the doors be shut upon him, that he may play
the fool nowhere but in's own house. Farewell.
Ophelia
135 O help him, you sweet heavens.
Hamlet
If thou dost marry, I'll give thee this plague for thy
dowry: be thou as chaste as ice, as pure as snow,
thou shalt not escape calumny. Get thee to a nunnery,
farewell. Or if thou wilt needs marry, marry a
140 fool; for wise men know well enough what monsters
you make of them. To a nunnery, go—and quickly
too. Farewell.
Ophelia
Heavenly powers, restore him.
Hamlet
I have heard of your paintings well enough. God
145 hath given you one face and you make yourselves
another. You jig and amble, and you lisp, you nickname God's creatures, and make your wantonness
your ignorance. Go to, I'll no more on't, it hath made
me mad. I say we will have no mo marriage. Those
150 that are married already—all but one—shall live;
the rest shall keep as they are. To a nunnery, go. [*Exit*
Ophelia
O, what a noble mind is here o'erthrown!
The courtier's, soldier's, scholar's, eye, tongue, sword,
Th'expectancy and rose of the fair state,
155 The glass of fashion and the mould of form,

156 *observ'd*: honoured, respected.
157 *deject*: dejected.
158 *music*: i.e. which were like music to her ears.
159 *most sovereign*: ruling over all other faculties.
161 *feature*: figure.
    blown: flowering.
162 *ecstasy*: madness.
164 *affections*: feelings.

167 *sits on brood*: is brooding over. The image is continued with 'hatch'.
168 *doubt*: fear.

171 *set it down*: decided. The King's plot against Hamlet's life is already set in motion.
172 *tribute*: The Danegeld had been paid in self-protection by the English kings since the tenth century; at the time of Queen Elizabeth I, the Danes made a fresh attempt to claim this payment.
173 *Haply*: perhaps.
    the seas: sea voyages were a recognized treatment for depression.
174 *variable objects*: different sights.
175 'Whatever it is that is upsetting him so much.'
176 *still*: constantly.
177 *fashion of himself*: his normal behaviour.
180 *neglected*: rejected.

185 *be round with*: speak plainly to.
186 *in the ear*: where I can listen to.
187 *find him*: find out what's wrong with him.

Th'observ'd of all observers, quite, quite down!
And I, of ladies most deject and wretched,
That suck'd the honey of his music vows,
Now see that noble and most sovereign reason
160 Like sweet bells jangled out of tune and harsh,
That unmatch'd form and feature of blown youth
Blasted with ecstasy. O woe is me
T'have seen what I have seen, see what I see.

Enter King *and* Polonius

King
Love? His affections do not that way tend,
165 Nor what he spake, though it lack'd form a little,
Was not like madness. There's something in his soul
O'er which his melancholy sits on brood,
And I do doubt the hatch and the disclose
Will be some danger; which for to prevent,
170 I have in quick determination
Thus set it down: he shall with speed to England
For the demand of our neglected tribute.
Haply the seas and countries different,
With variable objects, shall expel
175 This something settled matter in his heart,
Whereon his brains still beating puts him thus
From fashion of himself. What think you on't?
Polonius
It shall do well. But yet do I believe
The origin and commencement of his grief
180 Sprung from neglected love. How now, Ophelia?
You need not tell us what Lord Hamlet said,
We heard it all. My lord, do as you please,
But if you hold it fit, after the play
Let his queen-mother all alone entreat him
185 To show his grief, let her be round with him,
And I'll be plac'd, so please you, in the ear
Of all their conference. If she find him not,
To England send him; or confine him where
Your wisdom best shall think.
King   It shall be so.
190 Madness in great ones must not unwatch'd go.

                                                [Exeunt

Act 3　Scene 2

The scene begins in a relaxed mood as Hamlet gives instructions on acting techniques to the professional players. He has written some additional material for them to perform, and whilst the actors make their final preparations Hamlet confides in Horatio, his trusted friend. By this means the audience's attention is directed towards Claudius and his reaction to 'The Murder of Gonzago' — the play within the play of *Hamlet*. The tension builds up during an episode in which Hamlet taunts Polonius, both directly and in his words to Ophelia. And then the play begins. When the players enact the murder of a king, Claudius suddenly puts a stop to their performance by rushing out of the hall, followed by Gertrude. Hamlet is congratulating himself on the success of his plot, and triumphing over Rosencrantz and Guildenstern, when Polonius brings a message from the Queen. Hamlet is called to Gertrude's chamber, and for a moment he is alone again and speaks solemnly as he remembers the Ghost's charge.

1　*the speech*: Hamlet refers at first to the lines he has just written (see *2, 2, 534–6*), but soon proceeds to comment on the whole art of acting.
3　*your players*: these actors.
　　had as lief: would rather.
5　*use all gently*: be moderate in everything you do (like gentlemen).
7　*acquire and beget*: learn and develop.

Scene 2

Enter Hamlet *and three of the* Players

Hamlet
Speak the speech, I pray you, as I pronounced it to
you, trippingly on the tongue; but if you mouth it as
many of your players do, I had as lief the town-crier
spoke my lines. Nor do not saw the air too much with
5　your hand, thus, but use all gently; for in the very
torrent, tempest, and, as I may say, whirlwind of
your passion, you must acquire and beget a temper-
ance that may give it smoothness. O, it offends me
to the soul to hear a robustious periwig-pated fellow
10　tear a passion to tatters, to very rags, to split the ears
of the groundlings, who for the most part are capable
of nothing but inexplicable dumb-shows and noise.
I would have such a fellow whipped for o'erdoing
Termagant. It out-Herods Herod. Pray you avoid it.
First Player
15　I warrant your honour.
Hamlet
Be not too tame neither, but let your own discretion
be your tutor. Suit the action to the word,
the word to the action, with this special observance,
that you o'erstep not the modesty of nature. For
20　anything so o'erdone is from the purpose of playing,
whose end, both at the first and now, was and is to

9 *periwig-pated*: with a wig on his head. Wigs were not generally worn at this time.

11 *groundlings*: those who stood around the stage, in the cheapest area.

12 *inexplicable*: incomprehensible. Ophelia, speaking as the innocent spectator, does not understand the dumb-show later in this scene (lines 133ff.).

14 *Termagant*: a noisy heathen god, represented in medieval drama.
out-Herods Herod: is more like Herod than he was himself.
Herod: the biblical tyrant who was 'exceeding wrath' (St Matthew, 2:16) and represented in his rage in medieval plays.

16–17 *let . . . tutor*: judge for yourselves.

20 *from . . . playing*: contrary to the aims of drama.

22 *hold . . . nature*: show life as it really is.

23 *feature*: appearance.
scorn: that which is scorned.

23–4 *the very . . . time*: things as they really are at the time.

24 *his*: its.
pressure: shape (as an impression on wax).

25 *come tardy off*: done badly.

26 *unskilful*: uneducated.

27 *censure*: criticism.
the which one: the one judicious man.

28 *allowance*: estimation.

30 *not . . . profanely*: not to make a blasphemous joke about it (the blasphemy would be in the suggestion that some human beings have not been made by God).

31 *Christians*: ordinary decent people.

32 *man*: any human being.

34 *journeymen*: hired labourers.

36 *indifferently*: fairly well.

39 *set down*: written. Comic actors were notorious for their freedom with the author's text.

48 *presently*: at once.

hold as 'twere the mirror up to nature; to show virtue her feature, scorn her own image, and the very age and body of the time his form and pressure. Now
25 this overdone or come tardy off, though it makes the unskilful laugh, cannot but make the judicious grieve, the censure of the which one must in your allowance o'erweigh a whole theatre of others. O, there be players that I have seen play—and heard
30 others praise, and that highly—not to speak it profanely, that neither having th'accent of Christians, nor the gait of Christian, pagan, nor man, have so strutted and bellowed that I have thought some of Nature's journeymen had made men, and not made
35 them well, they imitated humanity so abominably.

First Player
I hope we have reformed that indifferently with us.

Hamlet
O reform it altogether. And let those that play your clowns speak no more than is set down for them—
40 for there be of them that will themselves laugh, to set on some quantity of barren spectators to laugh too, though in the meantime some necessary question of the play be then to be considered. That's villainous, and shows a most pitiful ambition in the
45 fool that uses it. Go make you ready.   [*Exeunt* Players

Enter Polonius, Rosencrantz, *and* Guildenstern

How now, my lord? Will the King hear this piece of work?

Polonius
And the Queen too, and that presently.

Hamlet
Bid the players make haste.   [*Exit* Polonius
50 Will you two help to hasten them?

Rosencrantz
Ay, my lord.   [*Exeunt* Rosencrantz *and* Guildenstern

Hamlet
What ho, Horatio!

Enter Horatio

54 *e'en*: indeed.
  just: sane, well-balanced. Hamlet finds in
  Horatio exactly the friend and confidant
  that he needs — someone who (unlike the
  men he has just dismissed) can be trusted.
55 *my . . . withal*: I had any dealings with.
60–63 Shakespeare images flattery as a spaniel,
  licking its master and grovelling at his feet
  in hope of reward.
60 *candied tongue*: flattering words.
61 *pregnant*: ready to bow or kneel.
62 *thrift*: reward.
63 *my dear soul*: The Elizabethans valued
  friendship very highly, regarding it as a
  spiritual relationship even more estimable
  than heterosexual love.
  mistress of her choice: could choose for
  herself (the soul is traditionally female).
64 *distinguish her election*: discriminate in her
  choice.
65 *seal'd*: claimed.
66 *in suff'ring . . . nothing*: Hamlet plays with
  different meanings of 'suffer', apparently
  praising Horatio as one who has endured
  much, but been harmed by nothing.
67 *buffets*: blows.
69 *blood*: hot passion — the opposite of cool
  reason.
  commeddled: mixed equally.
70 *pipe*: The image of the recorder (where
  different notes are produced by stopping up
  the holes) is developed in lines 355–63.

72 *wear*: hold.
78 *act*: episode.
79 *very comment*: closest scrutiny.
80 *occulted*: hidden.
81 *unkennel*: break out (like a dog).
  in one speech: i.e. the one which Hamlet has
  composed.
84 *Vulcan's stithy*: the forge of the classical god
  of blacksmiths — readily associated with
  the underworld and hence with a 'damned
  ghost'.
  heedful note: careful observation.
87 *censure of his seeming*: judging how he
  behaves.
88 *'a steal aught*: he gets away with anything.
89 *pay the theft*: answer for it.

Horatio
Here, sweet lord, at your service.
  Hamlet
Horatio, thou art e'en as just a man
55 As e'er my conversation cop'd withal.
  Horatio
O my dear lord.
  Hamlet   Nay, do not think I flatter,
For what advancement may I hope from thee
That no revenue hast but thy good spirits
To feed and clothe thee? Why should the poor be
  flatter'd?
60 No, let the candied tongue lick absurd pomp,
And crook the pregnant hinges of the knee
Where thrift may follow fawning. Dost thou hear?
Since my dear soul was mistress of her choice,
And could of men distinguish her election,
65 Sh'ath seal'd thee for herself; for thou hast been
As one, in suff'ring all, that suffers nothing,
A man that Fortune's buffets and rewards
Hast ta'en with equal thanks; and blest are those
Whose blood and judgment are so well commeddled
70 That they are not a pipe for Fortune's finger
To sound what stop she please. Give me that man
That is not passion's slave, and I will wear him
In my heart's core, ay, in my heart of heart,
As I do thee. Something too much of this.
75 There is a play tonight before the King:
One scene of it comes near the circumstance
Which I have told thee of my father's death.
I prithee, when thou seest that act afoot,
Even with the very comment of thy soul
80 Observe my uncle. If his occulted guilt
Do not itself unkennel in one speech,
It is a damned ghost that we have seen,
And my imaginations are as foul
As Vulcan's stithy. Give him heedful note;
85 For I mine eyes will rivet to his face,
And after we will both our judgments join
In censure of his seeming.
  Horatio   Well, my lord.
If 'a steal aught the whilst this play is playing
And scape detecting, I will pay the theft.

Enter Trumpets *and* Kettle-drums *and
sound a flourish*

Hamlet

90 They are coming to the play. I must be idle.
Get you a place.

Enter King, Queen, Polonius, Ophelia,
Rosencrantz, Guildenstern, *and other* Lords
attendant, with the King's Guard *carrying
torches*

King

How fares our cousin Hamlet?

Hamlet

Excellent, i'faith, of the chameleon's dish. I eat the
air, promise-crammed. You cannot feed capons so.

King

95 I have nothing with this answer, Hamlet. These
words are not mine.

Hamlet

No, nor mine now.—[*To* Polonius] My lord, you
played once i'th' university, you say?

Polonius

That did I, my lord, and was accounted a good
100 actor.

Hamlet

What did you enact?

Polonius

I did enact Julius Caesar. I was killed i'th' Capitol.
Brutus killed me.

Hamlet

It was a brute part of him to kill so capital a calf
105 there. Be the players ready?

Rosencrantz

Ay, my lord, they stay upon your patience.

Queen

Come hither, my dear Hamlet, sit by me.

Hamlet

No, good mother, here's metal more attractive.

Turns to Ophelia

Polonius

[*Aside to the* King] O ho! do you mark that?

90 *be idle*: look as though I am not doing
anything.

92 *fares*: The King means 'does'; but Hamlet
takes up the sense 'eats'.

93 *chameleon's dish*: It was believed that the
chameleon (a lizard that changes colour to
match its background) fed on air.

94 *promise-crammed*: stuffed full of promises.
We hear Claudius's promises to Hamlet, in
1, 2, 108–9, and later in *3, 2, 331–3*.
capons: chickens which are fattened for the
table.

95 *have nothing with*: don't understand.
96 *are not mine*: don't answer my question.

104 Hamlet's reply depends largely upon puns
for its wit: 'brute' develops from 'Brutus',
who killed Caesar in the Roman Capitol;
and the killing (in jest) of a calf was part of
traditional mumming entertainment; 'calf'
also means 'fool'.

108 *attractive*: with magnetic powers.

110 *lie in your lap*: The sexual innuendo is clear
— although Hamlet denies it in line 113. In
the Morality Plays the youth, by lying in
the lap of the temptress, puts himself in her
power.

115 *country matters*: sexual intercourse.

119 *Nothing*: i.e. her virginity. See *Hero &*
Leander by Christopher Marlowe:
          maids are nothing then,
  Without the sweet society of men.
                (255–6)

Hamlet

110 [*Lying down at* Ophelia's *feet*] Lady, shall I lie in your
lap?

Ophelia

No, my lord.

Hamlet

I mean, my head upon your lap.

Ophelia

Ay, my lord.

Hamlet

115 Do you think I meant country matters?

Ophelia

I think nothing, my lord.

Hamlet

That's a fair thought to lie between maids' legs.

Ophelia

What is, my lord?

Hamlet

Nothing.

Ophelia

120 You are merry, my lord.

Hamlet

Who, I?

Ophelia

Ay, my lord.

123 *your only jig-maker*: the best maker of comedies.

125 *within's*: within this.

126 *twice two months*: Ophelia's remark indicates — perhaps not accurately — that some time has passed between *Acts 1* and *2*.

128 *sables*: luxurious dark furs, traditionally worn in mourning.

131 *by'r lady*: by Our Lady (the Virgin Mary).

132 *'a suffer not thinking on*: he will have to put up with being forgotten.
hobby-horse: This was a traditional feature of the morris dance; Hamlet proceeds to sing (or quote) a line from a popular song.

133s.d. *dumb-show*: mime. Such a performance often preceded the main business of early — pre-Shakespearean — tragedies; it served as a kind of programme note to aid the understanding of the audience — although the more intelligent (perhaps like Claudius) ignored it.

135 *miching malicho*: sneaking mischief.

136 *argument*: plot.

137 *this fellow*: The dumb-shows were often accompanied by a presenter whose function was to explain their meaning to the audiences — although the present one is not very helpful.

138 *counsel*: secrets.

Hamlet

O God, your only jig-maker. What should a man
do but be merry? For look you how cheerfully my
mother looks and my father died within's two hours.

Ophelia

Nay, 'tis twice two months, my lord.

Hamlet

So long? Nay then, let the devil wear black, for I'll
have a suit of sables. O heavens, die two months ago
and not forgotten yet! Then there's hope a great
man's memory may outlive his life half a year. But
by'r lady 'a must build churches then, or else shall
'a suffer not thinking on, with the hobby-horse, whose
epitaph is 'For O, for O, the hobby-horse is forgot'.

The trumpets sound. A dumb-show follows

Enter a King *and a* Queen, *the* Queen *embracing him
and he her. She kneels, and makes show of protestation
unto him. He takes her up, and declines his head upon her
neck. He lies him down upon a bank of flowers. She,
seeing him asleep, leaves him. Anon comes in another*
Man, *takes off his crown, kisses it, pours poison in the
sleeper's ears, and leaves him. The* Queen *returns, finds
the* King *dead, makes passionate action. The* Poisoner
with some Three or Four *comes in again. They seem to
condole with her. The dead body is carried away. The*
Poisoner *woos the* Queen *with gifts. She seems harsh
awhile, but in the end accepts his love.*   [*Exeunt*

Ophelia

What means this, my lord?

Hamlet

Marry, this is miching malicho. It means mischief.

Ophelia

Belike this show imports the argument of the play.

Enter Prologue

Hamlet

We shall know by this fellow. The players cannot
keep counsel: they'll tell all.

Ophelia

Will 'a tell us what this show meant?

125

130

135

140 *any show*: Ophelia's reaction insists on Hamlet's indecency.	**Hamlet**
	140 Ay, or any show that you will show him. Be not you ashamed to show, he'll not shame to tell you what it means.
	Ophelia
143 *naught*: rubbish, offensive.	You are naught, you are naught. I'll mark the play.
	Prologue
	For us and for our tragedy,
	145 *Here stooping to your clemency,*
	We beg your hearing patiently. [*Exit*
	Hamlet
147 *posy for a ring*: motto engraved inside a ring.	Is this a prologue, or the posy of a ring?
	Ophelia
	'Tis brief, my lord.
	Hamlet
	As woman's love.

Enter the Player King *and* Queen

Player King

150 *Full thirty times hath Phoebus' cart gone round*

Neptune's salt wash and Tellus' orbed ground,

And thirty dozen moons with borrow'd sheen

About the world have times twelve thirties been

Since love our hearts and Hymen did our hands

155 *Unite commutual in most sacred bands.*

Player Queen

So many journeys may the sun and moon

Make us again count o'er ere love be done.

But woe is me, you are so sick of late,

So far from cheer and from your former state,

160 *That I distrust you. Yet though I distrust,*

Discomfort you, my lord, it nothing must;

For women's fear and love hold quantity,

In neither aught, or in extremity.

Now what my love is, proof hath made you know,

165 *And as my love is siz'd, my fear is so.*

Where love is great, the littlest doubts are fear;

Where little fears grow great, great love grows there.

Player King

Faith, I must leave thee, love, and shortly too:

My operant powers their functions leave to do;

170 *And thou shalt live in this fair world behind,*

Honour'd, belov'd; and haply one as kind

For husband shalt thou—

Left margin glosses:

150 *Phoebus' cart*: the chariot of the sun-god.

151 *Neptune's salt wash*: the sea, ruled by the god Neptune.
Tellus' orbed ground: the rounded sphere of the earth, dominion of Tellus.

152 *borrow'd sheen*: brightness reflected from the sun.

154 *Hymen*: the classical god of marriage.

155 *bands*: bonds.

160 *distrust*: am worried about.

162–3 *hold . . . extremity*: are in proportion to each other: there is nothing of either or else too much of both.

165 *siz'd*: measured.

169 *operant powers*: faculties.
leave to do: cease to work.

Player Queen   *O confound the rest.*
Such love must needs be treason in my breast.
In second husband let me be accurst;
175   *None wed the second but who kill'd the first.*
    Hamlet
[Aside] That's wormwood.
    Player Queen
The instances that second marriage move
Are base respects of thrift, but none of love.
A second time I kill my husband dead,
180   *When second husband kisses me in bed.*
    Player King
I do believe you think what now you speak;
But what we do determine, oft we break.
Purpose is but the slave to memory,
Of violent birth but poor validity,
185   *Which now, the fruit unripe, sticks on the tree,*
But fall unshaken when they mellow be.
Most necessary 'tis that we forget
To pay ourselves what to ourselves is debt.
What to ourselves in passion we propose,
190   *The passion ending, doth the purpose lose.*
The violence of either grief or joy
Their own enactures with themselves destroy.
Where joy most revels grief doth most lament;
Grief joys, joy grieves, on slender accident.
195   *This world is not for aye, nor 'tis not strange*
That even our loves should with our fortunes change,
For 'tis a question left us yet to prove,
Whether love lead fortune or else fortune love.
The great man down, you mark his favourite flies;
200   *The poor advanc'd makes friends of enemies;*
And hitherto doth love on fortune tend:
For who not needs shall never lack a friend,
And who in want a hollow friend doth try
Directly seasons him his enemy.
205   *But orderly to end where I begun,*
Our wills and fates do so contrary run
That our devices still are overthrown:
Our thoughts are ours, their ends none of our own.
So think thou wilt no second husband wed,
210   *But die thy thoughts when thy first lord is dead.*

---

175   *but who*: except those who.

176   *wormwood*: bitter. Hamlet's comment
(whether or not these are the lines which he
has written) seems to imply that his mother
has become associated with her first
husband's death through her second
marriage.
177   *instances*: motives, causes.
178   *base . . . thrift*: mean considerations of
worldly advantages.
181   *think*: mean.

183   *Purpose*: what we decide to do. The speech
of the Player King is a mere sequence of
platitudes, not always readily intelligible;
consequently Shakespeare's audience need
not deflect the focus of their attention from
Claudius.
    slave to memory: depends on what we
remember.
184   *validity*: staying-power.
187–8 'It is inevitable ('necessary') that we
should forget to pay the debts that we owe
only to ourselves.'
191–2 'All violent emotions are short-lived, and
so are the plans they determine on.'
194   *slender accident*: the slightest occasion.
195   *aye*: ever.

199   *down*: displaced.
200   *advanc'd*: put in a high position.
201   *hitherto*: up to this point. He is debating the
'question' stated in line 202.
202   *who not needs*: the person who has no need
of help.
203   *in want*: in trouble.
    hollow: insincere.
    try: put to the test.
204   *seasons him*: turns him into.
206   *wills and fates*: desires and destinies.
207   *devices*: designs.
    still: always.
208   *ends*: results.

Player Queen
Nor earth to me give food, nor heaven light,
Sport and repose lock from me day and night,
To desperation turn my trust and hope,
An anchor's cheer in prison be my scope,
215 *Each opposite, that blanks the face of joy,*
Meet what I would have well and it destroy,
Both here and hence pursue me lasting strife,
If, once a widow, ever I be a wife.

Hamlet
If she should break it now.

Player King
220 *'Tis deeply sworn. Sweet, leave me here awhile.*
My spirits grow dull, and fain I would beguile
The tedious day with sleep.

[*He sleeps*]

Player Queen   *Sleep rock thy brain,*
And never come mischance between us twain.   [*Exit*

Hamlet
Madam, how like you this play?

Queen
225 The lady doth protest too much, methinks.

Hamlet
O, but she'll keep her word.

King
Have you heard the argument? Is there no offence
in't?

Hamlet
No, no, they do but jest—poison in jest. No offence
230 i'th' world.

King
What do you call the play?

Hamlet
The Mousetrap—marry, how tropically! This play
is the image of a murder done in Vienna—Gonzago
is the Duke's name, his wife Baptista—you shall see
235 anon. 'Tis a knavish piece of work, but what o' that?
Your Majesty, and we that have free souls, it touches
us not. Let the galled jade wince, our withers are
unwrung.

Enter Lucianus

---

214   *anchor's cheer*: the living of a hermit (anchorite).
my scope: all that I ask for.

215-6   'May everything turn out opposite to my desires, wiping out my delight.'

217   *here and hence*: in this life and the next.

219   *break*: reveal; 'she' may refer either to the Player Queen or to Gertrude. Hamlet's interjection is timely, breaking into the hypnotic rhythms of the players.

223   *mischance*: ill-fortune.

225   *protest too much*: is making too many promises.

227   *Have . . . argument*: do you know what it is about. Claudius is getting suspicious.
no offence: anything objectionable. Hamlet deliberately mistakes the meaning when he repeats the word.

229   *jest*: pretend, make believe.
offence: crime.

232   *The Mousetrap*: Hamlet invents a new title for his altered version of 'The Murder of Gonzago' (see 2, 2, 532).
tropically: metaphorically. A 'trope' is a figure of speech.

233   *a murder done in Vienna*: The play does in fact 'image' something of a murder done in Urbino in 1538.

236   *free*: guiltless.

237   *the galled jade*: the horse which has a sore (usually caused by an ill-fitting saddle).
withers: shoulders (of a horse).

239   *nephew*: Hamlet declares himself as a threat to his uncle — the accuracy of his identification of the character is less important.

240   *chorus*: In early drama the figure of the Chorus was used to explain or 'interpret' the action of the play.

241–2   'I could supply words ('interpret') for you and your lover if I could see what was going on between you.' Hamlet could act as the 'interpreter' who supplies the words in a puppet-show.

243   *keen*: sharp.

244   *cost you a groaning*: make you cry.
       edge: sharp sexual desire.

245   *better, and worse*: more keen, and more objectionable.

246   Hamlet picks up an echo of the church marriage service, in which the partners vow to take each other 'for better, for worse'. His 'mis-take' seems to accuse women of treating the vow lightly — a variant reading in the Folio text is 'must take'.

248   *the . . . revenge*: Hamlet, impatient for the next stage in his plot, misquotes lines from an old play, the anonymous *True Tragedy of Richard III*.

249–54   Some critics assume this to be the speech written by Hamlet.

249   *apt*: ready.

250   *Confederate season*: the right time.

251   *midnight weeds collected*: herbs gathered at midnight.

252   *Hecate*: Hecate was the classical goddess of witchcraft, traditionally represented in three forms — hence 'thrice'.
       ban: curse.

254   *usurps*: takes possesion of.

255   *his name*: i.e. the sleeper's name.

256   *The story is extant*: Hamlet is probably correct — but Shakespeare's source has not been found. The method is the same as that used by Luigi Gonzaga to kill the Duke of Urbino — who was married to his sister, Baptista Gonzaga.

259   *rises*: Court protocol demands that the courtiers should also stand up, and the confusion of the scene is heightened by the calls for 'Lights'. The whole action of the play pivots on this point.

260   *false fire*: the report of guns firing blank cartridges.

This is one Lucianus, nephew to the King.

Ophelia
240   You are as good as a chorus, my lord.

Hamlet
I could interpret between you and your love if I could see the puppets dallying.

Ophelia
You are keen, my lord, you are keen.

Hamlet
It would cost you a groaning to take off my edge.

Ophelia
245   Still better, and worse.

Hamlet
So you mis-take your husbands.—Begin, murderer. Leave thy damnable faces and begin. Come, the croaking raven doth bellow for revenge.

Lucianus
Thoughts black, hands apt, drugs fit, and time agreeing,
250   *Confederate season, else no creature seeing,*
Thou mixture rank, of midnight weeds collected,
With Hecate's ban thrice blasted, thrice infected,
Thy natural magic and dire property
On wholesome life usurps immediately.

[*Pours the poison in the sleeper's ears*]

Hamlet
255   'A poisons him i'th' garden for his estate. His name's Gonzago. The story is extant, and written in very choice Italian. You shall see anon how the murderer gets the love of Gonzago's wife.

Ophelia
The King rises.

Hamlet
260   What, frighted with false fire?

Queen
How fares my lord?

Polonius
Give o'er the play.

King
Give me some light. Away.

Polonius
Lights, lights, lights.

[*Exeunt all but* Hamlet *and* Horatio

265 *strucken*: wounded. Hamlet quotes — or perhaps sings — a popular ballad.

267 *watch*: keep awake.

268 'That's how it is in life.'

269 *this*: i.e. the success of his theatrical venture.
    forest of feathers: mass of feathers in my hat (a fashion favoured by actors).

270 *turn Turk with me*: let me down.
    Provincial roses: rosettes from Provins (N. France).

271 *razed*: slashed (as decoration).
    cry: company (the word usually describes a pack of hounds).

273 *share*: A shareholder was part-owner of the theatrical company's assets and took a share of its profits; Shakespeare was one of the sharers of his own company, the King's Men.

275–8 Hamlet improvises another verse. 'Damon' was a popular name for shepherds in pastoral poetry; 'Jove', king of the gods, is clearly analogous to Hamlet's father, of whom the country has been deprived ('dismantled'); and Claudius is the 'pajock' (= low, base fellow). Horatio clearly expects the rhyme-word 'ass'.

286–7 Hamlet parodies lines from a well-known revenge play, Kyd's *The Spanish Tragedy*.

287 *perdie*: by God (French *pardieu*).

289 *vouchsafe*: permit.

Hamlet

265 Why, let the strucken deer go weep,
    The hart ungalled play;
  For some must watch while some must sleep,
    Thus runs the world away.
Would not this, sir, and a forest of feathers, if the rest
270 of my fortunes turn Turk with me, with Provincial
roses on my razed shoes, get me a fellowship in a cry
of players?

Horatio

Half a share.

Hamlet

A whole one, I.
275   For thou dost know, O Damon dear,
      This realm dismantled was
    Of Jove himself, and now reigns here
      A very, very—pajock.

Horatio

You might have rhymed.

Hamlet

280 O good Horatio, I'll take the ghost's word for a
thousand pound. Didst perceive?

Horatio

Very well, my lord.

Hamlet

Upon the talk of the poisoning?

Horatio

I did very well note him.

Hamlet

285 Ah ha! Come, some music; come, the recorders.
  For if the King like not the comedy,
    Why then, belike he likes it not, perdie.
Come, some music.

Enter Rosencrantz *and* Guildenstern

Guildenstern

Good my lord, vouchsafe me a word with you.

Hamlet

290 Sir, a whole history.

Guildenstern

The King, sir—

Hamlet

Ay, sir, what of him?

Guildenstern
Is in his retirement marvellous distempered.
Hamlet
With drink, sir?
Guildenstern
295 No, my lord, with choler.
Hamlet
Your wisdom should show itself more richer to
signify this to the doctor, for for me to put him to
his purgation would perhaps plunge him into more
choler.
Guildenstern
300 Good my lord, put your discourse into some frame,
and start not so wildly from my affair.
Hamlet
I am tame, sir. Pronounce.
Guildenstern
The Queen your mother, in most great affliction of
spirit, hath sent me to you.
Hamlet
305 You are welcome.
Guildenstern
Nay, good my lord, this courtesy is not of the right
breed. If it shall please you to make me a wholesome
answer, I will do your mother's commandment; if
not, your pardon and my return shall be the end of
310 my business.
Hamlet
Sir, I cannot.
Rosencrantz
What, my lord?
Hamlet
Make you a wholesome answer. My wit's diseased.
But sir, such answer as I can make, you shall com-
315 mand—or rather, as you say, my mother. Therefore
no more, but to the matter. My mother, you say—
Rosencrantz
Then thus she says: your behaviour hath struck her
into amazement and admiration.
Hamlet
O wonderful son, that can so stonish a mother! But
320 is there no sequel at the heels of this mother's admir-
ation? Impart.

293 *marvellous distempered*: extremely upset.
Hamlet deliberately misunderstands.

295 *choler*: anger. Hamlet again misunderstands, and takes the sense 'bile'.

297–8 *put . . . purgation*: attempt to treat his
disorder (physically, with laxatives or
bloodletting; spiritually, by urging
confession of his guilt).

300 *put . . . frame*: talk sense.
301 *start . . . affair*: don't change the subject so
suddenly.

307 *breed*: kind.
wholesome: sensible.

309 *your pardon*: your permission to depart.

318 *admiration*: astonishment.

322 *closet*: private chamber. Rosencrantz and
    Guildenstern activate the plot proposed by
    Polonius in *Act 3*, scene 1, 183ff.

325 *trade*: business; Hamlet is contemptuous.

327 *pickers and stealers*: i.e. hands. The Church
    catechism teaches the duty 'to keep (one's)
    hands from picking and stealing'.

329 *bar . . . liberty*: shut yourself up in your
    own trouble. Rosencrantz's advice might
    also be a threat.
330 *deny*: refuse to confide.
331 *advancement*: promotion.

332 *voice*: support (see *1, 2, 108*).

334 *the proverb*: i.e. 'while the grass grows, the
    horse starves'.
335 *something musty*: rather stale.
335s.d. *Players*: actors.

336 *withdraw*: have a private word (with
    Rosencrantz and Guildenstern).
337–8 'Why do you go such a roundabout way,
    like hunters who get upwind in order to
    drive their quarry into a snare ('toil').'
339–40 Guildenstern's smoothly evasive answer
    is not easily understandable; he seems to be
    saying that his great love for Hamlet is
    responsible for any apparent discourtesy.
341 *that*: i.e. how love can be 'unmannerly'.

347 *I know . . . it*: I don't know how to play it.

Rosencrantz
She desires to speak with you in her closet ere you go
to bed.
Hamlet
We shall obey, were she ten times our mother.
Have you any further trade with us?   325
Rosencrantz
My lord, you once did love me.
Hamlet
And do still, by these pickers and stealers.
Rosencrantz
Good my lord, what is your cause of distemper? You
do surely bar the door upon your own liberty if you
deny your griefs to your friend.   330
Hamlet
Sir, I lack advancement.
Rosencrantz
How can that be, when you have the voice of the
King himself for your succession in Denmark?
Hamlet
Ay, sir, but while the grass grows—the proverb is
something musty.   335

Enter the Players *with recorders*

O, the recorders. Let me see one.—To withdraw
with you, why do you go about to recover the wind
of me, as if you would drive me into a toil?
Guildenstern
O my lord, if my duty be too bold, my love is too
unmannerly.   340
Hamlet
I do not well understand that. Will you play upon
this pipe?
Guildenstern
My lord, I cannot.
Hamlet
I pray you.
Guildenstern
Believe me, I cannot.   345
Hamlet
I do beseech you.
Guildenstern
I know no touch of it, my lord.

Hamlet
It is as easy as lying. Govern these ventages with
your fingers and thumb, give it breath with your
350 mouth, and it will discourse most eloquent music.
Look you, these are the stops.

Guildenstern
But these cannot I command to any utterance of
harmony. I have not the skill.

Hamlet
Why, look you now, how unworthy a thing you
355 make of me. You would play upon me, you would
seem to know my stops, you would pluck out the
heart of my mystery, you would sound me from my
lowest note to the top of my compass; and there is
much music, excellent voice, in this little organ, yet
360 cannot you make it speak. 'Sblood, do you think I
am easier to be played on than a pipe? Call me what
instrument you will, though you fret me, you cannot
play upon me.

Enter Polonius

God bless you sir.

Polonius
365 My lord, the Queen would speak with you, and
presently.

Hamlet
Do you see yonder cloud that's almost in shape of
a camel?

Polonius
By th' mass and 'tis—like a camel indeed.

Hamlet
370 Methinks it is like a weasel.

Polonius
It is backed like a weasel.

Hamlet
Or like a whale.

Polonius
Very like a whale.

Hamlet
Then I will come to my mother by and by.—
375 [*Aside*] They fool me to the top of my bent.—I will
come by and by.

Polonius
I will say so.   · [*Exit*

348 *ventages*: stops, air-holes.

357 *sound*: fathom (with a pun on 'make
      sound').
358 *compass*: range.
359 *organ*: instrument.

362 *fret*: irritate: 'frets' are also the finger-
      positions on some stringed instruments.

366 *presently*: immediately.

375 *to the top of my bent*: as far as I can go. The
      'bent' is the full stretch of a bow.

379 *witching time*: the time when witches
appear.

380 *yawn*: gape. The graves open for the ghosts
to walk out.

381 *drink hot blood*: i.e. in diabolic parody of the
action of the mass.

384 *nature*: natural feeling.

385 *Nero*: the ancient Roman emperor who
killed his mother after she had poisoned her
husband.
firm: steadfast.

387 *speak daggers*: wound her with words.

388 'May my voice and my mind be
inconsistent on this subject.'

389 *somever*: soever.
shent: reproached.

390 'May my soul never agree to putting my
words into action.' An official seal is needed
before words (in a document or deed)
become legal.

Hamlet

'By and by' is easily said.—Leave me, friends.

                     [Exeunt all but Hamlet

'Tis now the very witching time of night,

380 When churchyards yawn and hell itself breathes out

Contagion to this world. Now could I drink hot blood,

And do such bitter business as the day

Would quake to look on. Soft, now to my mother.

O heart, lose not thy nature. Let not ever

385 The soul of Nero enter this firm bosom;

Let me be cruel, not unnatural.

I will speak daggers to her, but use none.

My tongue and soul in this be hypocrites:

How in my words somever she be shent,

390 To give them seals never my soul consent.   *[Exit*

Act 3   Scene 3

The frightened King is preparing to send Hamlet
away from Denmark: Rosencrantz and Guildenstern will accompany him to England. Polonius
hurries away to hide in the Queen's closet where
he can overhear Gertrude's conversation with
Hamlet. Claudius tries to pray, allowing the
audience to hear his admission of guilt, and
presenting Hamlet with an unexpected opportunity to avenge his father.

3 *dispatch*: deal with.

4 *shall along*: shall go along.

5 *terms of our estate*: my position (as king).

7 *brows*: threatening looks.
provide: equip.

9 *bodies*: i.e. the lives of the king's subjects.

11 *peculiar*: concerning only the individual.
The language — characteristically for
Rosencrantz — is pompous and imprecise
in its meaning.

13 *noyance*: harm.

14 *weal*: well-being.

15 *cess of majesty*: cessation of rule (when the
monarch dies or is dethroned).

16 *gulf*: whirlpool.

17 *massy wheel*: There are many pictures
which show the monarch at the top of
Fortune's wheel.

19 *lesser things*: e.g. courtiers and statesmen.

20 *mortised and adjoined*: closely joined (the
image is from carpentry).

Scene 3

Enter King, Rosencrantz *and* Guildenstern

      King

I like him not, nor stands it safe with us

To let his madness range. Therefore prepare you.

I your commission will forthwith dispatch,

And he to England shall along with you.

5 The terms of our estate may not endure

Hazard so near us as doth hourly grow

Out of his brows.

      Guildenstern   We will ourselves provide.

Most holy and religious fear it is

To keep those many many bodies safe

10 That live and feed upon your Majesty.

      Rosencrantz

The single and peculiar life is bound

With all the strength and armour of the mind

To keep itself from noyance; but much more

That spirit upon whose weal depends and rests

15 The lives of many. The cess of majesty

Dies not alone, but like a gulf doth draw

What's near it with it. Or it is a massy wheel

Fix'd on the summit of the highest mount,

To whose huge spokes ten thousand lesser things

20 Are mortis'd and adjoin'd, which when it falls,

21 *annexment*: thing which is joined on.
22 *Attends the boist'rous ruin*: accompanies the major disaster.

24 'Get ready to travel quickly.'
25 *this fear*: i.e. this cause of fear.

28 *convey*: secrete, hide.
29 *process*: what goes on.
    tax him home: speak plainly to him.
30 *as you said*: The suggestion in fact came from Polonius himself (see *3, 1, 186–7*).
31 *meet*: suitable.
33 *of vantage*: in addition; *or* from a good (concealed) position.
36 *rank*: rotten. Claudius for the first time reveals his thoughts to the audience, so that we understand the enormity of his deed — and the rightness of Hamlet's cause.
37 *primal eldest curse*: the curse of Cain, who became the world's first murderer by killing his brother (Genesis, 4:11–12).
39 *inclination*: natural desire.
    will: determination.
41 *double business bound*: with two jobs to do.
42 *in pause . . . begin*: still wondering which to do first.
43–6 The images in these lines have parallels in other plays of Shakespeare's (the bloody hand in *Macbeth*, and the raining mercy in *Merchant of Venice*). They combine with biblical references: 'How fair a thing is mercy in the time of anguish and trouble? It is like a cloud of rain that cometh in the time of drought' (Ecclesiasticus, 35:19); 'though your sins be as scarlet, they shall be as white as snow' (Isaiah, 1:18); *and* 'wash me, and I shall be whiter than snow' (Psalm 51:7).
46 *Whereto serves mercy*: what is mercy for.
47 *to confront . . . offence*: meet sin face to face.
48 *twofold force*: Claudius remembers the petitions of the Lord's prayer: 'Lead us not into temptation' *and* 'deliver us from evil' — *both* 'prevent us from sinning', *and* 'forgive us for the wrong we have already done'.
51 *My fault is past*: Claudius's sin has already been committed — he must pray for forgiveness now.

Each small annexment, petty consequence,
Attends the boist'rous ruin. Never alone
Did the King sigh, but with a general groan.

King
Arm you, I pray you, to this speedy voyage,
25 For we will fetters put about this fear
Which now goes too free-footed.

Rosencrantz   We will haste us.
            [*Exeunt* Rosencrantz *and* Guildenstern

        Enter Polonius

Polonius
My lord, he's going to his mother's closet.
Behind the arras I'll convey myself
To hear the process. I'll warrant she'll tax him home,
30 And as you said—and wisely was it said—
'Tis meet that some more audience than a mother,
Since nature makes them partial, should o'erhear
The speech of vantage. Fare you well, my liege.
I'll call upon you ere you go to bed,
35 And tell you what I know.

King   Thanks, dear my lord.
            [*Exit* Polonius
O, my offence is rank, it smells to heaven;
It hath the primal eldest curse upon't—
A brother's murder. Pray can I not,
Though inclination be as sharp as will,
40 My stronger guilt defeats my strong intent,
And, like a man to double business bound,
I stand in pause where I shall first begin,
And both neglect. What if this cursed hand
Were thicker than itself with brother's blood,
45 Is there not rain enough in the sweet heavens
To wash it white as snow? Whereto serves mercy
But to confront the visage of offence?
And what's in prayer but this twofold force,
To be forestalled ere we come to fall
50 Or pardon'd being down? Then I'll look up.
My fault is past—but O, what form of prayer
Can serve my turn? 'Forgive me my foul murder?'
That cannot be, since I am still possess'd
Of those effects for which I did the murder—
55 My crown, mine own ambition, and my queen.

56 *retain th'offence*: keep the results of the sin.

57 *currents*: courses of events.

58 *gilded*: gold-bearing. Shakespeare suggests both bribery and, through the pun, guilt.
    shove by: push aside.

59–60 'What has been gained by the crime is often used to buy off the law.'

61 *There*: i.e. 'above' – in heaven.
    shuffling: tricky dealing.

61–2 *Lies in his true nature*: is seen for what it really is.

62–4 *we ourselves . . . evidence*: when we are confronted with our sins, we are compelled to give evidence against ourselves.

64 *What rests*: what's the alternative.

65 *can*: can do.

68 *limed*: trapped. Birds were sometimes caught by smearing trees with lime.

69 *engag'd*: entangled.
    Make assay: come to my aid.

70 *strings of steel*: hardened (because of what he has done).

73 *pat*: smartly.

74 *And so 'a goes to heaven*: Hamlet assumes that his uncle, because he is able to pray, is in such a state of grace that his soul will not have to endure the purgatorial torments that Hamlet's father is suffering.

75 *scann'd*: interpreted.

77 *sole*: only.

79 *hire and salary*: i.e. payment (not punishment) for the deed.

80 *took my father grossly*: Hamlet's father had been unprepared for death, and was not able to purge his sins — through prayer and penance — before he died.

81 *crimes*: sins.
    broad blown: in full blossom.
    flush: full of life.

82 *audit*: reckoning.

83 *in . . . thought*: in the way that we on earth think about it.

84 *'Tis heavy with him*: things are bad for him.

85 *him*: i.e. Claudius.

86 *fit and season'd*: thoroughly prepared.
    passage: journey.

88 *Up*: away.
    know . . . hint: wait until you find a more fearful opportunity.

May one be pardon'd and retain th'offence?
In the corrupted currents of this world
Offence's gilded hand may shove by justice,
And oft 'tis seen the wicked prize itself
60 Buys out the law. But 'tis not so above:
There is no shuffling, there the action lies
In his true nature, and we ourselves compell'd
Even to the teeth and forehead of our faults
To give in evidence. What then? What rests?
65 Try what repentance can. What can it not?
Yet what can it, when one cannot repent?
O wretched state! O bosom black as death!
O limed soul, that struggling to be free
Art more engag'd! Help, angels! Make assay.
70 Bow, stubborn knees; and heart with strings of steel,
Be soft as sinews of the new-born babe.
All may be well.

He kneels

Enter Hamlet

Hamlet
Now might I do it pat, now 'a is a-praying.
And now I'll do't.

Draws his sword

            And so 'a goes to heaven;
75 And so am I reveng'd. That would be scann'd:
A villain kills my father, and for that
I, his sole son, do this same villain send
To heaven.
Why, this is hire and salary, not revenge.
80 'A took my father grossly, full of bread,
With all his crimes broad blown, as flush as May;
And how his audit stands who knows save heaven?
But in our circumstance and course of thought
'Tis heavy with him. And am I then reveng'd,
85 To take him in the purging of his soul,
When he is fit and season'd for his passage?
No.
Up, sword, and know thou a more horrid hent:
When he is drunk asleep, or in his rage,

90   Or in th'incestuous pleasure of his bed,
     At game a-swearing, or about some act
     That has no relish of salvation in't,
     Then trip him, that his heels may kick at heaven
     And that his soul may be as damn'd and black
95   As hell, whereto it goes. My mother stays.
     This physic but prolongs thy sickly days.   [*Exit*
          King
     My words fly up, my thoughts remain below.
     Words without thoughts never to heaven go.   [*Exit*

Act 3   Scene 4

Polonius tells the Queen how she must speak to
Hamlet, then he hides behind the arras and
overhears the beginning of the conversation. But,
fearing for the Queen's safety, he tries to raise the
alarm — and is stabbed through the concealing
curtain. Hamlet proceeds to confront his mother
with her guilt, and only the intervention of the
Ghost can stop his passionate outburst. After the
Ghost has left the stage, the mother listens to her
son's counsel; and the scene ends as Hamlet
prepares to embark for England.

91   *game*: gambling.
92   *relish*: taste.
93   *heels . . . heaven*: i.e. fall headlong into hell.

95   *stays*: is waiting.
96   *physic*: i.e. the praying.

1   *straight*: immediately.
     lay home to him: speak firmly to him (see
     'tax him home' 3, 3, 29).
2   *pranks*: rude behaviour.
     broad: outrageous.
4   *silence me*: hide myself in silence.
5   *be round*: speak plainly.
     war'nt: promise (warrant).

13   *forgot me*: forgotten who I am.
     by the rood: by the cross on which Christ
     was crucified.
14   *husband's brother's wife*: Such a marriage
     was forbidden by the church laws of that
     time as stated in *The Book of Common
     Prayer*.
15   *would*: I wish.

Scene 4

Enter Queen *and* Polonius

     Polonius
'A will come straight. Look you lay home to him,
Tell him his pranks have been too broad to bear with
And that your Grace hath screen'd and stood between
Much heat and him. I'll silence me even here.
5   Pray you be round.
          Queen   I'll war'nt you, fear me not.
     Withdraw, I hear him coming.
                    [Polonius *hides behind the arras*

     Enter Hamlet

          Hamlet
     Now, mother, what's the matter?
          Queen
     Hamlet, thou hast thy father much offended.
          Hamlet
     Mother, you have my father much offended.
          Queen
10   Come, come, you answer with an idle tongue.
          Hamlet
     Go, go, you question with a wicked tongue.
          Queen
     Why, how now, Hamlet?
          Hamlet   What's the matter now?
          Queen
     Have you forgot me?
          Hamlet   No, by the rood, not so.
     You are the Queen, your husband's brother's wife,
15   And, would it were not so, you are my mother.

16 This line gives Hamlet some cause for suspicion.

23 *A rat*: rats are well-known for drawing attention to themselves by squeaking.
    Dead for a ducat: I'll bet a ducat I've killed it.

29 *kill a king*: Gertrude's reaction declares her innocence of the murder.
32 *thy better*: i.e. Claudius.
33 *too busy*: interfering.
37 *custom*: habit.
    braz'd: brazened — hardened like brass.
38 *proof*: impenetrable (like armour).
    sense: feeling.
42 *rose*: emblem of perfect love.
44 *blister*: the sign of a whore, which was branded on the forehead.
45 *dicers*: gamblers (with dice).
46-7 'Reduces marriage to a legal contract, and marriage vows to empty words.'
48-51 Hamlet's own syntax seems to crack with the weight it utters: the sky glowers sadly (with 'tristful visage') over the whole earth ('this solidity and compound mass') as at impending doomsday ('against the doom'), and is sick at the thought of what has been done.

Queen
Nay, then I'll set those to you that can speak.
Hamlet
Come, come, and sit you down, you shall not budge.
You go not till I set you up a glass
Where you may see the inmost part of you.
Queen
20 What wilt thou do? Thou wilt not murder me?
Help, ho!
Polonius
[*Behind the arras*] What ho! Help!
Hamlet
How now? A rat! Dead for a ducat, dead.

Thrusts his rapier through the arras

Polonius
[*Behind*] O, I am slain.
Queen
25 O me, what hast thou done?
Hamlet   Nay, I know not.
Is it the King?

*Lifts up the arras and
discovers* Polonius, *dead*

Queen
O what a rash and bloody deed is this!
Hamlet
A bloody deed. Almost as bad, good mother,
As kill a king and marry with his brother.
Queen
30 As kill a king?
Hamlet   Ay, lady, it was my word.—
Thou wretched, rash, intruding fool, farewell.
I took thee for thy better. Take thy fortune:
Thou find'st to be too busy is some danger.—
Leave wringing of your hands. Peace, sit you down,
35 And let me wring your heart; for so I shall
If it be made of penetrable stuff,
If damned custom have not braz'd it so,
That it be proof and bulwark against sense.

52 *index*: the 'table of contents' at the beginning of a book.

53 *this picture*: In some productions Hamlet indicates portraits hanging on the wall; in others he shows miniatures, worn as lockets.

54 *counterfeit presentment*: representation in a portrait.

55 *this brow*: Hamlet's father has the qualities of the gods of classical mythology.

56 *Hyperion*: god of the sun.
front of Jove: forehead of the king of the gods.

58 *station . . . Mercury*: stance like the messenger of the gods (who was renowned for his posture).

59 *New-lighted*: just as he alights (Shakespeare seems to allude to such a description of Mercury in Virgil's *Aeneid*, iv.252–3).

60–61 'It was as though all the gods had combined to impress their likenesses on his form.'

62 'To show the world what a man ought to be.'

64 *mildew'd ear*: One ear of corn, infected with mildew, spreads the disease among the healthy ('wholesome') corn.

65 *Blasting*: infecting.

66 *leave*: cease.

67 *batten*: fatten yourself. The sense of these lines is clear enough (Hamlet is reproaching his mother for choosing to love his uncle after she had known his father); but the imagery is not easily explicable.

69 *heyday in the blood*: time of wild sexual passion.
humble: undemanding.

70 *waits upon*: is controlled by.

71–6 *Sense . . . difference*: ability to perceive through the five senses.

72 *motion*: Aristotle taught that some sense was present in all things which are capable of movement (e.g. animals and plants are sensible, but not stones).

73 *apoplex'd*: paralysed (as though by a stroke).
would not err: would not err in such a way.

74 *ecstasy*: madness, state of hallucination.
thrall'd: enslaved.

75 *quantity of choice*: ability to make a choice. ·

76 *serve . . . difference*: needed where there is such a difference (as in her choice between his father and his uncle).

77 *cozen'd*: deceived.
hoodman-blind: blind-man's buff.

Queen
What have I done, that thou dar'st wag thy tongue
40 In noise so rude against me?
    Hamlet   Such an act
That blurs the grace and blush of modesty,
Calls virtue hypocrite, takes off the rose
From the fair forehead of an innocent love
And sets a blister there, makes marriage vows
45 As false as dicers' oaths—O, such a deed
As from the body of contraction plucks
The very soul, and sweet religion makes
A rhapsody of words. Heaven's face does glow
O'er this solidity and compound mass
50 With tristful visage, as against the doom,
Is thought-sick at the act.
    Queen   Ay me, what act
That roars so loud and thunders in the index?
    Hamlet
Look here upon this picture, and on this,
The counterfeit presentment of two brothers.
55 See what a grace was seated on this brow,
Hyperion's curls, the front of Jove himself,
An eye like Mars to threaten and command,
A station like the herald Mercury
New-lighted on a heaven-kissing hill,
60 A combination and a form indeed
Where every god did seem to set his seal
To give the world assurance of a man.
This was your husband. Look you now what follows.
Here is your husband, like a mildew'd ear
65 Blasting his wholesome brother. Have you eyes?
Could you on this fair mountain leave to feed
And batten on this moor? Ha, have you eyes?
You cannot call it love; for at your age
The heyday in the blood is tame, it's humble,
70 And waits upon the judgment, and what judgment
Would step from this to this? Sense sure you have,
Else could you not have motion; but sure that sense
Is apoplex'd, for madness would not err
Nor sense to ecstasy was ne'er so thrall'd
75 But it reserv'd some quantity of choice
To serve in such a difference. What devil was't
That thus hath cozen'd you at hoodman-blind?
Eyes without feeling, feeling without sight,

79   *sans all*: without any of the other senses.

81   *mope*: be unaware.

82   *Rebellious hell*: i.e. the sexual passion which rebels against the controlling reason.

83   *mutine*: mutiny.
     matron: mature woman.

84–5   *flaming youth . . . fire*: Hamlet evokes the image of a wax candle, whose melted drops burn in its own flame.

86   *compulsive ardour*: irresistible passion.
     gives the charge: makes the attack.

87   *frost*: i.e. the cooler desires of the 'matron'.

88   *panders will*: is put to the service of passion.

90   *grained*: ingrained.

91   *will . . . tinct*: will not lose their colour (e.g. when washed).

92   *enseamed*: greasy.

93   *Stew'd*: steeped, soaked. Hamlet's disgust comes to its climax — characteristically, with a pun ('stews' = brothels).

95   *like daggers*: i.e. just as Hamlet promised at *3, 2, 387*.

97   *tithe*: tenth part.

98   *precedent lord*: previous husband.
     a vice: In Morality plays, the Vice was a clown who played comic scenes with the devil; Hamlet describes Claudius as a parody of kingship.

99   *cutpurse*: thief.

103   *of shreds and patches*: made of bits and pieces.

104–5   See Hamlet's appeal to the 'Angels and ministers of grace' at *1, 4, 39*.

107   *chide*: Ghosts, it was believed, would re-appear if their initial request was not performed promptly.

108   *laps'd in time and passion*: The exact meaning of these words is uncertain; Hamlet feels that he has let slip both the right moment and the right emotion for taking revenge on Claudius. Shakespeare is imprecise about time sequences here (and in most of his plays) but it is evident that

Ears without hands or eyes, smelling sans all,
80 Or but a sickly part of one true sense
Could not so mope. O shame, where is thy blush?
Rebellious hell,
If thou canst mutine in a matron's bones,
To flaming youth let virtue be as wax
85 And melt in her own fire; proclaim no shame
When the compulsive ardour gives the charge,
Since frost itself as actively doth burn
And reason panders will.
        Queen   O Hamlet, speak no more.
Thou turn'st my eyes into my very soul,
90 And there I see such black and grained spots
As will not leave their tinct.
        Hamlet   Nay, but to live
In the rank sweat of an enseamed bed,
Stew'd in corruption, honeying and making love
Over the nasty sty!
        Queen   O speak to me no more.
95 These words like daggers enter in my ears.
No more, sweet Hamlet.
        Hamlet   A murderer and a villain,
A slave that is not twentieth part the tithe
Of your precedent lord, a vice of kings,
A cutpurse of the empire and the rule,
100 That from a shelf the precious diadem stole
And put it in his pocket—
        Queen
No more.
        Hamlet
A king of shreds and patches—

        Enter Ghost

Save me and hover o'er me with your wings,
105 You heavenly guards! What would your gracious
        figure?
        Queen
Alas, he's mad.
        Hamlet
Do you not come your tardy son to chide,
That, laps'd in time and passion, lets go by
Th'important acting of your dread command?
110 O say.
        Ghost   Do not forget. This visitation

some weeks have elapsed since the Ghost's
first appearance to Hamlet.
109 *important*: urgent.
110 *Do not forget*: Once again (see *1*, 5, 91)
the Ghost stirs Hamlet's memory.
111 *whet*: sharpen (like a knife).
112 *amazement*: bewilderment. Gertrude is
unaware of the Ghost's presence.
114 *Conceit*: imagination.

117 *bend your eye*: fix your gaze.
118 *incorporal*: empty.
119 *Forth . . . peep*: your eyes stare wildly.
120 *in th'alarm*: when the alarm is sounded.
121-2 Gertrude describes the same pheno-
menon that Macbeth recalls:
            my fell of hair
Would at a dismal treatise rouse and stir
As life were in't. (*Macbeth*, 5, 5, 11–13).
excrements: outgrowths (which have no life
in them).
an: on.
126 *His form and cause*: his appearance and the
reason he has for appearing.
conjoin'd: joined together.
127 *capable*: sensible, able to respond.
128 *action*: movement.
129 *effects*: purposes.
130 *want true colour*: not look right — be done
for the wrong reason.
tears . . . blood: perhaps tears will be shed
rather than blood.

137 *in his habit as he liv'd*: dressed just as he
used to when he was alive (i.e. not in
armour). Q1, perhaps reflecting theatrical
practice, directs that the Ghost should enter
'in his night gown' (= a robe of undress) at
line 103.
138 *portal*: doorway.
139 *coinage*: invention.
140 *bodiless creation*: making something out of
nothing.
ecstasy: madness.
141 *cunning in*: clever at.
142 *temperately keep time*: beats regularly.

Is but to whet thy almost blunted purpose.
But look, amazement on thy mother sits.
O step between her and her fighting soul.
Conceit in weakest bodies strongest works.

115 Speak to her, Hamlet.

Hamlet
How is it with you, lady?

Queen   Alas, how is't with you,
That you do bend your eye on vacancy,
And with th'incorporal air do hold discourse?
Forth at your eyes your spirits wildly peep,

120 And, as the sleeping soldiers in th'alarm,
Your bedded hair, like life in excrements,
Start up and stand an end. O gentle son,
Upon the heat and flame of thy distemper
Sprinkle cool patience. Whereon do you look?

Hamlet
125 On him, on him. Look you how pale he glares.
His form and cause conjoin'd, preaching to stones,
Would make them capable.—Do not look upon me,
Lest with this piteous action you convert
My stern effects. Then what I have to do

130 Will want true colour—tears perchance for blood.

Queen
To whom do you speak this?

Hamlet
Do you see nothing there?

Queen
Nothing at all; yet all that is I see.

Hamlet
Nor did you nothing hear?

Queen
135 No, nothing but ourselves.

Hamlet
Why, look you there, look how it steals away.
My father, in his habit as he liv'd!
Look where he goes even now out at the portal.

                                    [*Exit* Ghost

Queen
This is the very coinage of your brain.
140 This bodiless creation ecstasy
Is very cunning in.

Hamlet
My pulse as yours doth temperately keep time,

143	*makes . . . music*: sounds as healthy.
145	*re-word*: repeat.
146	*gambol from*: shy away from, refuse to do.
147	*Lay*: apply. *flattering unction*: soothing ointment.
149	*skin and film*: put a skin over.
152	*what is to come*: future opportunities of sin.
154	*ranker*: grow even more. Hamlet develops the 'unweeded garden' metaphor from *1, 2, 135–7*.
155	*fatness*: grossness. *pursy*: (morally) flabby.
157	*curb*: bow. *him*: i.e. vice.
162	*Assume*: acquire.
163–7	The gist of Hamlet's words (which in one early edition are confused, and in others omitted) is that whilst custom destroys our sense of the evil in bad habits, it does have the virtue of making good habits easily formed — as Hamlet proceeds to exemplify.
166	*gives . . . livery*: creates a habit.
167	*aptly*: readily.
168	*shall*: i.e. must necessarily.
170	*use*: habitual practice. *stamp of nature*: inborn characteristics.
171	*[lodge]*: Modern editors must supply some word meaning 'entertain hospitably' to balance 'or throw him out'.
173–4	'When you are ready to ask for God's blessing, then I will ask for your blessing' (as a son should do when he takes leave of his mother).
174	*lord*: i.e. Polonius. Hamlet appears to believe that the murder of Polonius was ordained by Providence.
177	*their scourge and minister*: i.e. the instrument of divine power.
178	*bestow*: dispose of. *answer well*: atone for, justify.
181	*This*: i.e. the death of Polonius. *remains behind*: is still to come.

And makes as healthful music. It is not madness
That I have utter'd. Bring me to the test,
145 And I the matter will re-word, which madness
Would gambol from. Mother, for love of grace,
Lay not that flattering unction to your soul,
That not your trespass but my madness speaks.
It will but skin and film the ulcerous place,
150 Whiles rank corruption, mining all within,
Infects unseen. Confess yourself to heaven,
Repent what's past, avoid what is to come;
And do not spread the compost on the weeds
To make them ranker. Forgive me this my virtue;
155 For in the fatness of these pursy times
Virtue itself of vice must pardon beg,
Yea, curb and woo for leave to do him good.
   Queen
O Hamlet, thou hast cleft my heart in twain.
   Hamlet
O throw away the worser part of it
160 And live the purer with the other half.
Good night. But go not to my uncle's bed.
Assume a virtue if you have it not.
That monster, custom, who all sense doth eat
Of habits evil, is angel yet in this,
165 That to the use of actions fair and good
He likewise gives a frock or livery
That aptly is put on. Refrain tonight,
And that shall lend a kind of easiness
To the next abstinence, the next more easy;
170 For use almost can change the stamp of nature,
And either [lodge] the devil or throw him out
With wondrous potency. Once more, good night,
And when you are desirous to be blest,
I'll blessing beg of you. For this same lord
175 I do repent; but heaven hath pleas'd it so,
To punish me with this and this with me,
That I must be their scourge and minister.
I will bestow him, and will answer well
The death I gave him. So, again, good night.
180 I must be cruel only to be kind.
This bad begins, and worse remains behind.
One word more, good lady.
   Queen   What shall I do?

184 *bloat*: flabby. Hamlet's disgust returns, with his irony.

185 *wanton*: wantonly.
     mouse: a common term of endearment.

186 *a pair*: a few.
     reechy: filthy.

187 *paddling in*: pawing.

188 *ravel . . . out*: disentangle the whole business for him.

190 *in craft*: in cunning.
     'Twere good: The sarcasm increases.

192 *paddock . . . gib*: toad, bat, or tom-cat. Hamlet abuses Claudius, associating him with the familiar spirits of witchcraft.

193 *dear concernings*: matters that concern him so closely.

195–9 Hamlet's allusions are not very clear — but their intention is not hard to grasp. Birds released from a basket are impossible to catch — like cats let out of bags. The ape's fame has not survived: presumably the animal crept into the basket hoping to imitate the birds, but instead of flying it fell from the housetop and was killed. Hamlet is warning the Queen not to reveal his secrets or try to imitate his cleverness.
     try conclusions: see what will happen.

203 *concluded*: decided.

205 *fang'd*: with venomous fangs; Hamlet is now fully alert to the danger presented by Rosencrantz and Guildenstern.

206 *sweep my way*: escort me.

207 *marshal me to knavery*: lead me into some trap.

208 *enginer*: maker of military 'engines'.

209 *Hoist . . . petard*: blown up with his own bomb.
     and . . . hard: unless I'm very unlucky.

210 *delve . . . mines*: dig a countermine a whole yard deeper.

212 'When two plots meet head-on.'

213 *set me packing*: get me going; the murder of Polonius will serve to start off Hamlet's plot.

214 *lug*: Perhaps Hamlet drags Polonius by the heels.
     neighbour: adjoining.

215 *indeed*: i.e. for the last time.

217 *prating*: chattering; the couplet forms an epitaph for Polonius.

218 *draw toward an end*: finish my business.

Hamlet
Not this, by no means, that I bid you do:
Let the bloat King tempt you again to bed,
185 Pinch wanton on your cheek, call you his mouse,
And let him, for a pair of reechy kisses,
Or paddling in your neck with his damn'd fingers,
Make you to ravel all this matter out
That I essentially am not in madness,
190 But mad in craft. 'Twere good you let him know,
For who that's but a queen, fair, sober, wise,
Would from a paddock, from a bat, a gib,
Such dear concernings hide? Who would do so?
No, in despite of sense and secrecy,
195 Unpeg the basket on the house's top,
Let the birds fly, and like the famous ape,
To try conclusions, in the basket creep,
And break your own neck down.
     Queen
Be thou assur'd, if words be made of breath,
200 And breath of life, I have no life to breathe
What thou hast said to me.
     Hamlet
I must to England, you know that?
     Queen   Alack,
I had forgot. 'Tis so concluded on.
     Hamlet
There's letters seal'd, and my two schoolfellows,
205 Whom I will trust as I will adders fang'd—
They bear the mandate, they must sweep my way
And marshal me to knavery. Let it work;
For 'tis the sport to have the enginer
Hoist with his own petard, and't shall go hard
210 But I will delve one yard below their mines
And blow them at the moon. O, 'tis most sweet
When in one line two crafts directly meet.
This man shall set me packing.
I'll lug the guts into the neighbour room.
215 Mother, good night indeed. This counsellor
Is now most still, most secret, and most grave,
Who was in life a foolish prating knave.
Come, sir, to draw toward an end with you.
Good night, mother.
                                   [*Exit lugging in* Polonius.

The Queen *remains*

Act 4

Act 4   Scene 1

Claudius questions the Queen about Hamlet's madness, and Gertrude tells him of the death of Polonius. The King is more determined than ever that Hamlet must be sent to England. The action in this scene immediately follows that of the preceding scene in Gertrude's closet — the King has come to find his wife and hear the outcome of the plot which was suggested by Polonius at the end of *Act 3*, scene 1.

1   *matter in*: a reason for.
    heaves: sighs.
2   *translate*: put it into words.
4   *Bestow this place*: leave us alone. The brief appearance of Rosencrantz and Guildenstern is a useful reminder of their part in the King's plot.

8   *lawless*: uncontrollable.

11   *brainish apprehension*: mental seizure.

13   *had been*: would have been.
     us: The King (using the royal plural) thinks first of his own safety.

16   *answer'd*: explained.

18   *short*: under control.
     haunt: circulation.

22   *divulging*: being known.
23   *pith*: essential substance.

Scene 1

Enter King, *with* Rosencrantz *and* Guildenstern, *to the* Queen

King
There's matter in these sighs, these profound heaves,
You must translate. 'Tis fit we understand them.
Where is your son?
        Queen
Bestow this place on us a little while.
                [*Exeunt* Rosencrantz *and* Guildenstern
5   Ah, mine own lord, what have I seen tonight!
        King
What, Gertrude, how does Hamlet?
        Queen
Mad as the sea and wind when both contend
Which is the mightier. In his lawless fit,
Behind the arras hearing something stir,
10   Whips out his rapier, cries 'A rat, a rat',
And in this brainish apprehension kills
The unseen good old man.
        King   O heavy deed!
It had been so with us had we been there.
His liberty is full of threats to all—
15   To you yourself, to us, to everyone.
Alas, how shall this bloody deed be answer'd?
It will be laid to us, whose providence
Should have kept short, restrain'd, and out of haunt
This mad young man. But so much was our love,
20   We would not understand what was most fit,
But like the owner of a foul disease,
To keep it from divulging, let it feed
Even on the pith of life. Where is he gone?

25-7 Gertrude describes (what we never see) Hamlet weeping over the body of Polonius — and in this, she claims, his madness shows itself to be the real thing, just as gold ('ore') shines out in a mine ('mineral') of base metals.

29   'As soon as it is daybreak.' Claudius reminds us that it is still the middle of the night.

32   *countenance*: accept responsibility for.

33   *join . . . aid*: get some more assistance.

36   *speak fair*: be tactful about it.

40   *untimely*: unfortunately.
      [So envious slander]: Half a line is missing from this speech, and the sense demands its completion. Claudius is observing that malicious gossip has the deadly accuracy of a cannon.
41   *the world's diameter*: across the whole world.
42   *level*: direct.
      blank: target.
44   *woundless*: invulnerable.

Queen
To draw apart the body he hath kill'd,
25 O'er whom—his very madness, like some ore
Among a mineral of metals base,
Shows itself pure—'a weeps for what is done.
    King
O Gertrude, come away.
The sun no sooner shall the mountains touch
30 But we will ship him hence; and this vile deed
We must with all our majesty and skill
Both countenance and excuse.—Ho, Guildenstern!

Enter Rosencrantz *and* Guildenstern

Friends both, go join you with some further aid.
Hamlet in madness hath Polonius slain,
35 And from his mother's closet hath he dragg'd him.
Go seek him out—speak fair—and bring the body
Into the chapel. I pray you haste in this.
    [*Exeunt* Rosencrantz *and* Guildenstern
Come, Gertrude, we'll call up our wisest friends,
And let them know both what we mean to do
40 And what's untimely done. [So envious slander],
Whose whisper o'er the world's diameter,
As level as the cannon to his blank,
Transports his poison'd shot, may miss our name
And hit the woundless air. O come away,
45 My soul is full of discord and dismay.   [*Exeunt*

Act 4   Scene 2

Hamlet refuses to tell Rosencrantz and Guildenstern where he has hidden the body of Polonius.

1   *stowed*: stowed away, hidden.

Scene 2

Enter Hamlet

Hamlet
Safely stowed.

Calling within

But soft, what noise? Who calls on Hamlet? O, here they come.

Enter Rosencrantz, Guildenstern, *and* Others

Rosencrantz
What have you done, my lord, with the dead body?
Hamlet
5 Compounded it with dust, whereto 'tis kin.
Rosencrantz
Tell us where 'tis, that we may take it thence and
bear it to the chapel.
Hamlet
Do not believe it.
Rosencrantz
Believe what?
Hamlet
10 That I can keep your counsel and not mine own.
Besides, to be demanded of a sponge—what replica-
tion should be made by the son of a king?
Rosencrantz
Take you me for a sponge, my lord?
Hamlet
Ay, sir, that soaks up the King's countenance, his
15 rewards, his authorities. But such officers do the
King best service in the end: he keeps them, like an
ape, in the corner of his jaw—first mouthed, to be
last swallowed. When he needs what you have
gleaned, it is but squeezing you and, sponge, you
20 shall be dry again.
Rosencrantz
I understand you not, my lord.
Hamlet
I am glad of it. A knavish speech sleeps in a foolish
ear.
Rosencrantz
My lord, you must tell us where the body is and go
25 with us to the King.
Hamlet
The body is with the King, but the King is not with
the body. The King is a thing—
Guildenstern
A thing, my lord?
Hamlet
Of nothing. Bring me to him.   [*Exeunt*

---

5 *Compounded*: mixed. Although Hamlet has not in fact buried the body.
whereto 'tis kin: see Genesis, 3:19: 'dust thou art, and unto dust shalt thou return'.

10 *counsel*: advice. Hamlet plays on another sense of the word (= secret) in a typically evasive answer.
11 *demanded of*: asked questions by.
12 *replication*: reply. Hamlet uses a legal term.

14 *countenance*: favour.
15 *authorities*: powers.
16 *like an ape*: One of the early texts (Q1) reads 'as an ape doth keep nuts'; Hamlet seems to be warning — or threatening — the King's spies.
17 *mouthed*: put into the mouth.
19 *gleaned*: picked up.

22 'Sarcasm is wasted on fools.'

26 Hamlet's riddling answer is capable of several interpretations — e.g. 'the body of Polonius is here in the palace with Claudius, but Claudius, not being dead, is not with Polonius'.
27 *a thing*: Hamlet might be starting to make a profound remark about the nature of kingship; or (as Guildenstern perhaps anticipates) a slanderous comment on Claudius.
29 *Of nothing*: of no importance, worthless.

Act 4   Scene 3

Hamlet is brought before the King, and tells
Claudius where he may find the body of Polonius.
Claudius, who is now very worried about his
nephew, tells Hamlet that he must leave
immediately for England.

4   *distracted*: unreasoning.

5   *like*: choose.

6–7   *th'offender's scourge . . . the offence*: they
criticize the punishment and never think
about the crime.

7   *To bear . . . even*: to keep everything quiet.

9   *Deliberate pause*: a calculated consideration.

9–10   *Diseases . . . reliev'd*: A proverb: serious
illnesses need drastic treatment.

11   Apparently Guildenstern is absent.

20   *convocation*: assembly. Hamlet proceeds to
a clever play with words and ideas,
combining a familiar aphorism observing
that even an emperor must become a meal
for worms, and an allusion to the Diet (=
council) held by the Emperor Charles V in
the German city of Worms (which was
especially famous for its treatment of
Luther in 1521).
politic: scheming.

24   *variable service*: different courses at a
meal.

Scene 3

Enter King *and two or three* Lords

King
I have sent to seek him and to find the body.
How dangerous is it that this man goes loose!
Yet must not we put the strong law on him:
He's lov'd of the distracted multitude,
5   Who like not in their judgment but their eyes,
And where 'tis so, th'offender's scourge is weigh'd,
But never the offence. To bear all smooth and even,
This sudden sending him away must seem
Deliberate pause. Diseases desperate grown
10   By desperate appliance are reliev'd,
Or not at all.

Enter Rosencrantz *and* Others

How now, what hath befall'n?
Rosencrantz
Where the dead body is bestow'd, my lord,
We cannot get from him.
King   But where is he?
Rosencrantz
Without, my lord, guarded, to know your pleasure.
King
15   Bring him before us.
Rosencrantz   Ho! Bring in the lord.

Enter Hamlet *with* Guards

King
Now, Hamlet, where's Polonius?
Hamlet
At supper.
King
At supper? Where?
Hamlet
Not where he eats, but where 'a is eaten. A cer-
20   tain convocation of politic worms are e'en at him.
Your worm is your only emperor for diet: we fat all
creatures else to fat us, and we fat ourselves for
maggots. Your fat king and your lean beggar is but
variable service—two dishes, but to one table.
25   That's the end.

King
Alas, alas.

Hamlet
A man may fish with the worm that hath eat of a
king, and eat of the fish that hath fed of that worm.

King
What dost thou mean by this?

Hamlet
30 Nothing but to show you how a king may go a
progress through the guts of a beggar.

King
Where is Polonius?

Hamlet
In heaven. Send thither to see. If your messenger
find him not there, seek him i'th'other place your-
35 self. But if indeed you find him not within this
month, you shall nose him as you go up the stairs into
the lobby.

King
[*To some* Attendants] Go seek him there.

Hamlet
'A will stay till you come.   [*Exeunt* Attendants

King
40 Hamlet, this deed, for thine especial safety—
Which we do tender, as we dearly grieve
For that which thou hast done—must send thee hence
With fiery quickness. Therefore prepare thyself.
The bark is ready, and the wind at help,
45 Th'associates tend, and everything is bent
For England.

Hamlet
For England?

King
Ay, Hamlet.

Hamlet
Good.

King
50 So is it, if thou knew'st our purposes.

Hamlet
I see a cherub that sees them. But come, for
England. Farewell, dear mother.

King
Thy loving father, Hamlet.

31   *progress*: state journey, royal tour.

34   *th'other place*: hell.

36   *nose*: smell.

41   *tender*: have a care for.

44   *bark*: ship.
     at help: in the right quarter.
45   *Th'associates tend*: your companions wait.
     bent: directed.

47   *For England*: Hamlet is not surprised — he
     told his mother his destination in *3, 4, 202*.

51   *cherub*: The Old Testament prophet Ezekiel
     described the celestial Cherubim as being
     'full of eyes' (Ezekiel, 10:12).

55 *man and wife*: see St Mark, 10:8: 'they twain shall be one flesh'.

57 *at foot*: closely.
59–60 'Everything else connected with this business has been got ready.'
61 *England*: i.e. King of England; Claudius addresses himself to the monarch.
    hold'st at aught: value at all.
62–5 'Our power should have taught you to value us, since you are still smarting from the wounds inflicted on you, and you are still paying tribute (the Danegeld) to us.'
63 *cicatrice*: scar.
64 *free awe*: respect given willingly.
65 *coldly set*: value lightly.
66 *sovereign process*: royal command.
    imports at full: gives full directions.
67 *congruing to*: in accordance with.
68 *present death*: immediate execution. The King's purpose is now revealed.
69 *hectic*: fever.
71 *Howe'er my haps*: whatever else happens.

Hamlet
My mother. Father and mother is man and wife,
55 man and wife is one flesh; so my mother. Come, for
England.   [*Exit*
King
Follow him at foot. Tempt him with speed aboard,
Delay it not—I'll have him hence tonight.
Away, for everything is seal'd and done
60 That else leans on th'affair. Pray you make haste.
                                    [*Exeunt all but the* King
And England, if my love thou hold'st at aught—
As my great power thereof may give thee sense,
Since yet thy cicatrice looks raw and red
After the Danish sword, and thy free awe
65 Pays homage to us—thou mayst not coldly set
Our sovereign process, which imports at full,
By letters congruing to that effect,
The present death of Hamlet. Do it, England;
For like the hectic in my blood he rages,
70 And thou must cure me. Till I know 'tis done,
Howe'er my haps, my joys were ne'er begun.   [*Exit*

Act 4   Scene 4

A change of mood and location as an army of Norwegian soldiers marches across the stage. At their head is young Fortinbras, brisk and purposeful; and the watching Hamlet is moved to further meditation on his own inactivity.

2 *by his licence*: see 2, 2, 77–8.

3 *conveyance*: safe conduct.

6 *express . . . eye*: pay our respects to his person.

8 *softly*: quietly. The soldiers are to behave respectfully.

9 *powers*: soldiers.

Scene 4

Enter Fortinbras *with his* Army, *marching over the stage*

Fortinbras
Go, captain, from me greet the Danish king.
Tell him that by his licence Fortinbras
Craves the conveyance of a promis'd march
Over his kingdom. You know the rendezvous.
5 If that his Majesty would aught with us,
We shall express our duty in his eye;
And let him know so.
Captain   I will do't, my lord.
Fortinbras
Go softly on.   [*Exeunt all but the* Captain

Enter Hamlet, Rosencrantz *and* Others

Hamlet
Good sir, whose powers are these?

Captain

10   They are of Norway, sir.

Hamlet

How purpos'd, sir, I pray you?

Captain

Against some part of Poland.

Hamlet

Who commands them, sir?

Captain

The nephew to old Norway, Fortinbras.

Hamlet

15   Goes it against the main of Poland, sir,
Or for some frontier?

Captain

Truly to speak, and with no addition,
We go to gain a little patch of ground
That hath in it no profit but the name.

20   To pay five ducats—five—I would not farm it;
Nor will it yield to Norway or the Pole
A ranker rate should it be sold in fee.

Hamlet

Why, then the Polack never will defend it.

Captain

Yes, it is already garrison'd.

Hamlet

25   Two thousand souls and twenty thousand ducats
Will not debate the question of this straw!
This is th'impostume of much wealth and peace,
That inward breaks, and shows no cause without
Why the man dies. I humbly thank you, sir.

Captain

30   God buy you, sir.   [*Exit*

Rosencrantz   Will't please you go, my lord?

Hamlet

I'll be with you straight. Go a little before.

[*Exeunt all but* Hamlet

How all occasions do inform against me,
And spur my dull revenge. What is a man
If his chief good and market of his time

35   Be but to sleep and feed? A beast, no more.
Sure he that made us with such large discourse,
Looking before and after, gave us not
That capability and godlike reason

12   *Against*: to attack.

14   *old Norway*: the old King of Norway.

15   *the main*: the central part.
16   *frontier*: fortress on the boundary.

17   *addition*: exaggeration.

19   *the name*: i.e. of conqueror. Fortinbras is fighting just for the sake of his reputation.
20   *farm*: rent.

22   *ranker*: better interest.
in fee: outright.

23   *the Polack*: the King of Poland.

25   Hamlet estimates the cost — in lives and money — of this expedition.
26   'Will not settle this trivial matter.'
27   *th'impostume . . . peace*: the abscess of the affluent society. Shakespeare often suggests that corruption spreads through a peaceful society, and eventually erupts into war.
28   *without*: externally.

32–3 Hamlet muses on the chance happenings — the encounter with the players, and now the meeting with Fortinbras — which seem to reproach him for his indecisiveness.
34   *his chief . . . time*: all he does with his time.
36   *large discourse*: fine power of reasoning.
37   *Looking before and after*: i.e. learning from the past and planning for the future.
38   *godlike reason*: The power of reasoning is what separates man from the rest of creation.

39 *fust*: go mouldy.
40 *Bestial oblivion*: an animal's forgetfulness.
41 *Of*: resulting from.
  too precisely: in too much detail.
  event: the outcome.
44 *To do*: to be done.
45 *Sith*: since.
  cause: motive.
46 *gross*: as weighty.
47 *mass and charge*: size and expense.
48 *delicate*: sensitive.
  tender: young.
49 *puff'd*: blown up.
50 *Makes mouths at*: pulls faces at, scorns.
  the invisible event: unpredictable outcome.
53–4 'To refuse to do anything unless there is a
  good cause to fight for is *not* what makes a
  man truly great.' In these lines the '*not*'
  must be taken in a double sense.
55–6 'What is truly great is to fight over an
  apparently worthless cause (as Fortinbras is
  doing) when it affects one's honour.'
58 *Excitements of*: incentives for. In Hamlet's
  case, both mind and emotions should be
  affected.
60 *twenty thousand men*: The numbers of
  ducats and of men (estimated in line 25)
  have got confused.
61 *fantasy and trick*: trifling illusion.
62 *like beds*: i.e. willingly.
63 'Not big enough to hold those who are
  fighting for it.'
64 *tomb . . . continent*: a big enough grave and
  container.
66 Hamlet's resolution may be compared with
  that of Macbeth, who determines:
              from this moment
  The very firstlings of my heart shall be
  The firstlings of my hand.
              (*Macbeth, 4*, 1, 146–8)

To fust in us unus'd. Now whether it be
40 Bestial oblivion, or some craven scruple
Of thinking too precisely on th'event—
A thought which, quarter'd, hath but one part wisdom
And ever three parts coward—I do not know
Why yet I live to say this thing's to do,
45 Sith I have cause, and will, and strength, and means
To do't. Examples gross as earth exhort me,
Witness this army of such mass and charge,
Led by a delicate and tender prince,
Whose spirit, with divine ambition puff'd,
50 Makes mouths at the invisible event,
Exposing what is mortal and unsure
To all that fortune, death, and danger dare,
Even for an eggshell. Rightly to be great
Is not to stir without great argument,
55 But greatly to find quarrel in a straw
When honour's at the stake. How stand I then,
That have a father kill'd, a mother stain'd,
Excitements of my reason and my blood,
And let all sleep, while to my shame I see
60 The imminent death of twenty thousand men
That, for a fantasy and trick of fame,
Go to their graves like beds, fight for a plot
Whereon the numbers cannot try the cause,
Which is not tomb enough and continent
65 To hide the slain? O, from this time forth
My thoughts be bloody or be nothing worth.   [*Exit*

The Queen is told that Ophelia, anguished by the death of her father, has gone out of her mind. The girl herself appears, showing all the signs we have been told about; and both Gertrude and Claudius — for different reasons — are deeply distressed. Ophelia sings, and speaks in riddles: the form of her madness is not unlike Hamlet's — except that hers is real. When Ophelia has left the stage, Claudius voices his fear that the murder of Polonius will have serious consequences for them all. Immediately afterwards, news is brought of the arrival of Laertes, who is demanding retribution for the killing of Polonius. Ophelia returns to the stage, and Laertes' grief is redoubled at the sight of his sister's madness.

2 *distract*: distracted.
   mood: state of mind.
   will needs be: must be.
3 *would she have*: does she want.
5 *tricks i'th'world*: strange dealings about.
   hems: says 'Mmm'.
6 *Spurns . . . straws*: takes offence at the least little thing.
   in doubt: ambiguously.
7 *nothing*: nonsense.
8 *unshaped use*: disorganized manner.
9 *collection*: try to sort it out.
   aim: guess.
11 *Which*: i.e. her words.
   yield: represent.
12 'Although we cannot be certain, there may be such that is dangerous.'
15 *ill-breeding*: mischief-making.
17 *sick*: guilty. Hamlet's reproaches have had the desired effect.
18 *toy*: trifle.
   amiss: misfortune. The rhymed couplets here mark off the proverbial nature of the thought or *sententia*.
19 *artless jealousy*: uncontrolled suspicion.
20 *spills*: destroys.
21 *beauteous Majesty*: Presumably Ophelia refers to the Queen.
22s.d. *sings*: Ophelia's grief, as expressed in her songs (which are snatches of old ballads), seems to mourn both for her father's death and for the loss of Hamlet, her own 'true love'. (See p.137).

Scene 5

Enter Queen, Horatio, *and a* Gentleman

Queen
I will not speak with her.
Gentleman   She is importunate,
Indeed distract. Her mood will needs be pitied.
Queen
What would she have?
Gentleman
She speaks much of her father, says she hears
5 There's tricks i'th' world, and hems, and beats her heart,
Spurns enviously at straws, speaks things in doubt
That carry but half sense. Her speech is nothing,
Yet the unshaped use of it doth move
The hearers to collection. They aim at it,
10 And botch the words up fit to their own thoughts,
Which, as her winks and nods and gestures yield them,
Indeed would make one think there might be thought,
Though nothing sure, yet much unhappily.
Horatio
'Twere good she were spoken with, for she may strew
15 Dangerous conjectures in ill-breeding minds.
Queen
Let her come in.   [*Exit* Gentleman
[*Aside*] To my sick soul, as sin's true nature is,
Each toy seems prologue to some great amiss.
So full of artless jealousy is guilt,
20 It spills itself in fearing to be spilt.

Enter Ophelia

Ophelia
Where is the beauteous Majesty of Denmark?
Queen
How now, Ophelia?

Ophelia

[*Sings*]   *How should I your true love know*
                  From another one?
25   *By his cockle hat and staff*
                  And his sandal shoon.

Queen

Alas, sweet lady, what imports this song?

Ophelia

Say you? Nay, pray you mark.

[*Sings*]   *He is dead and gone, lady,*
30   *He is dead and gone,*
                  At his head a grass-green turf,
                  At his heels a stone.

O ho!

Queen

Nay, but Ophelia—

Ophelia

35 Pray you mark.

[*Sings*]   *White his shroud as the mountain snow—*

Enter King

Queen

Alas, look here, my lord.

Ophelia

[*Sings*]   *Larded with sweet flowers*
                  Which bewept to the grave did not go
40   *With true-love showers.*

King

How do you, pretty lady?

Ophelia

Well, good dild you. They say the owl was a baker's
daughter. Lord, we know what we are, but know
not what we may be. God be at your table.

King

45 Conceit upon her father.

25–6   The lover is depicted as a pilgrim,
wearing in his hat a 'cockle' or scallop shell
(the sign of a pilgrim visiting the shrine of
St James at Compostela), carrying a
pilgrim's walking-staff, and clad in
sandalled shoes ('shoon' is an archaic plural
form).

28   *mark*: listen.

38   *Larded*: sprinkled all over.
39   *did not go*: Ophelia stumbles in her song,
violating its rhythm but describing the
burial of Polonius more exactly (see lines
84, 210–12).
42   *good dild you*: may God yield (i.e. reward)
you.
       the owl: A folk-tale tells of a baker's
daughter turned into an owl because she
gave short weight.
43–4   *we know . . . we may be*: See 1 John, 3:2:
'Now are we the sons of God, and it doth
not yet appear what we may be.'
44   *at your table*: with you.
45   *Conceit upon*: distressed about.

Ophelia
Pray let's have no words of this, but when they ask
you what it means, say you this.
[*Sings*]   *Tomorrow is Saint Valentine's day,*
             All in the morning betime,
50   *And I a maid at your window,*
             To be your Valentine.
             Then up he rose, and donn'd his clo'es,
             And dupp'd the chamber door,
             Let in the maid that out a maid
55   *Never departed more.*
          King
Pretty Ophelia—
          Ophelia
Indeed, without an oath, I'll make an end on't.
             By Gis and by Saint Charity,
             Alack and fie for shame,
60   *Young men will do't if they come to't—*
             By Cock, they are to blame.
             Quoth she, 'Before you tumbled me,
             You promis'd me to wed.'
He answers,
65   *'So would I a done, by yonder sun,*
             And thou hadst not come to my bed.'
          King
How long hath she been thus?
          Ophelia
I hope all will be well. We must be patient. But I
cannot choose but weep to think they would lay
70 him i'th' cold ground. My brother shall know of it.
And so I thank you for your good counsel. Come,
my coach. Good night, ladies, good night. Sweet
ladies, good night, good night.   [*Exit*
          King
Follow her close; give her good watch, I pray you.
                                                  [*Exit* Horatio
75 O, this is the poison of deep grief: it springs
All from her father's death. And now behold—
O Gertrude, Gertrude,
When sorrows come, they come not single spies,
But in battalions. First, her father slain;
80 Next, your son gone, and he most violent author
Of his own just remove; the people muddied,

48 *St Valentine's day*: 14 February. Tradition
    held that young men and women alike
    would find a true lover in the first person of
    the opposite sex to be encountered on this
    day.
49 *betime*: early.
52 *clo'es*: clothes.
53 *dupp'd*: opened.

58 *Gis*: Jesus.
    Charity: the personification of the virtue.

60 *do't . . . to't*: take advantage of a girl if they
    are given the chance.
61 *Cock*: God — but there is also a pun on
    'cock' = penis.
62 *tumbled me*: i.e. took my virginity.

65 *a done*: have done.
66 *And*: if.

74 *close*: immediately.
    give her good watch: watch her carefully.
78 *When . . . battalions*: i.e. it never rains but
    it pours. Claudius offers a variant on a
    common saying; 'spies' were single soldiers
    sent ahead of the general army to
    reconnoitre.
81 *his . . . remove*: Claudius shifts the blame
    for the Prince's departure on to Hamlet
    himself.
    muddied: confused — like water in a stream
    or fountain that has been stirred up.

82	*Thick and unwholesome*: troubled and suspicious.
83	*we*: I. Again Claudius uses the royal plural. *greenly*: foolishly.
84	*hugger-mugger*: secretly and in haste.
85	'Beside herself, out of her mind.'
86	*which*: i.e. judgement. *pictures*: only images of men.
87	*as much containing*: just as serious.
89	*Feeds on this wonder*: broods over his bewilderment. *keeps . . .clouds*: holds himself aloof.
90	*wants not*: does not lack. *buzzers*: scandal-mongers.
92	*necessity*: the need to blame someone. *of matter beggar'd*: being short of hard facts.
93	'Won't hesitate to accuse me.'
94	*In ear and ear*: to one person after another. *this*: this whole business.
95	*murd'ring-piece*: gun (e.g. cannon) which scatters its shot and kills many at once.
96	*gives me superfluous death*: is killing me several times over.
97	*Switzers*: bodyguard (dressed in the red and yellow uniform of the Swiss mercenary soldiers).
99–108	Such announcements were set-pieces in classical drama and in Elizabethan tragedies; their formal rhetoric marks them off from the usual verse.
99	*overpeering*: rising above. *his list*: its limits.
100	*flats*: low-lying coastal area, where the rising tide races inland. *impetuous*: violent.
101	*in a riotous head*: advancing with a gang of rebels.
103–5	'As if a new world was just about to begin, rejecting the traditions and established customs which are essential to support "every word" of civilised rule.'
106	*Choose we*: let *us* choose. Denmark was an elective monarchy — in which the king, though nominated by his predecessor, had to be ratified in his election by the voice of the people.
107	*Caps*: i.e. thrown in the air.
109	*cry*: give voice (like hounds that have picked up a scent).
110	*counter*: the wrong way.
111	*broke*: forced open.

Thick and unwholesome in their thoughts and
    whispers
For good Polonius' death—and we have done but
    greenly
In hugger-mugger to inter him; poor Ophelia
85 Divided from herself and her fair judgment,
Without the which we are pictures, or mere beasts;
Last, and as much containing as all these,
Her brother is in secret come from France,
Feeds on this wonder, keeps himself in clouds,
90 And wants not buzzers to infect his ear
With pestilent speeches of his father's death,
Wherein necessity, of matter beggar'd,
Will nothing stick our person to arraign
In ear and ear. O my dear Gertrude, this,
95 Like to a murd'ring-piece, in many places
Gives me superfluous death.

A noise within

              Attend!
Where is my Switzers? Let them guard the door.

Enter a Messenger

What is the matter?
   Messenger   Save yourself, my lord.
The ocean, overpeering of his list,
100 Eats not the flats with more impetuous haste
Than young Laertes, in a riotous head,
O'erbears your officers. The rabble call him lord,
And, as the world were now but to begin,
Antiquity forgot, custom not known—
105 The ratifiers and props of every word—
They cry, 'Choose we! Laertes shall be king.'
Caps, hands, and tongues applaud it to the clouds,
'Laertes shall be king, Laertes king.'
   Queen
How cheerfully on the false trail they cry.
110 O, this is counter, you false Danish dogs.

A noise within

   King
The doors are broke.

Enter Laertes *with* Followers

112 *this*: Laertes is contemptuous.

113 *give me leave*: if you don't mind. Laertes is
    politely dismissive.

118 *brands the harlot*: See *3, 4, 42–4*.
119 *Even here*: i.e. here of all places.

121 *looks so giant-like*: makes such a show of
    violence. The classical rebellion myth
    describes how the giants, by piling Mt
    Pelion on top of Mt Ossa, assailed the
    Greek gods in heaven.
122 *fear*: be afraid for.
123 *such divinity . . . a king*: The Elizabethans
    believed that the king was God's represen-
    tative on earth, and was protected in his
    function by the power of the Almighty;
    Claudius is never more regal than at this
    moment.
124 *but peep . . . would*: only gets a glimpse of
    what it would like to do.
125 *his will*: what it wants.

130 *juggled with*: played with.
132 *grace*: Laertes forswears the love of God,
    necessary for salvation.
    profoundest pit: hell. For the 'bottomless pit'
    see Revelation, 9:1.
133 *To this point I stand*: I have reached this
    position.
134 *both . . . negligence*: I don't care what
    happens to me in this world or the next.
136 *throughly*: thoroughly.
    stay: prevent.
137 *the world's*: i.e. the world's will.

Laertes
Where is this king?—Sirs, stand you all without.
    Followers
No, let's come in.
    Laertes   I pray you give me leave.
    Followers
We will, we will.
    Laertes
115 I thank you. Keep the door.   [*Exeunt* Followers
                      O thou vile king,
Give me my father.
    Queen
[*Holding him*]   Calmly, good Laertes.
    Laertes
That drop of blood that's calm proclaims me bastard,
Cries cuckold to my father, brands the harlot
Even here between the chaste unsmirched brow
120 Of my true mother.
    King   What is the cause, Laertes,
That thy rebellion looks so giant-like?—
Let him go, Gertrude. Do not fear our person.
There's such divinity doth hedge a king
That treason can but peep to what it would,
125 Acts little of his will.—Tell me, Laertes,
Why thou art thus incens'd.—Let him go, Gertrude.
—Speak, man.
    Laertes
Where is my father?
    King   Dead.
    Queen   But not by him.
    King
Let him demand his fill.
    Laertes
130 How came he dead? I'll not be juggled with.
To hell, allegiance! Vows to the blackest devil!
Conscience and grace, to the profoundest pit!
I dare damnation. To this point I stand,
That both the worlds I give to negligence,
135 Let come what comes, only I'll be reveng'd
Most throughly for my father.
    King   Who shall stay you?
    Laertes
My will, not all the world's.

138 *husband*: manage, take care of.

139 *go far with little*: A commonplace saying: 'make a little go a long way.'

141 *writ*: laid down, prescribed.

142 *swoopstake*: as in a sweepstake — where the winner takes all the stakes. Claudius asks if Laertes will use no discrimination. *draw*: take from.

144 *Will you*: do you want to.

146–7 The pelican, showing natural feeling ('kind') was thought to nourish ('Repast') its brood ('kind') with its own blood. The extravagant image is typical of the inflated sentiments of Laertes.

150 *sensibly*: feelingly.

151 *level*: plainly. *'pear*: appear.

154–5 Laertes would willingly (in his characteristic exaggeration) lose his mind and his sight.

155 *virtue*: power.

157 *turn the beam*: tilt the balance; i.e. his revenge will exceed the injury.

161–3 'The sensitivity of human love is such that it sends something of itself (which is precious) after the beloved who has gone away.'

162 *instance*: token.

164 For the songs, see p.137.

167 *persuade*: urge me to.

168 *move*: persuade.

And for my means, I'll husband them so well,
They shall go far with little.
    King   Good Laertes,
140 If you desire to know the certainty
Of your dear father, is't writ in your revenge
That, swoopstake, you will draw both friend and foe,
Winner and loser?
    Laertes
None but his enemies.
    King   Will you know them then?
    Laertes
145 To his good friends thus wide I'll ope my arms,
And, like the kind life-rend'ring pelican,
Repast them with my blood.
    King   Why, now you speak
Like a good child and a true gentleman.
That I am guiltless of your father's death
150 And am most sensibly in grief for it,
It shall as level to your judgment 'pear
As day does to your eye.

A noise within. Ophelia *is heard singing*

Let her come in.
    Laertes
How now, what noise is that?

Enter Ophelia

O heat, dry up my brains. Tears seven times salt
155 Burn out the sense and virtue of mine eye.
By heaven, thy madness shall be paid with weight
Till our scale turn the beam. O rose of May!
Dear maid—kind sister—sweet Ophelia—
O heavens, is't possible a young maid's wits
160 Should be as mortal as an old man's life?
Nature is fine in love, and where 'tis fine
It sends some precious instance of itself
After the thing it loves.
    Ophelia
[*Sings*]   *They bore him bare-fac'd on the bier,*
165   *And in his grave rain'd many a tear—*
Fare you well, my dove.
    Laertes
Hadst thou thy wits and didst persuade revenge,
It could not move thus.

169   *You must sing*: Ophelia instructs the
        bystanders to sing a refrain to her song
        (which is apparently in two parts).
170   *wheel*: change in rhythm.
171   *the false steward*: The story (perhaps a
        ballad) has not been traced.
172   'This nonsense says more than words could
        do.'
173–83 Symbolic meanings are attributed to
        plants, and Ophelia distributes her
        offerings (either real or imaginary) to the
        other characters — 'fennel and
        columbines', representing flattery and
        marital infidelity; 'rue', the herb signifying
        repentance; 'a daisy', the flower of unhappy
        love; and 'violets', the flowers of
        faithfulness.

176   *document*: lesson.
177   *fitted*: appropriately given to him.
180   *a*: on.
181   *with a difference*: The phrase is heraldic,
        referring to a variation in a coat-of-arms.
184   A line from a popular song.
185   *Thought*: sadness.
        passion: suffering.
186   *favour*: charm.
193   'The hair on his head was pale as flax.'
195   *cast away moan*: grieve uselessly.
197   *of*: on.
199   *commune with*: share in.
200   *Go but apart*: hold off a moment.
201   *whom*: whichever.
203   *direct . . . hand*: our own hand, or the hand
        of an agent.
204   *touch'd*: i.e. with guilt.
206   *satisfaction*: recompense.
208   *jointly labour*: share the cause.
210   *obscure funeral*: Laertes is angry because his
        father has been buried 'in hugger-mugger'
        — without the conventional displays of
        mourning, which he now lists.
211   *trophy*: memorial.

Ophelia
You must sing *A-down a-down*, and you *Call him*
170   *a-down-a*. O, how the wheel becomes it! It is the
false steward that stole his master's daughter.
Laertes
This nothing's more than matter.
Ophelia
There's rosemary, that's for remembrance—pray
you, love, remember. And there is pansies, that's for
175   thoughts.
Laertes
A document in madness: thoughts and remembrance
fitted.
Ophelia
There's fennel for you, and columbines. There's
rue for you. And here's some for me. We may call it
180   herb of grace a Sundays. You must wear your rue
with a difference. There's a daisy. I would give you
some violets, but they withered all when my father
died. They say 'a made a good end.
[*Sings*] *For bonny sweet Robin is all my joy.*
Laertes
185   Thought and affliction, passion, hell itself
She turns to favour and to prettiness.
Ophelia
[*Sings*]   *And will 'a not come again?*
                     And will 'a not come again?
                        No, no, he is dead,
190   *Go to thy death-bed,*
                     He never will come again.

                     His beard was as white as snow,
                     All flaxen was his poll.
                        He is gone, he is gone,
195   *And we cast away moan.*
                     God a mercy on his soul.
And of all Christian souls. God buy you.   [*Exit*
Laertes
Do you see this, O God?
King
Laertes, I must commune with your grief,
200   Or you deny me right. Go but apart,
Make choice of whom your wisest friends you will,
And they shall hear and judge 'twixt you and me.

hatchment o'er his bones: painting of coat-of-arms displayed outside the house of mourning, and later over the tomb.

212   *ostentation*: ceremony.
214   *That*: so that.
      call't in question: demand an explanation.
216   *go with me*: Claudius has made an ally of the rebel.

> If by direct or by collateral hand
> They find us touch'd, we will our kingdom give,
> 205   Our crown, our life, and all that we call ours
> To you in satisfaction; but if not,
> Be you content to lend your patience to us,
> And we shall jointly labour with your soul
> To give it due content.
>   **Laertes**   Let this be so.
> 210   His means of death, his obscure funeral—
> No trophy, sword, nor hatchment o'er his bones,
> No noble rite, nor formal ostentation—
> Cry to be heard, as 'twere from heaven to earth,
> That I must call't in question.
>   **King**   So you shall.
> 215   And where th'offence is, let the great axe fall.
> I pray you go with me.   [*Exeunt*

Act 4   Scene 6

Horatio is approached by sailors, who bring letters from Hamlet.

8   *and*: if it.
9   *th'ambassador*: Apparently Hamlet did not disclose his real identity to the sailors.

Scene 6

Enter Horatio *and a* Servant

Horatio
What are they that would speak with me?
     Servant
Seafaring men, sir. They say they have letters for you.
     Horatio
Let them come in.   [*Exit* Servant
I do not know from what part of the world
5   I should be greeted, if not from Lord Hamlet.

Enter Sailors

     First Sailor
God bless you, sir.
     Horatio
Let him bless thee too.
     First Sailor
'A shall, sir, and please him. There's a letter for
you, sir. It came from th'ambassador that was bound
10   for England—if your name be Horatio, as I am let
to know it is.

12 *overlooked*: read through.
13 *means*: i.e. means of access.
14 *Ere . . . sea*: before we had been two days at sea.
15 *warlike appointment*: prepared to do battle. In Shakespeare's day the seas around Denmark were infested with pirates.
16 *put on . . . valour*: we were forced to fight them.
17 *in the grapple*: The pirates would have thrown grappling irons to draw alongside the Danish ship — thus allowing Hamlet to cross over easily (and in fact escape from Rosencrantz and Guildenstern).
19 *thieves of mercy*: Hamlet adapts the familiar expression 'angels of mercy' to suit his present need.
    what they did: what they were doing — i.e. they had their own reasons for treating him well.
20 *a turn*: a service.
21 *repair*: come and join.
22–4 *I have . . . matter*: Hamlet's words, though they would astound Horatio ('make thee dumb'), cannot do justice to the subject; the metaphor is of a shot too small for the bore of the gun.
29 *way*: access.

Act 4   Scene 7

Laertes and the King are now in league against Hamlet. The letters delivered by the seamen are brought in, and Claudius, sharing the news with Laertes, learns of Hamlet's return to Denmark. A plot is laid — after the King has prepared Laertes, by flattery, to be his instrument. The Queen brings more news: Ophelia is drowned.

1 *my acquittance seal*: agree that I am not guilty.
3 *Sith*: since.
   knowing: knowledgeable.
5 *Pursu'd my life*: tried to kill me (see *4, 1,* 13).
6 *proceeded not*: did not do something about.
   feats: wicked deeds.
7 *crimeful*: criminal.
   capital: punishable by death.
8 *safety*: care for your own safety.
9 *mainly*: mightily.
10 *much unsinew'd*: very feeble.

Horatio [*Reads the letter*]
Horatio, when thou shalt have overlooked this, give these fellows some means to the King. They have letters for him. Ere we were two days old at
15 *sea, a pirate of very warlike appointment gave us chase. Finding ourselves too slow of sail, we put on a compelled valour, and in the grapple I boarded them. On the instant they got clear of our ship, so I alone became their prisoner. They have dealt with me like thieves of mercy. But they*
20 *knew what they did: I am to do a turn for them. Let the King have the letters I have sent, and repair thou to me with as much speed as thou wouldest fly death. I have words to speak in thine ear will make thee dumb; yet are they much too light for the bore of the matter. These good*
25 *fellows will bring thee where I am. Rosencrantz and Guildenstern hold their course for England; of them I have much to tell thee. Farewell.*
                    He that thou knowest thine,
                                Hamlet.
Come, I will give you way for these your letters,
30 And do't the speedier that you may direct me
To him from whom you brought them.   [*Exeunt*

Scene 7

Enter King *and* Laertes

King
Now must your conscience my acquittance seal,
And you must put me in your heart for friend,
Sith you have heard, and with a knowing ear,
That he which hath your noble father slain
5 Pursu'd my life.
    Laertes   It well appears. But tell me
Why you proceeded not against these feats,
So crimeful and so capital in nature,
As by your safety, wisdom, all things else
You mainly were stirr'd up.
        King   O, for two special reasons,
10 Which may to you perhaps seem much unsinew'd,
But yet to me th'are strong. The Queen his mother

13 *be it either which*: whichever it is.
14 *conjunctive*: closely linked.
15 *his sphere*: According to Ptolemy, the separate planets were carried round the earth in individual, transparent, crystalline spheres.
16 Claudius sees Gertrude as the sphere which contains and empowers his movement.
17 *count*: reckoning.
18 *the general gender*: the common people.
20 *like the spring*: Several such springs are known in England; their rich mineral deposits petrify the objects placed ('dipped') in the waters.
21 *gyves*: deformities (literally, shackles). The hard *g* is alliterative with 'graces'.
22 *Too slightly timber'd*: with too light a shaft.
26 *desp'rate terms*: a condition of desperation.
27 *go back again*: i.e. to what she used to be.
28 'Was easily able to beat anyone now living.' *on mount*: conspicuously (like the king on top of a mountain).

30 *Break not your sleeps*: don't lose any sleep — i.e. don't worry.
32 *let . . . danger*: allow ourselves to be insulted with threats.
33 *hear more*: Perhaps Claudius expects news from England — but not the letters that have just arrived.

42 *High and mighty*: Hamlet's form of address is correct, although the phraseology lends itself to sarcasm.
     naked: stripped of belongings.
43 *your kingly eyes*: your Majesty in person.

Lives almost by his looks, and for myself—
My virtue or my plague, be it either which—
She is so conjunctive to my life and soul
15 That, as the star moves not but in his sphere,
I could not but by her. The other motive
Why to a public count I might not go
Is the great love the general gender bear him,
Who, dipping all his faults in their affection,
20 Work like the spring that turneth wood to stone,
Convert his gyves to graces; so that my arrows,
Too slightly timber'd for so loud a wind,
Would have reverted to my bow again,
But not where I had aim'd them.
     Laertes
25 And so have I a noble father lost,
A sister driven into desp'rate terms,
Whose worth, if praises may go back again,
Stood challenger on mount of all the age
For her perfections. But my revenge will come.
     King
30 Break not your sleeps for that. You must not think
That we are made of stuff so flat and dull
That we can let our beard be shook with danger
And think it pastime. You shortly shall hear more.
I lov'd your father, and we love ourself,
35 And that, I hope, will teach you to imagine—

Enter a Messenger *with letters*

     Messenger
These to your Majesty, this to the Queen.
     King
From Hamlet! Who brought them?
     Messenger
Sailors, my lord, they say. I saw them not.
They were given me by Claudio. He receiv'd them
40 Of him that brought them.
          King   Laertes, you shall hear them.—
Leave us.   [*Exit* Messenger
[*Reads*] *High and mighty, you shall know I am set naked*
on your kingdom. Tomorrow shall I beg leave to see your
kingly eyes, when I shall, first asking your pardon,
45 *thereunto recount the occasion of my sudden and more*
strange return.
          Hamlet.

47   *abuse*: deception.

49   *character*: handwriting.

52   *devise me*: explain this to me.

57   The King seems momentarily baffled, but
     immediately regains his composure as he
     sets to work to flatter and persuade Laertes.

61   *checking at*: stopping in the course of
     (shying like a horse).

63   *now . . . device*: which I have just thought
     out.

66   *uncharge the practice*: make excuses for the
     trick.

72   *your sum of parts*: all your accomplishments
     taken together.

74–5 *in my regard . . . siege*: which I do not rate
     very highly ('siege' = rank, status).
76   *very ribbon*: mere decoration.
77–80 'It is good to see young men appearing *as*
     young men, just as it is appropriate for
     older men to show their maturity.'
78   *careless*: carefree.
     livery: uniform.
79   *sables . . . weeds*: furred clothing in sober
     colours.

What should this mean? Are all the rest come back?
Or is it some abuse, and no such thing?

Laertes
Know you the hand?

King   'Tis Hamlet's character.
50   'Naked'—
And in a postscript here he says 'Alone'.
Can you devise me?

Laertes
I am lost in it, my lord. But let him come.
It warms the very sickness in my heart
55   That I shall live and tell him to his teeth,
'Thus diest thou'.

King   If it be so, Laertes—
As how should it be so, how otherwise?—
Will you be rul'd by me?

Laertes   Ay, my lord,
So you will not o'errule me to a peace.

King
60   To thine own peace. If he be now return'd,
As checking at his voyage, and that he means
No more to undertake it, I will work him
To an exploit, now ripe in my device,
Under the which he shall not choose but fall;
65   And for his death no wind of blame shall breathe,
But even his mother shall uncharge the practice
And call it accident.

Laertes   My lord, I will be rul'd,
The rather if you could devise it so
That I might be the organ.

King   It falls right.
70   You have been talk'd of since your travel much,
And that in Hamlet's hearing, for a quality
Wherein they say you shine. Your sum of parts
Did not together pluck such envy from him
As did that one, and that, in my regard,
75   Of the unworthiest siege.

Laertes   What part is that, my lord?
King
A very ribbon in the cap of youth—
Yet needful too, for youth no less becomes
The light and careless livery that it wears
Than settled age his sables and his weeds

80   *health*: well-being.

82   *serv'd*: fought.

83   *can well*: have great skill.

84   *Had witchcraft*: was a magician.
     grew unto his seat: sat so well on horseback.

86   *incorps'd and demi-natur'd*: made into one
     body and possessed of half the nature —
     i.e. like a centaur.

87–9 'He was so much better than I would ever
     have thought possible, that I could not even
     imagine the movements he performed.'
     The mysterious Lamord seems to have
     been demonstrating dressage.

92   *brooch*: jewel (usually worn in the hat).

94   *made confession of you*: said he knew you.
96   *defence*: fencing.
97   *rapier*: The weapon favoured by gentlemen.

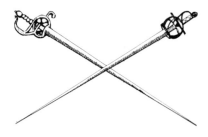

99   *if one could match you*: if there were anyone
     capable of giving you a match.
     scrimers: fencers (French *escrimeurs*).
100 *motion*: action.
104 *sudden*: immediate.
     play: fight a duel.
110–22 The King's speech, with its observations
     on the effects of time, develops a dominant
     theme in the play (see the reflections of the
     Player King, 3, 2, 182–94).
110 *begun by time*: i.e. created by
     circumstances.
111 *passages of proof*: good examples.
112 *qualifies*: modifies, diminishes.

80 Importing health and graveness. Two months since
    Here was a gentleman of Normandy—
    I have seen myself, and serv'd against, the French,
    And they can well on horseback, but this gallant
    Had witchcraft in't. He grew unto his seat,
85 And to such wondrous doing brought his horse
    As had he been incorps'd and demi-natur'd
    With the brave beast. So far he topp'd my thought
    That I in forgery of shapes and tricks
    Come short of what he did.

        Laertes   A Norman was't?

        King

90 A Norman.

        Laertes

    Upon my life, Lamord.

        King   The very same.

        Laertes

    I know him well. He is the brooch indeed
    And gem of all the nation.

        King

    He made confession of you,
95 And gave you such a masterly report
    For art and exercise in your defence,
    And for your rapier most especial,
    That he cried out 'twould be a sight indeed
    If one could match you. The scrimers of their nation
100 He swore had neither motion, guard, nor eye,
    If you oppos'd them. Sir, this report of his
    Did Hamlet so envenom with his envy
    That he could nothing do but wish and beg
    Your sudden coming o'er to play with you.
105 Now out of this—

        Laertes   What out of this, my lord?

        King

    Laertes, was your father dear to you?
    Or are you like the painting of a sorrow,
    A face without a heart?

        Laertes   Why ask you this?

        King

    Not that I think you did not love your father,
110 But that I know love is begun by time,
    And that I see, in passages of proof,
    Time qualifies the spark and fire of it.

114	*snuff*: the burnt portion of the candle's wick, which eventually dims the flame that creates it.
115	*still*: always.
116	*pleurisy*: excess (the word was for a time wrongly held to derive from the Latin *plus*).
117	*his*: its. *That we would do*: whatever it is that we want to do.
118	*We . . . would*: we should do it whilst we still have the desire. *would*: desire.
120	*tongues . . . accidents*: i.e. to dissuade or prevent the desire.
121	*this 'should'*: this awareness of what we ought to do (but never actually doing it). *spendthrift*: wasteful — because the act of sighing was thought to draw blood from the heart (whose heaviness was relieved by the sigh).
122	*quick of th'ulcer*: heart of the matter. The 'quick' is the most sensitive spot.
126	*sanctuarize*: give sanctuary (i.e. protection) to.
128	*Will you do this*: if you are going to do this. *keep close*: stay hidden.
130	*put on*: appoint.
131	*varnish*: polish.
132	*in fine*: finally.
133	*wager o'er your heads*: lay bets on you. *remiss*: carelessly trusting.
134	*generous*: magnanimous. *contriving*: deceitful practices.
135	*peruse the foils*: inspect the weapons.
136	*shuffling*: The King's own words condemn his underhand practices.
137	*unbated*: not tipped, unblunted. *pass of practice*: Claudius seems to be recommending some foul play.
139	*anoint*: put poison on.
140	*unction*: ointment. *of a mountebank*: from some quack. Such 'doctors' sold their wares from a bench or platform.
141	*mortal*: deadly.
142	*cataplasm*: plaster.
143	*simples*: medicinal herbs, which were thought to have even more power ('virtue') if they were gathered in moonlight.
146	*gall*: graze.
149	*our shape*: the part we are to play. The metaphor is theatrical.
150	*drift*: scheme, intention. *look*: be visible.

There lives within the very flame of love
A kind of wick or snuff that will abate it;
115 And nothing is at a like goodness still,
For goodness, growing to a pleurisy,
Dies in his own too-much. That we would do,
We should do when we would: for this 'would' changes
And hath abatements and delays as many
120 As there are tongues, are hands, are accidents,
And then this 'should' is like a spendthrift sigh
That hurts by easing. But to the quick of th'ulcer:
Hamlet comes back; what would you undertake
To show yourself in deed your father's son
125 More than in words?

Laertes   To cut his throat i'th' church.

King
No place indeed should murder sanctuarize;
Revenge should have no bounds. But good Laertes,
Will you do this, keep close within your chamber;
Hamlet, return'd, shall know you are come home;
130 We'll put on those shall praise your excellence,
And set a double varnish on the fame
The Frenchman gave you, bring you, in fine, together,
And wager o'er your heads. He, being remiss,
Most generous, and free from all contriving,
135 Will not peruse the foils, so that with ease—
Or with a little shuffling—you may choose
A sword unbated, and in a pass of practice
Requite him for your father.

Laertes   I will do't.
And for that purpose, I'll anoint my sword.
140 I bought an unction of a mountebank
So mortal that but dip a knife in it,
Where it draws blood, no cataplasm so rare,
Collected from all simples that have virtue
Under the moon, can save the thing from death
145 That is but scratch'd withal. I'll touch my point
With this contagion, that if I gall him slightly,
It may be death.

King   Let's further think of this,
Weigh what convenience both of time and means
May fit us to our shape. If this should fail,
150 And that our drift look through our bad performance,

152 *back*: back-up.

153 *blast in proof*: fail when put to the test.

154 *your cunnings*: your respective skills.

156 *motion*: action.

159 *A chalice for the nonce*: a cup of wine specially for this purpose.
160 *stuck*: thrust (a fencing term).

165 *There is a willow*: The emblem of rejected or forsaken lovers. The Queen's speech has a detached eloquence which divides the message from the messenger.
askant: slanting over.
166 *his*: its.
hoary: The grey underside of the leaves of the green willow is reflected in the water.
167 *Therewith*: i.e. using the leaves of the willow tree.
fantastic: cleverly made.
168 *crow-flowers*: pink campion.
long purples: the flowers of the wild orchis, which has a purple spike and long pale tubers.
169 *liberal*: loose-tongued.
grosser: cruder.
170 *cold*: chaste.
171 *crownet weeds*: weeds made into a wreath.
172 *envious*: malicious.
174 *clothes*: Ophelia is wearing the farthingale of an Elizabethan court lady.
176 *lauds*: songs of praise.
177 *incapable*: insensible.
178–9 *native . . . element*: born and equipped to live in water.

185 *forbid*: restrain.

'Twere better not essay'd. Therefore this project
Should have a back or second that might hold
If this did blast in proof. Soft, let me see.
We'll make a solemn wager on your cunnings—
155 I ha't!
When in your motion you are hot and dry—
As make your bouts more violent to that end—
And that he calls for drink, I'll have prepar'd him
A chalice for the nonce, whereon but sipping,
160 If he by chance escape your venom'd stuck,
Our purpose may hold there. But stay, what noise?

Enter Queen

Queen
One woe doth tread upon another's heel,
So fast they follow. Your sister's drown'd, Laertes.
  Laertes
Drown'd? O, where?
  Queen
165 There is a willow grows askant the brook
That shows his hoary leaves in the glassy stream.
Therewith fantastic garlands did she make
Of crow-flowers, nettles, daisies, and long purples,
That liberal shepherds give a grosser name,
170 But our cold maids do dead men's fingers call them.
There on the pendent boughs her crownet weeds
Clamb'ring to hang, an envious sliver broke,
When down her weedy trophies and herself
Fell in the weeping brook. Her clothes spread wide,
175 And mermaid-like awhile they bore her up,
Which time she chanted snatches of old lauds,
As one incapable of her own distress,
Or like a creature native and indued
Unto that element. But long it could not be
180 Till that her garments, heavy with their drink,
Pull'd the poor wretch from her melodious lay
To muddy death.
  Laertes   Alas, then she is drown'd.
  Queen
Drown'd, drown'd.
  Laertes
Too much of water hast thou, poor Ophelia,
185 And therefore I forbid my tears. But yet

186 *our trick*: only natural.
187 *Let . . . will*: however embarrassing it may
     be.
     these: i.e. his tears.
188 *The woman will be out*: I shall have no more
     of woman's weakness in me.
189 *douts*: quenches.

It is our trick; nature her custom holds,
Let shame say what it will. [*Weeps*] When these are
   gone,
The woman will be out. Adieu, my lord,
I have a speech o' fire that fain would blaze
190 But that this folly douts it.   [*Exit*
   King   Let's follow, Gertrude.
How much I had to do to calm his rage.
Now fear I this will give it start again.
Therefore let's follow.   [*Exeunt*

Act 5

Act 5   Scene 1

A grave-digger enlivens his gloomy task by jesting with his companion. Hamlet enters, with Horatio, and joins in the black comedy with his sardonic wit, commenting satirically on society and mortality. Hamlet retreats when the funeral procession approaches; but when he learns who is to be buried, he bursts out among the mourners and declares his love for the dead Ophelia in a confrontation with her brother, Laertes.

s.d. *two Clowns*: The scene is written for a comic actor and a 'straight man', identified here, as in Q2 and F, as 'Other'.

1 *Christian burial*: Christian funeral rites were denied to suicides, and their bodies were not buried in consecrated ground, until the 19th century.

2 *salvation*: The Grave-digger means 'damnation', although he says the opposite: such comic verbal substitutions often characterize Shakespeare's clowns. The Queen's speech (4, 7, 171–82) has told *the audience* the truth about the mad Ophelia's accidental death — but other characters in the play have no such assurance.

3 *straight*: immediately — with a pun on 'strait' (= narrow).

4 *crowner*: coroner (a common variant). The findings of the inquest were necessary to give warrant for the burial.
Christian burial: i.e. the verdict was not 'suicide'.

7 *her own defence*: The Grave-digger mistakes again; self-defence is an admissible plea in a homicide case.

9 *se offendendo*: i.e. *se defendendo*.

10 *if I drown myself*: Shakespeare parodies documents in a real-life legal case of drowning in 1554.

11 *branches*: divisions.

12 *argal*: Latin *ergo* = therefore. The mistaken pronunciation allows a pun on the name of an Elizabethan logician, John Argall.

Scene 1

Enter two Clowns [—*the* Grave-digger *and* Another]

Grave-digger
Is she to be buried in Christian burial, when she wilfully seeks her own salvation?

Other
I tell thee she is, therefore make her grave straight. The crowner hath sat on her and finds it Christian
5 burial.

Grave-digger
How can that be, unless she drowned herself in her own defence?

Other
Why, 'tis found so.

Grave-digger
It must be *se offendendo*, it cannot be else. For here
10 lies the point: if I drown myself wittingly, it argues an act, and an act hath three branches—it is to act, to do, to perform; argal, she drowned herself wittingly.

Other
Nay, but hear you, Goodman Delver—

Grave-digger
15 Give me leave. Here lies the water—good. Here stands the man—good. If the man go to this water and drown himself, it is, will he nill he, he goes, mark you that. But if the water come to him and drown him, he drowns not himself. Argal, he that is
20 not guilty of his own death shortens not his own life.

Other
But is this law?

14 *Goodman*: A title used particularly when addressing a man by his occupation.
17 *will he nill he*: whether he wants to or not.
22 *quest*: inquest.
23 *an't*: of it.

27 *countenance*: privilege.
28 *even-Christen*: fellow-Christians (who are all equal in the sight of God).
29 *my spade*: i.e. give me my spade.

31 *hold up*: carry on.
Adam's profession: Adam had to care for the garden of Eden (Genesis, 3:23).

33 *bore arms*: had a gentleman's coat of arms. The Grave-digger enjoys his joke.
38–39 *If . . . thyself*: if you can't give me the answer, admit that I have beaten you. The common saying was 'Confess and be hanged'.

40 *Go to*: get on with it.

43 *frame*: structure.

45 *does well*: is a good answer.

Grave-digger
Ay, marry is't, crowner's quest law.
Other
Will you ha' the truth an't? If this had not been a gentlewoman, she should have been buried out o'
25 Christian burial.
Grave-digger
Why, there thou say'st. And the more pity that great folk should have countenance in this world to drown or hang themselves more than their even-Christen. Come, my spade. There is no ancient
30 gentlemen but gardeners, ditchers, and gravemakers —they hold up Adam's profession.

He digs

Other
Was he a gentleman?
Grave-digger
'A was the first that ever bore arms.
Other
Why, he had none.
Grave-digger
35 What, art a heathen? How dost thou understand the Scripture? The Scripture says Adam digged. Could he dig without arms? I'll put another question to thee. If thou answerest me not to the purpose, confess thyself—
Other
40 Go to.
Grave-digger
What is he that builds stronger than either the mason, the shipwright, or the carpenter?
Other
The gallows-maker, for that frame outlives a thousand tenants.
Grave-digger
45 I like thy wit well in good faith, the gallows does well. But how does it well? It does well to those that do ill. Now, thou dost ill to say the gallows is built stronger than the church; argal, the gallows may do well to thee. To't again, come.
Other
50 Who builds stronger than a mason, a shipwright, or a carpenter?

52   *unyoke*: have done with it (like oxen freed from the yoke at the end of the day).

55   *Mass*: by the mass.

57   *mend his pace*: go any better.

60   *Yaughan*: perhaps the name [?Johan] of the local publican.
stoup: flagon.

63   The Grave-digger punctuates his song with the grunting — 'O' and 'a' — of his digging efforts.
contract: pass.
behove: advantage.

65   *feeling of his business*: respect for his occupation.
'a: that he.
67   'He is accustomed to the job.'
69   *daintier sense*: more sensitive feeling.
72   *intil*: to.
73   *such*: i.e. 'in youth'.
75   *jowls*: dashes.
76   *Cain's jawbone*: Cain's fratricide was the prototype for the crime of Claudius (see *3, 3, 37*); tradition has it that he killed Abel with the jawbone of an ass.
77   *politician*: schemer.
this ass: i.e. the Grave-digger.
78   *o'er-offices*: lords it over (by virtue of his office as gravedigger).
circumvent God: cheat even God.
87   *chopless*: lacking a jaw.
88   *mazard*: headpiece.
89   *revolution*: turn-around (like the wheel of Fortune, coming full circle).
trick: knack.
90   'Were these bones only bred for this purpose.'
91   *loggets*: a game where pieces of wood were tossed at a target.

Grave-digger

Ay, tell me that and unyoke.
Other
Marry, now I can tell.
Grave-digger
To't.
Other
55   Mass, I cannot tell.
Grave-digger
Cudgel thy brains no more about it, for your dull ass will not mend his pace with beating. And when you are asked this question next, say 'A gravemaker'. The houses he makes lasts till doomsday.
60   Go, get thee to Yaughan; fetch me a stoup of liquor.
[Exit the Other Clown

The Grave-digger *continues digging*

[*Sings*]   *In youth when I did love, did love,*
                  Methought it was very sweet:
        To contract—O—the time for—a—my behove,
        O methought there—a—was nothing—a—meet.

Enter Hamlet *and* Horatio

Hamlet
65   Has this fellow no feeling of his business 'a sings in grave-making?
Horatio
Custom hath made it in him a property of easiness.
Hamlet
'Tis e'en so, the hand of little employment hath the daintier sense.
Grave-digger
70   [*Sings*]   *But age with his stealing steps*
                  Hath claw'd me in his clutch,
              And hath shipp'd me intil the land,
                  As if I had never been such.

[He throws up a skull]

Hamlet
That skull had a tongue in it, and could sing once.
75   How the knave jowls it to th' ground, as if 'twere Cain's jawbone, that did the first murder. This

93 *For and*: and moreover (a regular ballad idiom).

97–110 Hamlet develops an oration on a traditional theme *Ubi sunt?*, asking 'Where are they now?'.

97 *quiddities*: quibbling arguments about what things really mean (*quidditas* = essential nature of a thing); 'quillities' is Hamlet's playful variant.

98 *tenures*: terms on which property is held.

100 *sconce*: head.

101 *action of battery*: i.e. that he is liable for an action for assault.
in's time: when he was alive.

102 *buyer of land*: In Shakespeare's time, many old properties were being sold, and lawyers were often accused of using their legal expertise for their personal advantage in such dealings.

102–4 *statutes . . . recoveries*: These legal terms describe bonds and actions relating to property and debt: 'statutes' secure the debts upon the debtor's land; 'recognizances' acknowledge the debt; 'fines' are actions leading to an agreement; 'double vouchers' involve a third party in the transaction; and 'recoveries' are suits for obtaining possession.

104 *fine*: final result. Hamlet plays on the different senses of the word 'fine'.

105 *the recovery*: the whole gain.

106 *vouch*: assure.

107–8 *the length . . . indentures*: the actual extent of the documents used in the conveyancing. The deed was duplicated on a single sheet, which was divided by a jagged cut so that the two parts (hence 'pair'), when pieced together, would prove the genuineness of a claim.

109 *conveyances*: documents relating to ownership of land or property.
this box: the coffin (compared to a deed-box).

might be the pate of a politician which this ass now o'er-offices, one that would circumvent God, might it not?

Horatio

80 It might, my lord.

Hamlet

Or of a courtier, which could say, 'Good morrow, sweet lord. How dost thou, sweet lord?' This might be my Lord Such-a-one, that praised my Lord Such-a-one's horse when 'a meant to beg it, might it

85 not?

Horatio

Ay, my lord.

Hamlet

Why, e'en so, and now my Lady Worm's, chopless, and knocked about the mazard with a sexton's spade. Here's fine revolution and we had the trick to see't.

90 Did these bones cost no more the breeding but to play at loggets with 'em? Mine ache to think on't.

Grave-digger

[*Sings*]   *A pickaxe and a spade, a spade,*
        For and a shrouding-sheet,
        O a pit of clay for to be made
95   *For such a guest is meet.*

[*Throws up another skull*]

Hamlet

There's another. Why, may not that be the skull of a lawyer? Where be his quiddities now, his quillities, his cases, his tenures, and his tricks? Why does he suffer this mad knave now to knock him about the

100 sconce with a dirty shovel, and will not tell him of his action of battery? Hum, this fellow might be in's time a great buyer of land, with his statutes, his recognizances, his fines, his double vouchers, his recoveries. Is this the fine of his fines and the

105 recovery of his recoveries, to have his fine pate full of fine dirt? Will his vouchers vouch him no more of his purchases, and double ones too, than the length and breadth of a pair of indentures? The very conveyances of his lands will scarcely lie in this box, and

110 *th'inheritor*: the man who acquires the 'box'.

114 *sheep and calves*: i.e. fools.
assurance: certainty of possession — *and* the deed securing this.
116 *sirrah*: sir (a form used only to address inferiors).

119 *thine*: Hamlet speaks to the Grave-digger using the familiar second person singular, while the Grave-digger replies with the polite (second person plural) form.
120 *You lie*: The pun is expected.

123 *quick*: living.

129 *none*: no woman.

133 *absolute*: strict in his use of language, pedantic.
134 *card*: book — literally, a shipman's navigation chart.
equivocation: ambiguity.
undo: ruin.
135 *these . . . note of it*: I have watched it happening over the past few years.
136 *the age*: people nowadays.
grown so picked: become so refined.

110 must th'inheritor himself have no more, ha?

Horatio
Not a jot more, my lord.
Hamlet
Is not parchment made of sheepskins?
Horatio
Ay, my lord, and of calveskins too.
Hamlet
They are sheep and calves which seek out assurance
115 in that. I will speak to this fellow.—Whose grave's
this, sirrah?
Grave-digger
Mine, sir.
[*Sings*]   *O a pit of clay for to be made—*
Hamlet
I think it be thine indeed, for thou liest in't.
Grave-digger
120 You lie out on't, sir, and therefore 'tis not yours.
For my part, I do not lie in't, yet it is mine.
Hamlet
Thou dost lie in't, to be in't and say 'tis thine. 'Tis
for the dead, not for the quick: therefore thou liest.
Grave-digger
'Tis a quick lie, sir, 'twill away again from me to
125 you.
Hamlet
What man dost thou dig it for?
Grave-digger
For no man, sir.
Hamlet
What woman then?
Grave-digger
For none neither.
Hamlet
130 Who is to be buried in't?
Grave-digger
One that was a woman, sir; but rest her soul, she's
dead.
Hamlet
How absolute the knave is. We must speak by the
card or equivocation will undo us. By the Lord,
135 Horatio, this three years I have took note of it, the
age is grown so picked that the toe of the peasant

136–8 *the toe . . . kibe*: there's not much difference between poor and rich — one comes so close to the other that he rubs ('galls') his chilblain ('kibe').

143 *young Hamlet was born*: From the evidence presented in this scene, various critics have attempted to calculate Hamlet's age; but precise chronology seems unimportant.

150 *as mad as he*: The madness of the English became a national joke.

160 *pocky*: diseased.
       hold: survive.
161 *laying in*: i.e. burying.

comes so near the heel of the courtier he galls his
kibe.—How long hast thou been grave-maker?

Grave-digger

Of all the days i'th' year I came to't that day that
our last King Hamlet o'ercame Fortinbras.   140

Hamlet

How long is that since?

Grave-digger

Cannot you tell that? Every fool can tell that. It
was that very day that young Hamlet was born—he
that is mad and sent into England.

Hamlet

Ay, marry. Why was he sent into England?   145

Grave-digger

Why, because 'a was mad. 'A shall recover his wits
there. Or if 'a do not, 'tis no great matter there.

Hamlet

Why?

Grave-digger

'Twill not be seen in him there. There the men are
as mad as he.   150

Hamlet

How came he mad?

Grave-digger

Very strangely, they say.

Hamlet

How 'strangely'?

Grave-digger

Faith, e'en with losing his wits.

Hamlet

Upon what ground?   155

Grave-digger

Why, here in Denmark. I have been sexton here,
man and boy, thirty years.

Hamlet

How long will a man lie i'th' earth ere he rot?

Grave-digger

Faith, if 'a be not rotten before 'a die—as we have
many pocky corses nowadays that will scarce hold   160
the laying in—'a will last you some eight year or nine
year. A tanner will last you nine year.

Hamlet

Why he more than another?

166 *whoreson*: An expression of contemptuous familiarity.

167 *lien*: been lying. The 'you' is merely for emphasis.

174 *Rhenish*: Rhine wine.

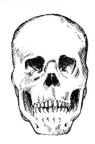

179 *fancy*: imagination.

181 *my gorge rises*: I feel sick at the sight.

186 *chop-fallen*: down in the mouth.

188 *to . . . come*: she will end up looking like this.

191 *Alexander*: Alexander the Great (356–323 BC) was the greatest conqueror known to the classical world, and often cited in meditations on Death the Leveller; he was also noted for the beauty of his body.

Grave-digger

Why, sir, his hide is so tanned with his trade that
165 'a will keep out water a great while, and your water
is a sore decayer of your whoreson dead body. Here's
a skull now hath lien you i'th' earth three and twenty
years.

Hamlet

Whose was it?

Grave-digger

170 A whoreson mad fellow's it was. Whose do you
think it was?

Hamlet

Nay, I know not.

Grave-digger

A pestilence on him for a mad rogue! 'A poured a
flagon of Rhenish on my head once. This same
175 skull, sir, was Yorick's skull, the King's jester.

Hamlet

This?

Takes the skull

Gravedigger

E'en that.

Hamlet

Alas, poor Yorick. I knew him, Horatio, a fellow
of infinite jest, of most excellent fancy. He hath bore
180 me on his back a thousand times, and now—how
abhorred in my imagination it is. My gorge rises at
it. Here hung those lips that I have kissed I know not
how oft. Where be your gibes now, your gambols,
your songs, your flashes of merriment, that were
185 wont to set the table on a roar? Not one now to mock
your own grinning? Quite chop-fallen? Now get you
to my lady's chamber and tell her, let her paint an
inch thick, to this favour she must come. Make her
laugh at that.—Prithee, Horatio, tell me one thing.

Horatio

190 What's that, my lord?

Hamlet

Dost thou think Alexander looked o' this fashion
i'th' earth?

Horatio

E'en so.

Hamlet
And smelt so? Pah!

Puts down the skull

Horatio
195 E'en so, my lord.
Hamlet
To what base uses we may return, Horatio! Why,
may not imagination trace the noble dust of
Alexander till 'a find it stopping a bung-hole?
Horatio
'Twere to consider too curiously to consider so.
Hamlet
200 No, faith, not a jot, but to follow him thither with
modesty enough, and likelihood to lead it. Alexander
died, Alexander was buried, Alexander returneth
to dust, the dust is earth, of earth we make loam, and
why of that loam whereto he was converted might
205 they not stop a beer-barrel?
Imperious Caesar, dead and turn'd to clay,
Might stop a hole to keep the wind away.
O that that earth which kept the world in awe
Should patch a wall t'expel the winter's flaw.
210 But soft, but soft awhile. Here comes the King,
The Queen, the courtiers.

Enter Bearers *with a Coffin, a* Priest, King,
Queen, Laertes, Lords *Attendant*

Who is this they follow?
And with such maimed rites? This doth betoken
The corse they follow did with desp'rate hand
Fordo it own life. 'Twas of some estate.
215 Couch we awhile and mark.
Laertes
What ceremony else?
Hamlet
That is Laertes, a very noble youth. Mark.
Laertes
What ceremony else?
Priest
Her obsequies have been as far enlarg'd
220 As we have warranty. Her death was doubtful;

---

199 *curiously*: ingeniously.

201 *modesty*: moderation.
likelihood to lead it: consideration of what is likely.
203 *loam*: plaster (made with clay and water).

206 *Imperious Caesar*: The emperor Julius Caesar was often cited together with Alexander; the rhyme seems to be Hamlet's own.
209 *flaw*: storm.

212 *maimed rites*: i.e. the minimum of ceremony.

214 *Fordo*: destroy.
it: its.
estate: worldly position.
215 *Couch we*: let's hide ourselves.

219 *enlarg'd*: extended.
220 *have warranty*: As the Priest explains, some additional sanction (other than the findings of the coroner) was necessary when there was any doubt of the cause of death.

221 *o'ersways*: overrules.
order: normal practice.
223 *last trumpet*: i.e. the end of the world.
for: instead of. In most human societies, suicide is seen as a rejection and violation of that society's ethics, and consequently punished by deprivation of the social rites.
224 *Shards*: pieces of broken pottery.
225 *virgin crants*: wreath worn as a sign of virginity, hung in the church after the burial.
226 *maiden strewments*: flowers strewn on the grave as a sign of chastity.
bringing home: i.e. to the grave, her final resting-place.
227 *Of bell and burial*: with the tolling of the church bell and the solemnities of burial.
230 *sage requiem*: a solemn requiem mass, praying for the repose of the soul.
231 *peace-parted souls*: the souls of those who have died with the blessing of the church and at peace with God.
233 *violets*: flowers of perfect love (see *4, 5, 182*) and chastity.

234 *minist'ring angel*: see the 'angels and ministers of grace' invoked by Hamlet in *1, 4, 39*.
235 *howling*: i.e. among the damned in hell.
238 *bride-bed*: Gertrude refers to the Elizabethan custom whereby the marriage-bed was decorated ('deck'd') with flowers.
241 *ingenious*: alert.
243 *caught her*: The coffin would have been open, so that Laertes could actually catch hold of the body of Ophelia.
244 *quick*: living.
245 *flat*: plain, level ground.
246 *Pelion*: The mountain which, in Greek mythology, was piled on top of Mt Ossa when the giants attempted to storm the home of the gods on Mt Olympus.
248 *Bears . . . emphasis*: is expressed so passionately.

And but that great command o'ersways the order,
She should in ground unsanctified been lodg'd
Till the last trumpet: for charitable prayers
Shards, flints, and pebbles should be thrown on her.
225 Yet here she is allow'd her virgin crants,
Her maiden strewments, and the bringing home
Of bell and burial.
    Laertes
Must there no more be done?
    Priest   No more be done.
We should profane the service of the dead
230 To sing sage requiem and such rest to her
As to peace-parted souls.
    Laertes   Lay her i'th' earth,
And from her fair and unpolluted flesh
May violets spring. I tell thee, churlish priest,
A minist'ring angel shall my sister be
235 When thou liest howling.
    Hamlet   What, the fair Ophelia!
    Queen
[*Scattering flowers*] Sweets to the sweet. Farewell.
I hop'd thou shouldst have been my Hamlet's wife:
I thought thy bride-bed to have deck'd, sweet maid,
And not have strew'd thy grave.
    Laertes   O, treble woe
240 Fall ten times treble on that cursed head
Whose wicked deed thy most ingenious sense
Depriv'd thee of.—Hold off the earth awhile,
Till I have caught her once more in mine arms.

       Leaps in the grave

Now pile your dust upon the quick and dead,
245 Till of this flat a mountain you have made
T'o'ertop old Pelion or the skyish head
Of blue Olympus.
    Hamlet   What is he whose grief
Bears such an emphasis, whose phrase of sorrow
Conjures the wand'ring stars and makes them stand
250 Like wonder-wounded hearers? This is I,
Hamlet the Dane.
    Laertes
[*Grappling with him*] The devil take thy soul!

249   'Casts a spell on the planets, and makes
       them stand still in their courses.' Planets
       were called 'wand'ring stars' to distinguish
       them from the 'fixed stars' of the
       firmament.

251s.d. The comments of the bystanders suggest
       that this fight takes place on the stage, not
       in the grave (which would be represented
       by a trap-door in the stage).

254   *splenative*: hot-tempered (caused by excess
       of spleen).
262   *wag*: flutter (show the least sign of life).
268   *forbear him*: leave him alone.
269   *thou't*: thou wilt. Hamlet uses the 'thou' of
       insult.
270   *Woo't*: wilt thou.
271   *eisel*: vinegar.
       crocodile: Perhaps because these were said
       to shed false tears?
274   *quick*: alive.
276   *our ground*: i.e. where we are buried, the
       'flat' of line 245.
277   *his*: its.
       burning zone: the sphere of the sun.
278   *Ossa*: See line 246; Hamlet will outdo
       Laertes — even in the vehemence of his
       rhetoric.
282   *golden couplets*: twin chicks.
       disclos'd: hatched.

Hamlet   Thou pray'st not well.
I prithee take thy fingers from my throat,
For though I am not splenative and rash,
255 Yet have I in me something dangerous,
Which let thy wiseness fear. Hold off thy hand.
     King
Pluck them asunder.
     Queen
Hamlet! Hamlet!
     All
Gentlemen!
     Horatio
260 Good my lord, be quiet.
     Hamlet
Why, I will fight with him upon this theme
Until my eyelids will no longer wag.
     Queen
O my son, what theme?
     Hamlet
I lov'd Ophelia. Forty thousand brothers
265 Could not with all their quantity of love
Make up my sum. What wilt thou do for her?
     King
O, he is mad, Laertes.
     Queen
For love of God forbear him.
     Hamlet
'Swounds, show me what thou't do.
270 Woo't weep, woo't fight, woo't fast, woo't tear thyself,
Woo't drink up eisel, eat a crocodile?
I'll do't. Dost come here to whine,
To outface me with leaping in her grave?
Be buried quick with her, and so will I.
275 And if thou prate of mountains, let them throw
Millions of acres on us, till our ground,
Singeing his pate against the burning zone,
Make Ossa like a wart. Nay, and thou'lt mouth,
I'll rant as well as thou.
     Queen   This is mere madness,
280 And thus awhile the fit will work on him.
Anon, as patient as the female dove
When that her golden couplets are disclos'd,
His silence will sit drooping.

285 *ever*: always.
286 *Hercules*: the superman of Greek
    mythology, who was dramatically
    presented with roaring speeches. Hamlet,
    returning to the simple phrases of everyday
    use, threatens more effectively.
287 'A cat cannot be silenced for ever, and even
    a dog cannot always be kept down.'
288 *wait upon him*: look after him.
289 *in our last night's speech*: by thinking of what
    we talked about last night.
290 *to the present push*: into action immediately.
292 *living*: everlasting. But Claudius may
    intend — and Laertes understand — a
    more sinister meaning.

Hamlet		Hear you, sir,

What is the reason that you use me thus?
285 I lov'd you ever. But it is no matter.
Let Hercules himself do what he may,
The cat will mew, and dog will have his day.   [*Exit*
     King
I pray thee, good Horatio, wait upon him.
                                        [*Exit* Horatio
[*To* Laertes] Strengthen your patience in our last
    night's speech:
290 We'll put the matter to the present push.—
Good Gertrude, set some watch over your son.
This grave shall have a living monument.
An hour of quiet shortly shall we see;
Till then in patience our proceeding be.   [*Exeunt*

Act 5   Scene 2

Hamlet tells Horatio all the facts behind his
sudden return to Denmark. A courtier, Osric,
brings information of Laertes' challenge, which is
readily accepted by Hamlet. The duel is
immediately arranged, and we see the King
preparing the chalices. Hamlet and Laertes fight.
There is confusion, and the swords are
exchanged; Hamlet is wounded, and the Queen
drinks from the poisoned chalice prepared for her
son. The truth is revealed, and Hamlet's revenge
is complete. The play ends with the arrival of
Young Fortinbras.

 1 *see the other*: i.e. as he promised in *4, 6,
    22–3*.
 6 *mutines in the bilboes*: mutineers in shackles
    (which were attached to a fixed bar on
    board ship).
 7 *let us know*: let us remember. Hamlet
    never fails to meditate on his experience.
 9 *pall*: falter.
    learn us: teach us.
10–11 Hamlet's metaphor is from building,
    where the workmen cut ('rough-hew') the
    stone or timber which is then shaped by the
    master-craftsman.
    divinity: divine power.
    ends: purposes; *and* their results. The
    master-craftsman both directs and
    completes the work of the labourers.

Scene 2

Enter Hamlet *and* Horatio

   Hamlet
So much for this, sir. Now shall you see the other.
You do remember all the circumstance?
   Horatio
Remember it, my lord!
   Hamlet
Sir, in my heart there was a kind of fighting
5 That would not let me sleep. Methought I lay
Worse than the mutines in the bilboes. Rashly—
And prais'd be rashness for it: let us know
Our indiscretion sometime serves us well
When our deep plots do pall; and that should learn us
10 There's a divinity that shapes our ends,
Rough-hew them how we will—
   Horatio   That is most certain.

13 *sea-gown*: This is described as 'a coarse, high-collared, and short-sleeved gown, reaching down to the mid-leg'.
    scarf'd: wrapped round (not properly put on).
14 *them*: i.e. Rosencrantz and Guildenstern.
15 *Finger'd*: got my hands on.
    in fine: finally.
20 *Larded*: garnished.
21 *Importing*: concerning.
    health: well-being, security.
22 *bugs and goblins*: i.e. imaginary dangers.
    in my life: if I remain alive.
23 *on the supervise*: as soon as the letter is read.
    no leisure bated: without wasting time.
24 *stay*: wait for.
    grinding: sharpening.
29 *benetted*: entangled.
30–31 'My brains had started to work before I had even started to think what had to be done.' A 'prologue' outlines the action of the play which is to be performed.
32 *fair*: in a clerk's handwriting.
33–34 'I used to think, as statesmen ('statists') think, that only clerks need to have good handwriting.'
36 *yeoman's service*: trustworthy, loyal service — although untrained — such as the English yeomen gave their feudal lords in times of war.
37 *Th'effect . . . wrote?*: what I said in my letter?
38 *conjuration*: injunction.
39 *As England*: because England.
40 *As love*: so that love.
    like the palm: See Psalm, 92:12: 'The righteous shall flourish like the palm-tree'. Hamlet successfully imitates the orotundity of the King's style.
41 *wheaten garland*: the symbol of plenty and prosperity.
42 'Peace should be a close link between the friendly kingdoms, just as a comma links parts of a sentence.'
43 *such-like . . . charge*: such clauses (beginning with 'as') of great significance. Hamlet perhaps indicates a pun on 'heavily burdened asses'.
44 *view and knowing*: reading and understanding.
45 *without . . . less*: without further argument and doing exactly what was ordered.

Hamlet
Up from my cabin,
My sea-gown scarf'd about me, in the dark
Grop'd I to find out them, had my desire,
15   Finger'd their packet, and in fine withdrew
To mine own room again, making so bold,
My fears forgetting manners, to unseal
Their grand commission; where I found, Horatio—
Ah, royal knavery!—an exact command,
20   Larded with many several sorts of reasons
Importing Denmark's health, and England's too,
With ho! such bugs and goblins in my life,
That on the supervise, no leisure bated,
No, not to stay the grinding of the axe,
25   My head should be struck off.
    Horatio   Is't possible?
    Hamlet
Here's the commission, read it at more leisure.
But wilt thou hear now how I did proceed?
    Horatio
I beseech you.
    Hamlet
Being thus benetted round with villainies—
30   Or I could make a prologue to my brains,
They had begun the play—I sat me down,
Devis'd a new commission, wrote it fair—
I once did hold it, as our statists do,
A baseness to write fair, and labour'd much
35   How to forget that learning, but, sir, now
It did me yeoman's service. Wilt thou know
Th'effect of what I wrote?
    Horatio   Ay, good my lord.
    Hamlet
An earnest conjuration from the King,
As England was his faithful tributary,
40   As love between them like the palm might flourish,
As peace should still her wheaten garland wear
And stand a comma 'tween their amities,
And many such-like 'as'es of great charge,
That on the view and knowing of these contents,
45   Without debatement further more or less,

46 *sudden*: immediate.

47 *Not shriving-time allow'd*: without allowing
    them to confess their sins — just as
    Hamlet's father was sent to his death
    'Unhousel'd, disappointed, unanel'd' (*1*, 5,
    77).

48 *ordinant*: ordaining, controlling. Hamlet
    sees the shaping hand of 'divinity' (line 10)
    in even the smallest details.

49 *signet*: signet ring.

50 *model . . . seal*: exact likeness of that well-
    known royal Danish coat of arms.

51 *writ*: writing.

52 *Subscrib'd*: signed.
    impression: i.e. the impression of the seal on
    the wax.

53 *changeling*: substitute — literally, a baby
    substituted by fairies to replace the child
    they have stolen.

54 *what . . . sequent*: what followed this.

56 *go to't*: are going to their deaths. Horatio is
    disapproving.

57 *they . . . employment*: Hamlet seems to
    think that they were willing participants in
    the King's plots (although the text does not
    bear this out). A new, ruthless Hamlet is
    emerging.

58 *They . . . conscience*: I don't feel guilty
    about them.

59 *insinuation*: poking their fingers in,
    intruding.

60–62 'It is dangerous when little people get
    mixed up in the fighting of powerful
    opponents.'

60 *baser*: lowlier.

61 *pass*: sword-thrust.
    fell: cruel.
    points: i.e. sword-points.

62 *opposites*: opponents.

63 *stand me now upon*: now oblige me.

65 Hamlet now makes it appear that Claudius
    has somehow defrauded him of his right to
    succeed his father; Shakespeare is
    deliberately (I think) vague about the
    Danish monarchy.

66 *angle*: fish-hook.
    proper: own.

67 *coz'nage*: trickery. There is, of course,
    word-play with *cousinage* = kinship.
    perfect conscience: with a clear conscience.

68 *quit him*: pay him back.

69 *canker*: spreading sore.

72 *issue*: outcome.

He should those bearers put to sudden death,
Not shriving-time allow'd.

   Horatio   How was this seal'd?

   Hamlet

Why, even in that was heaven ordinant.
I had my father's signet in my purse,

50 Which was the model of that Danish seal,
Folded the writ up in the form of th'other,
Subscrib'd it, gave't th'impression, plac'd it safely,
The changeling never known. Now the next day
Was our sea-fight, and what to this was sequent

55 Thou knowest already.

   Horatio

So Guildenstern and Rosencrantz go to't.

   Hamlet

Why, man, they did make love to this employment.
They are not near my conscience, their defeat
Does by their own insinuation grow.

60 'Tis dangerous when the baser nature comes
Between the pass and fell incensed points
Of mighty opposites.

   Horatio   Why, what a king is this!

   Hamlet

Does it not, think thee, stand me now upon—
He that hath kill'd my king and whor'd my mother,

65 Popp'd in between th'election and my hopes,
Thrown out his angle for my proper life
And with such coz'nage—is't not perfect conscience
To quit him with this arm? And is't not to be damn'd
To let this canker of our nature come

70 In further evil?

   Horatio

It must be shortly known to him from England
What is the issue of the business there.

73 *The interim is mine*: I can act in this short
    time.
74 Hamlet is cryptic, perhaps referring to
    counting as far as the number one, or
    speaking the word 'one' — by which a
    fencer indicates that he has hit his
    opponent.
77 *image of my cause*: judging by my own case.
    Hamlet can see that Laertes must take
    revenge for his father's death; but *we* can
    also appreciate that Hamlet himself is the
    object of Laertes' hatred.
78 *court his favours*: try to make friends with
    him.
79 *bravery*: bravado.
83 *water-fly*: mosquito. The change into prose
    signals a momentary lightening of mood.
85 *gracious*: blessed.
86–8 *Let . . . mess*: As long as a man owns
    great possessions (though he is no better
    than the creatures he owns) he will be
    entertained at court.
87 *crib*: food-box.
88 *at the king's mess*: in the king's company (at
    a banquet).
    chuff: boor, peasant. (But one who was
    well-to-do.)
    spacious in the possession: owning much
    property.
89 *dirt*: land.
90 *Sweet lord*: A common courtly greeting.
92 *diligence*: attentiveness.
93 *bonnet . . . use*: put your hat on.
    Elizabethan hats were worn indoors, but
    removed in greeting; in the presence of a
    social superior, the hat would only be
    replaced with permission — although Osric
    seems reluctant to avail himself of Hamlet's
    condescension.

Hamlet
It will be short. The interim is mine.
And a man's life's no more than to say 'one'.
75 But I am very sorry, good Horatio,
That to Laertes I forgot myself;
For by the image of my cause I see
The portraiture of his. I'll court his favours.
But sure the bravery of his grief did put me
80 Into a tow'ring passion.
    Horatio   Peace, who comes here?

Enter Osric, *a Courtier*

Osric
Your Lordship is right welcome back to Denmark.
    Hamlet
I humbly thank you sir.—Dost know this
water-fly?
    Horatio
No, my good lord.
    Hamlet
85 Thy state is the more gracious, for 'tis a vice to
know him. He hath much land and fertile. Let a
beast be lord of beasts and his crib shall stand at the
king's mess. 'Tis a chuff, but, as I say, spacious in the
possession of dirt.
    Osric
90 Sweet lord, if your lordship were at leisure, I should
impart a thing to you from his Majesty.
    Hamlet
I will receive it, sir, with all diligence of spirit.
Your bonnet to his right use: 'tis for the head.

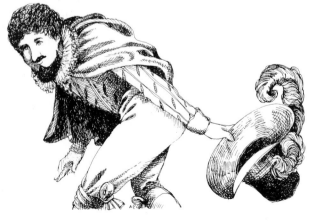

94   *very hot*: Osric is unwilling to offend court
      etiquette, and offers an excuse for not
      replacing his hat.
96   *indifferent*: rather.
98   *for my complexion*: for one of my
      constitution.
104   *remember*: i.e. remember your courtesy —
      which demands that the hat should be
      replaced after the greeting.
105   *for my ease*: I keep it off for my own
      comfort.
107   *absolute*: perfect.
108   *differences*: distinctions.
      soft society: pleasing manners.
      great showing: distinguished appearance.
109   *speak feelingly*: tell you the truth.
      card: model; 'calendar' has much the same
      meaning.
110   *gentry*: gentlemanly behaviour.
111   *the continent . . . see*: whatever it is that you
      would want to see in a gentleman.
      ('continent' = container.)
112   *his definement . . . in you*: he does not
      suffer from your description. Hamlet
      counters Osric's high-flown language.
113   *divide him inventorially*: list his attributes
      separately.
114   *dozy*: stupefy.
114–5 'Not be able to keep up with him.' A
      sailing-ship is said to 'yaw' when it loses the
      wind and wavers in its course.
115–6 *verity of extolment*: praising him
      truthfully. Hamlet's language must be
      appreciated more for sound than sense.
116   *article*: theme.
117   *infusion*: quality.
      dearth: rarity.
118   *make true diction*: speak truly.
      his semblable . . . mirror: only his reflection
      in the mirror looks anything like him.
119   *trace him*: follow in his footsteps.
      umbrage: shadow.

122–3 Hamlet asks what this is all about.

Osric
I thank your lordship, it is very hot.
Hamlet
95 No, believe me, 'tis very cold, the wind is northerly.
Osric
It is indifferent cold, my lord, indeed.
Hamlet
But yet methinks it is very sultry and hot for my
complexion.
Osric
Exceedingly, my lord, it is very sultry—as 'twere—
100 I cannot tell how. My lord, his Majesty bade me
signify to you that 'a has laid a great wager on your
head. Sir, this is the matter—
Hamlet
[*Signing to him to put on his hat*] I beseech you
remember—
Osric
105 Nay, good my lord, for my ease, in good faith.
Sir, here is newly come to court Laertes—believe
me, an absolute gentleman, full of most excellent
differences, of very soft society and great showing.
Indeed, to speak feelingly of him, he is the card or
110 calendar of gentry; for you shall find in him the
continent of what part a gentleman would see.
Hamlet
Sir, his definement suffers no perdition in you,
though I know to divide him inventorially would
dozy th'arithmetic of memory, and yet but yaw
115 neither, in respect of his quick sail. But, in the verity
of extolment, I take him to be a soul of great article
and his infusion of such dearth and rareness as, to
make true diction of him, his semblable is his mirror
and who else would trace him his umbrage, nothing
120 more.
Osric
Your lordship speaks most infallibly of him.
Hamlet
The concernancy, sir? Why do we wrap the gentleman
in our more rawer breath?
Osric
Sir?

125 'Can you not understand this language (i.e. although you can speak in it)?'
126 *will to't*: must try harder.

127 'Why are you speaking of this man?'; Hamlet rephrases the question of line 122.

129–30 *all's . . . spent*: he has used up all his fine language.

134 *not much approve me*: not be much of a compliment. Osric's opinion is not worth much.

136–8 Hamlet seems to be saying that he cannot admit ('confess') Laertes' excellence without implying that he himself has the same quality; before one knows another, one must know oneself.
139 *imputation*: estimation.
140 *by them in his meed*: by people who should know.
     unfellowed: unequalled.
142 *Rapier and dagger*: The fashionable weapons *c.* 1600. The dagger (or 'poniard', line 146) was held in the left hand to ward off the opponent's rapier.

Horatio
Is't not possible to understand in another tongue?
You will to't, sir, really.   125
            Hamlet
What imports the nomination of this gentleman?
            Osric
Of Laertes?
            Horatio
His purse is empty already, all's golden words are
spent.   130
            Hamlet
Of him, sir.
            Osric
I know you are not ignorant—
            Hamlet
I would you did, sir. Yet in faith if you did, it would
not much approve me. Well, sir?
            Osric
You are not ignorant of what excellence Laertes is—   135
            Hamlet
I dare not confess that, lest I should compare with
him in excellence; but to know a man well were to
know himself.
            Osric
I mean, sir, for his weapon; but in the imputation
laid on him, by them in his meed, he's unfellowed.   140
            Hamlet
What's his weapon?
            Osric
Rapier and dagger.

Hamlet

That's two of his weapons. But well.

Osric

145 The King, sir, hath wagered with him six Barbary horses, against the which he has impawned, as I take it, six French rapiers and poniards, with their assigns, as girdle, hanger, and so. Three of the carriages, in faith, are very dear to fancy, very responsive to the hilts, most delicate carriages, and of

150 very liberal conceit.

Hamlet

What call you the carriages?

Horatio

I knew you must be edified by the margin ere you had done.

Osric

The carriages, sir, are the hangers.

Hamlet

155 The phrase would be more german to the matter if we could carry a cannon by our sides—I would it might be hangers till then. But on. Six Barbary horses against six French swords, their assigns, and three liberal-conceited carriages—that's the French

160 bet against the Danish. Why is this—impawned, as you call it?

Osric

The King, sir, hath laid, sir, that in a dozen passes between yourself and him he shall not exceed you three hits; he hath laid on twelve for nine. And it

165 would come to immediate trial if your lordship would vouchsafe the answer.

Hamlet

How if I answer no?

Osric

I mean, my lord, the opposition of your person in trial.

Hamlet

170 Sir, I will walk here in the hall. If it please his Majesty, it is the breathing time of day with me. Let the foils be brought, the gentleman willing, and the King hold his purpose, I will win for him and I can; if not, I will gain nothing but my shame and

175 the odd hits.

144–5 *Barbary horses*: Arab horses, valued for speed and breeding.

145 *impawned*: staked.

147 *assigns*: accessories.
hanger: an arrangement of straps and a pad which attached the sword to its owner's girdle.

148 *dear to fancy*: well-designed.

149 *responsive to the hilts*: in keeping with the hilts of the swords.
delicate: finely wrought.

150 *liberal conceit*: richly decorated. Hamlet, in line 159, uses the phrase to mean 'highly imaginative'.

151 *What call you*: what do you mean by.

152 *must be . . . margin*: would need an explanation. In learned books an explanatory note or gloss might be printed in the margin.

155 *german*: appropriate. Cannons are properly said to be mounted and transported on 'carriages'.

159–60 'What Laertes has brought back from France staked against the home-bred horses.'

162 *laid*: bet.
passes: bouts.

162–4 The exact terms of the King's wager are obscure — although an Elizabethan audience would probably understand easily enough.

166 *vouchsafe the answer*: accept the challenge — although Hamlet pretends to understand a more literal meaning.

171 *breathing . . . me*: my time for exercise.

173 *hold his purpose*: keep his word (about the bet — but the audience can appreciate a more sinister sense).
and: if.

175 *the odd hits*: i.e. the extra three he will have received (line 164).

176 *deliver you so*: return this as your reply.

177 *after what flourish*: with whatever fancy touches.

179 *commend*: present. But in line 181 Hamlet gives another meaning (= praise) to Osric's courtesy.

180 *Yours*: Hamlet acknowledges Osric's departure.

181–2 *no tongues . . . turn*: nobody else's voice to do it for him.

183 *lapwing*: The young lapwing (a wading bird, of the plover family) leaves the nest within a few hours of hatching — and is proverbially a type of youthful folly. Perhaps Osric's hat suggests the egg-shell to Horatio.

184 *comply with his dug*: pay formal courtesies to his wet-nurse's breast.

185 *bevy*: batch (Hamlet's word, usually used of birds, was perhaps suggested by 'lapwing').

186 *the drossy age*: these degenerate times. *got the tune*: learned the way they talk.

187 *out . . . encounter*: through meeting with it regularly.

188 *yeasty collection*: bubbly conversation. *carries them through*: enables them to meet with.

189 *the most . . . opinions*: men of well-tried and carefully considered ideas.

190 *blow . . . trial*: put them to the test — prick the 'bubbles' and they burst: the fine phrases are empty of thought.

197 *I am . . . purposes*: true to my word. Hamlet is now thoroughly resolved on his course of action.

198 *If . . . ready*: I am ready when he is.

201 *In happy time*: how fortunate; a polite formula of welcome.

202 *use . . . entertainment*: show some courtesy. Hamlet shows a gracious obedience in his speech to Laertes, lines 222–40.

Osric
Shall I deliver you so?

Hamlet
To this effect, sir, after what flourish your nature will.

Osric
I commend my duty to your lordship.

Hamlet
180 Yours.   [*Exit* Osric
'A does well to commend it himself, there are no tongues else for's turn.

Horatio
This lapwing runs away with the shell on his head.

Hamlet
'A did comply with his dug before 'a sucked it. Thus
185 has he—and many more of the same bevy that I know the drossy age dotes on—only got the tune of the time and, out of an habit of encounter, a kind of yeasty collection, which carries them through and through the most fanned and winnowed opinions;
190 and do but blow them to their trial, the bubbles are out.

Enter a Lord

Lord
My lord, his Majesty commended him to you by young Osric, who brings back to him that you attend him in the hall. He sends to know if your
195 pleasure hold to play with Laertes or that you will take longer time.

Hamlet
I am constant to my purposes, they follow the King's pleasure. If his fitness speaks, mine is ready. Now or whensoever, provided I be so able as now.

Lord
200 The King and Queen and all are coming down.

Hamlet
In happy time.

Lord
The Queen desires you to use some gentle entertainment to Laertes before you fall to play.

Hamlet
She well instructs me.   [*Exit* Lord

207 *at the odds*: the 'three hits' of line 164.
208 *how ill all's here*: how worried I am about it.

211 *gaingiving*: misgiving.

213 *forestall their repair*: stop them from coming.

215–20 Hamlet assumes the royal plural — or perhaps includes Horatio in a general refusal to be panicked out of a calm acceptance of what is to happen.
215–6 Hamlet affirms the teaching of St Matthew's gospel (10:29) about God's providence: 'Are not two sparrows sold for a farthing? and one of them shall not fall to the ground without your Father.'
216 *it*: i.e. death.
218 *readiness*: See St Matthew, (24:44): 'Be ye also ready.'
218–20 'Since no man knows what he is leaving behind when he dies, what does it matter if he dies early ('betimes')?'
220s.d. *State*: court.
   foils and daggers: As specified in line 142.
222–40 See line 202. After asking a formal pardon from Laertes, Hamlet disclaims responsibility for his actions and blames the madness that possessed him; he was not himself!

224 *presence*: royal assembly.
225 'That I am suffering from some severe mental affliction.'

227 *nature*: natural (filial) feelings.
   exception: disapproval.

Horatio
205 You will lose, my lord.
Hamlet
I do not think so. Since he went into France, I have
been in continual practice. I shall win at the odds.
Thou wouldst not think how ill all's here about my
heart; but it is no matter.
Horatio
210 Nay, good my lord.
Hamlet
It is but foolery, but it is such a kind of gaingiving
as would perhaps trouble a woman.
Horatio
If your mind dislike anything, obey it. I will forestall
their repair hither and say you are not fit.
Hamlet
215 Not a whit. We defy augury. There is special providence in the fall of a sparrow. If it be now, 'tis not to
come; if it be not to come, it will be now; if it be not
now, yet it will come. The readiness is all. Since no
man, of aught he leaves, knows aught, what is't to
220 leave betimes? Let be.

A table prepared. Trumpets, Drums, *and* Officers *with
cushions. Enter* King, Queen, Laertes, Osric, *and all
the* State, *and* Attendants *with foils and daggers*

King
Come, Hamlet, come, and take this hand from me.

Puts Laertes's *hand into* Hamlet's

Hamlet
Give me your pardon, sir. I have done you wrong;
But pardon't as you are a gentleman.
This presence knows, and you must needs have heard,
225 How I am punish'd with a sore distraction.
What I have done
That might your nature, honour, and exception
Roughly awake, I here proclaim was madness.
Was't Hamlet wrong'd Laertes? Never Hamlet.
230 If Hamlet from himself be ta'en away,
And when he's not himself does wrong Laertes,
Then Hamlet does it not, Hamlet denies it.
Who does it then? His madness. If't be so,

236 *in this audience*: in the presence of these
   listeners. We are reminded that this is a
   'public' speech — neither a soliloquy nor an
   ordinary conversation — and calculated for
   different hearers.

237 *purpos'd*: intended.

239–40 Once released from the bow, an arrow
   may fly much farther than it was meant to
   do, and inflict unintended harm. The
   ambivalence of Hamlet's relationship with
   Laertes is focused in 'brother'.

240 *in nature*: i.e. as a son. Laertes' private
   feelings are satisfied, but he must still think
   about his public 'image' — his 'terms of
   honour'.

241–2 'Which (i.e. filial duty) should be the
   strongest motive for revenge.'

243 *stand aloof*: hold back.
   will: desire.

245 *voice and precedent*: an authoritative
   pronouncement, quoting precedents.

246 *name ungor'd*: reputation unharmed.

248 *will not wrong it*: Laertes' hypocrisy is
   emphasized by Hamlet's next lines.
   freely: without reservation.

249 *frankly*: honestly.

252 *foil*: background against which a jewel
   shows more brightly.

254 *Stick fiery off*: shine out brilliantly.

258 *laid the odds*: backed.

260 *he is better'd*: they say he is better.

261 *too heavy*: Whilst the fighters are choosing
   their weapons Laertes can find the
   'unbated' foil, and poison the sword's
   point.

262 *likes me well*: suits me.
   have all a length: are all the same length.

Hamlet is of the faction that is wrong'd;
235 His madness is poor Hamlet's enemy.
Sir, in this audience,
Let my disclaiming from a purpos'd evil
Free me so far in your most generous thoughts
That I have shot my arrow o'er the house
240 And hurt my brother.

   Laertes   I am satisfied in nature,
Whose motive in this case should stir me most
To my revenge; but in my terms of honour
I stand aloof, and will no reconcilement
Till by some elder masters of known honour
245 I have a voice and precedent of peace
To keep my name ungor'd. But till that time
I do receive your offer'd love like love
And will not wrong it.

   Hamlet   I embrace it freely,
And will this brothers' wager frankly play.—
250 Give us the foils.

   Laertes
Come, one for me.

   Hamlet
I'll be your foil, Laertes. In mine ignorance
Your skill shall like a star i'th' darkest night
Stick fiery off indeed.

   Laertes   You mock me, sir.

   Hamlet
255 No, by this hand.

   King
Give them the foils, young Osric. Cousin Hamlet,
You know the wager?

   Hamlet   Very well, my lord.
Your Grace has laid the odds o'th' weaker side.

   King
I do not fear it. I have seen you both,
260 But since he is better'd, we have therefore odds.

   Laertes
This is too heavy. Let me see another.

   Hamlet
This likes me well. These foils have all a length?

   Osric
Ay, my good lord.

They prepare to play

Enter Servants *with flagons of wine*

King
Set me the stoups of wine upon that table.
If Hamlet give the first or second hit,
Or quit in answer of the third exchange,
Let all the battlements their ordnance fire:
The King shall drink to Hamlet's better breath,
And in the cup an union shall he throw
Richer than that which four successive kings
In Denmark's crown have worn—give me the cups—
And let the kettle to the trumpet speak,
The trumpet to the cannoneer without,
The cannons to the heavens, the heaven to earth,
'Now the King drinks to Hamlet.' Come, begin.
And you, the judges, bear a wary eye.
Hamlet
Come on, sir.
Laertes
Come, my lord.

They play

Hamlet
One.
Laertes
No.
Hamlet
Judgment.
Osric
A hit, a very palpable hit.
Laertes
Well, again.
King
Stay, give me drink. Hamlet this pearl is thine.
Here's to thy health.

Drums; trumpets; and shot goes off

Give him the cup.

265
270
275
280
285

266 *quit . . . exchange*: draw level in the third
bout. The King's meaning is not clear —
but he obviously intends that Hamlet
should drink from the poisoned chalice as
soon as possible.
267 *ordnance*: We know the King's drinking
habits from the descriptions in *1, 2, 125–8*
and *1, 4, 8–12.*
268 *better breath*: renewed vigour.
269 *an union*: a very precious pearl, so called
because each one was unique — such as
might be worn in a royal crown. The
extravagant gesture (pearls dissolve in
wine) could conceal the King's murderous
intention.

272 *kettle*: kettledrum. Claudius gives
instructions with his final preparations: the
cups are to be ready, and the salute fired,
for the toast when the King drinks to
Hamlet. Such elaborate arrangements
intensify the suspense for the audience,
who are waiting for the fatal duel to begin.

Hamlet
I'll play this bout first. Set it by awhile.
Come.   *They play again*
Another hit. What say you?
Laertes
I do confess't.
King
Our son shall win.
Queen   He's fat and scant of breath.
Here, Hamlet, take my napkin, rub thy brows.
The Queen carouses to thy fortune, Hamlet.
Hamlet
Good madam.
King
Gertrude, do not drink.
Queen
I will, my lord, I pray you pardon me.

She drinks and offers the cup to Hamlet

King
[*Aside*] It is the poison'd cup. It is too late.
Hamlet
I dare not drink yet, madam—by and by.
Queen
Come, let me wipe thy face.
Laertes
My lord, I'll hit him now.
King   I do not think't.
Laertes
[*Aside*] And yet it is almost against my conscience.
Hamlet
Come for the third, Laertes. You do but dally.
I pray you pass with your best violence.
I am afeard you make a wanton of me.
Laertes
Say you so? Come on.

289 *confess't*: admit it.

290 *fat*: sweating.
scant of breath: breathless.

291 *napkin*: handkerchief.

293 *Good madam*: Hamlet acknowledges the Queen's salutation.

302 *pass*: thrust.

303 *make a wanton of me*: are just fooling around with me. Hamlet's taunt dispels Laertes' momentary wavering.

290

295

300

They play

Osric

305 Nothing neither way.

Laertes

Have at you now.

Laertes *wounds* Hamlet; *then, in scuffling,*
they change rapiers

King

Part them; they are incensed.

Hamlet

Nay, come again.

He wounds Laertes. *The* Queen *falls*

Osric

Look to the Queen there, ho!

Horatio

310 They bleed on both sides. How is it, my lord?

Osric

How is't, Laertes?

Laertes

Why, as a woodcock to mine own springe, Osric.
I am justly kill'd with mine own treachery.

Hamlet

How does the Queen?

King   She swoons to see them bleed.

Queen

315 No, no, the drink, the drink! O my dear Hamlet!
The drink, the drink! I am poison'd.   [*Dies*

Hamlet

O villainy! Ho! Let the door be lock'd.
Treachery! Seek it out.   [*Exit* Osric

Laertes

It is here, Hamlet. Hamlet, thou art slain.

320 No medicine in the world can do thee good;
In thee there is not half an hour's life.
The treacherous instrument is in thy hand,
Unbated and envenom'd. The foul practice
Hath turn'd itself on me. Lo, here I lie,

325 Never to rise again. Thy mother's poison'd.

312 *woodcock*: a proverbially foolish bird.
to mine own springe: caught in my own trap
(see *1*, 3, 115).

323 *Unbated and envenom'd*: See *4*, 7, 136–47.
practice: trickery.

327 *to thy work*: Hamlet finally achieves revenge
— although the King must be doubly
punished, to pay for his second crime in
causing Gertrude's death.

I can no more. The King—the King's to blame.

Hamlet
The point envenom'd too! Then, venom, to thy work.

Wounds the King

All
Treason! treason!

King
O yet defend me, friends. I am but hurt.

Hamlet
330 Here, thou incestuous, murd'rous, damned Dane,
Drink off this potion. Is thy union here?
Follow my mother.   [King *dies*

331 *thy union*: i.e. the pearl. And Hamlet also
puns on 'union' (= marriage) as he forces
the King to drink from his poisoned
chalice.
333 *temper'd*: concocted.
334 *Exchange forgiveness*: As he asks for
Hamlet's forgiveness, also forgiving
Hamlet for killing Polonius, Laertes
acquires some of the Prince's nobility.
335 *come not upon thee*: i.e. you are not
responsible for.
337 *make thee free*: absolve you.

Laertes   He is justly serv'd.
It is a poison temper'd by himself.
Exchange forgiveness with me, noble Hamlet.
335 Mine and my father's death come not upon thee,
Nor thine on me.   [*Dies*

Hamlet
Heaven make thee free of it. I follow thee.
I am dead, Horatio. Wretched Queen, adieu.
You that look pale and tremble at this chance,

339 *chance*: happening.
340 *mutes*: actors without speaking parts.
341–2 *this . . . arrest*: The personification of
Death as an officer of the law — a sergeant-
at-arms — is not uncommon in Elizabethan
drama.
341 *fell*: stern, cruel.
342 *strict*: just, inescapable.
I could tell you: Elizabethans believed that
those near death had the gift of prophecy.
344 *unsatisfied*: those who are ignorant.
346 *antique*: ancient. The pre-Christian Romans
preferred to commit suicide rather than live
an ignoble life.

340 That are but mutes or audience to this act,
Had I but time—as this fell sergeant, Death,
Is strict in his arrest—O, I could tell you—
But let it be. Horatio, I am dead,
Thou livest. Report me and my cause aright
345 To the unsatisfied.

Horatio   Never believe it.
I am more an antique Roman than a Dane.
Here's yet some liquor left.

Hamlet   As th'art a man
Give me the cup. Let go, by Heaven I'll ha't.
O God, Horatio, what a wounded name,

351 *hold me in thy heart*: love me.
352 *Absent . . . awhile*: i.e. do not die yet. For
Hamlet now, death is seen as the end of a
painful life and the beginning of eternal
bliss.

350 Things standing thus unknown, shall I leave behind
     me.
If thou didst ever hold me in thy heart,
Absent thee from felicity awhile,
And in this harsh world draw thy breath in pain
To tell my story.

A march afar off and shot within

What warlike noise is this?

Enter Osric

Osric

355 Young Fortinbras, with conquest come from Poland,
To the ambassadors of England gives
This warlike volley.
    Hamlet   O, I die, Horatio.
The potent poison quite o'ercrows my spirit.
I cannot live to hear the news from England,
360 But I do prophesy th'election lights
On Fortinbras. He has my dying voice.
So tell him, with th'occurrents more and less
Which have solicited—the rest is silence.   [*Dies*
    Horatio
Now cracks a noble heart. Good night, sweet prince,
365 And flights of angels sing thee to thy rest.

March within

Why does the drum come hither?

    Enter Fortinbras, *and the English*
    Ambassadors, *and* Soldiers *with drum and*
    colours

    Fortinbras
Where is this sight?
    Horatio   What is it you would see?
If aught of woe or wonder, cease your search.
    Fortinbras
This quarry cries on havoc. O proud Death,
370 What feast is toward in thine eternal cell,
That thou so many princes at a shot
So bloodily hast struck?
    First Ambassador   The sight is dismal;
And our affairs from England come too late.
The ears are senseless that should give us hearing
375 To tell him his commandment is fulfill'd,
That Rosencrantz and Guildenstern are dead.
Where should we have our thanks?
    Horatio   Not from his mouth,
Had it th'ability of life to thank you.
He never gave commandment for their death.
380 But since, so jump upon this bloody question,
You from the Polack wars and you from England

---

358 *o'ercrows*: triumphs over (like a victorious fighting-cock).

360 *election*: i.e. for the new king of Denmark.
    lights: favours, chooses.

361 *my dying voice*: my deathbed vote. Hamlet was himself promised the 'voice' of Claudius (*3, 2, 332–3*).

362 *occurrents more and less*: everything that has happened.

363 *solicited*: persuaded me to speak for him.

365 Horatio voices a common Christian sentiment: 'May you be carried to eternal rest by angels, who sing as they fly'.

366 *the drum*: i.e. the marching soldiers following the drum.

366s.d. *colours*: standards, banners.

368 *woe or wonder*: sorrow or disaster.

369 *quarry*: heap of dead bodies (e.g. deer killed in a hunt).
    cries on havoc: proclaims wholesale slaughter.

370 *toward*: being prepared.

372 *dismal*: full of terror.

374 *The ears*: i.e. the King's ears.

378 *Had . . . life*: even if he were alive.

380 *so jump upon*: so precisely at the right moment.
    question: business.

383 *stage*: platform. Horatio is asking for a public inquiry, open 'to the view' of all.

386 *carnal*: i.e. the marriage of Gertrude and Claudius.
387 *accidental judgments*: divine justice in what looked like accidents.
casual: happening (apparently) by chance.
388 *put on*: contrived.
forc'd: faked.
389 *this upshot*: i.e. the final outcome.

394 *of memory*: unforgotten.
395 'This seems a good time to claim them.'

397 *draw on more*: persuade other voices.
398 *this same*: i.e. the inquiry.
presently: immediately.
399 *wild*: agitated.
400 *On*: on top of, in addition to.
401 *stage*: platform (see line 383).
402 *put on*: put to the test.
403 *for his passage*: to mark his passing.

407 *Becomes the field*: is suitable for the battlefield.

Are here arriv'd, give order that these bodies
High on a stage be placed to the view,
And let me speak to th'yet unknowing world
385 How these things came about. So shall you hear
Of carnal, bloody, and unnatural acts,
Of accidental judgments, casual slaughters,
Of deaths put on by cunning and forc'd cause,
And, in this upshot, purposes mistook
390 Fall'n on th'inventors' heads. All this can I
Truly deliver.
   Fortinbras   Let us haste to hear it,
And call the noblest to the audience.
For me, with sorrow I embrace my fortune.
I have some rights of memory in this kingdom,
395 Which now to claim my vantage doth invite me.
   Horatio
Of that I shall have also cause to speak,
And from his mouth whose voice will draw on more.
But let this same be presently perform'd
Even while men's minds are wild, lest more mischance
400 On plots and errors happen.
   Fortinbras   Let four captains
Bear Hamlet like a soldier to the stage,
For he was likely, had he been put on,
To have prov'd most royal; and for his passage,
The soldier's music and the rite of war
405 Speak loudly for him.
Take up the bodies. Such a sight as this
Becomes the field, but here shows much amiss.
Go, bid the soldiers shoot.
              [*Exeunt marching, bearing off the bodies,
              after which a peal of ordnance is shot off*

The songs in *Hamlet*

The songs in Shakespeare's plays have attracted much attention in recent years. Sometimes they are versions of the 'pop songs' of the day, whose original tunes can be found in contemporary music-books. Detailed studies have been made by Dr F.W. Sternfeld, and published in his *Music in Shakespearian Tragedy* (1963) and *Songs from Shakespeare's Tragedies* (1964).

How should I your true love know
Hamlet, Act IV

Shakespeare's text

Ballad tune: *Walsingham*
harmonized by Francis Cutting

```
OPHELIA
1. How should I    your    true  love  know  From a - no - ther    one?
2. He  is  dead  and    gone,  la  - dy,   He  is  dead  and     gone;
3. White his shroud as  the  moun - tain  snow,*  Lar - ded  all  with sweet flowers;

By  his  cock  -  le     hat  and   staff,__  And  his  san - dal   shoon.
At  his  head   a    grass - green  turf, __  At   his  heels  a     stone.
Which be - wept  to the grave  did not  go __  With his true - love  showers.
```

*[Singing interrupted:] (QUEEN) Alas, look here, my lord.

Tomorrow is Saint Valentine's day
Hamlet, Act IV

Shakespeare's text   Linley: *Shakespeare's Dramatic Songs*

1. 'To-mor-row is Saint Va-len-tine's day, All in the morn-ing be-time, And I a maid at your win-dow, To be your Va-len-tine'.

2. Then up he rose and donn'd his clothes
   And dupp'd the chamber door,
   Let in the maid, that out a maid
   Never departed more.

3. By Gis and by Saint Charity,
   Alack, and fie for shame!
   Young men will do't if they come to't,
   By Cock, they are to blame.

4. Quoth she, 'Before you tumbled me,
   You promis'd me to wed.'
   [*He answers:*] 'So would I ha' done, by yonder sun,
   An thou hadst not come to my bed.'

They bore him bare-faced
Hamlet, Act IV

Shakespeare's text   Ballad tunes: *Walsingham*
                                      and *Bandalashot* (adapted)

They bore him bare-faced on the bier, Hey non non-ny, non-ny, hey non-ny; And in his grave rained ma-ny a tear,

[*Singing stops:*]
(OPHELIA) Fare you well, my dove.
(LAERTES) Hadst thou thy wits, and
           didst persuade revenge,
           It could not move thus.

You must sing, down a-down, and you call him a-down-a.

For bonny sweet Robin
Hamlet, Act IV

Shakespeare's text   Ballet Lute Book

For bon - ny sweet_ Ro - bin is all_____ my joy.

And will he not come again?
Hamlet, Act IV

Shakespeare's text   Linley: *Shakespeare's Dramatic Songs*

1st stanza: And will he not come a - gain?_____ And will he not come_ a -
2nd stanza: His beard _ as white as snow, _____ All fla - xen was_ his
             They bore _ him bare - faced on the bier, Hey non non-ny, non - ny, hey

gain? ____ No, no, -gain? _____ No, no, no, he is dead, Go
poll, ____ He is poll, ____ He is gone, he is gone, And we
non - ny, And _____ non - ny, And _ in his grave rained

to thy death - bed, [and] He ne - ver will come a - gain. _____
cast a - way moan, Gra - mer - cy on his soul! _____
ma ny a tear...

In youth when I did love
Hamlet, Act V

Shakespeare's text   Nott: *Songs and Sonnets*

1. In youth when_ I did love, did love, Me -
2. But age with his steal - ing steps _____ Hath
3. A pick - axe _____ and a spade, a spade, For

- thought it was ve - ry sweet: To con - tract O! the time for - a
claw'd me in his clutch: And _ hath _____ shipp'd me in -
and a _ shroud - ing sheet; O! a pit _____ of clay for_

my be - hove, O! me - thought there a was no - thing - a meet.
- til the land, As _____ if there had ne - ver been _____ such.
to be made, For such _____ a guest is _____ meet.

Classwork and Examinations

The works of Shakespeare are studied all over the world, and this classroom edition is being used in many different countries. Teaching methods vary from school to school and there are many different ways of examining a student's work. Some teachers and examiners expect detailed knowledge of Shakespeare's text, others ask for imaginative involvement with his characters and their situations, and there are some teachers who want their students to share in the theatrical experiences of directing and performing a play. Most people use a variety of methods. This section of the book offers a few suggestions for approaches to *Hamlet* which could be used in school and colleges to help with students' understanding and *enjoyment* of the play.

A   Discussion
B   Character Study
C   Activities
D   Context Questions
E   Comprehension Questions
F   Essays
G   Projects

A   Discussion   Talking about the play—about the issues it raises and the characters who are involved—is one of the most rewarding and pleasurable aspects of the study of Shakespeare. It makes sense to discuss each scene as it is read, sharing impressions—and perhaps correcting misapprehensions. It can be useful to compare aspects of this play with other fictions—plays, novels, films—or with modern life.

Sample topics

A1   How does Shakespeare create the 'atmosphere' for his ghost story in *Act 1*, Scene 1? Would modern theatre or film techniques be able to help him at all?

A2   In *Act 1*, Scene 4 we see a father (Polonius) giving advice to his children. How do you rate Polonius as a father? How would you react to the kind of advice that he gives to Laertes and Ophelia?

A3 How would you, as a director, stage the Ghost in its *Act 1* appearances? Consider *both* the resources of the Elizabethan theatre *and* those of modern stage/film technology, and compare this Ghost with other fictional apparitions.

A4 Do you blame Hamlet for stabbing the spy behind the arras? Would you feel the same if the listener had been Claudius and not Polonius?

A5 Suppose Hamlet had killed Claudius when he found him at the end of *Act 3*, Scene 3. Would you have more, or less, respect for the Prince?

A6 Why should a king—or other head of state—take more care of him/her self, and be better protected, than any other citizen (see *3, 3, 8–23*)?

A7 How would you, as a director, stage the episode in the closet when the Ghost appears to Hamlet?

A8 Can you share Hamlet's admiration for Fortinbras and his 'divine ambition' (*4, 4, 49*)?

A9 At the burial of Ophelia, Laertes asks 'What ceremony else?' (*5, 1, 126*). Discuss the importance which this play attaches to the rites and ceremonies of death.

A10 At the beginning of the play, Hamlet said that 'The time is out of joint' and that he 'was born to set it right' (*1, 5, 196–7*). In your opinion, has he done this?

A11 Hamlet believes that 'There is a special providence in the fall of a sparrow' (*5, 2, 215*). Does Providence have any part in this play?

A12 *Hamlet* is a very long play, and most directors find it necessary to make cuts. Where would you choose to cut?

B Character Study   Shakespeare is famous for his creation of characters, who seem like real people. We can judge their actions and we can try to understand their thoughts and feelings—just as we try to understand and criticize the people we know. As the play progresses, we learn to like or dislike, love or hate, them—just as though they lived in *our* world.

Characters can be studied *from the outside*, by observing what they do, and listening sensitively to what they say. This is the scholar's method; the scholar—or any reader—has access to the whole play, and can see the function of every character within the whole scheme of that play.

Another approach works *from the inside*, taking a single character and looking at the action and the other characters from his/her point of view. This is an actor's technique, creating a character—who can have only a partial view of what is going on—and it asks for a student's inventive imagination. The two methods—both useful in different ways—are really complementary to each other.

Suggestions—a)   from 'outside' the character

B1   What do we learn of the character and function of Horatio in the first act of the play?

B2   In Shakespeare's plays, the style of a person's speech often tells us a lot about his character. Show how true this is of Polonius.

B3   Consider the characters of Laertes and/or Fortinbras, and suggest how they compare and contrast with Hamlet.

B4   Describe the character of Ophelia, remembering the scenes at the beginning of the play where she was present with her brother and her father, the middle scenes with Prince Hamlet, and her final appearance before her death. Did her madness surprise you?

B5   'Despite all that he tells us about himself, Hamlet still remains a mystery—we can never feel that we fully understand him.' How well do you understand Hamlet? Write an account of his character, and compare your account with those of other students.

b)   from 'inside' a character

B6   Assuming the character of Horatio, write an account of your attitude to ghosts and describe how this was changed by your experience in *Act 1*. You could perhaps be writing a diary entry, or a letter to a friend at university, or a paper for publication in a learned journal.

B7   Imagine yourself to have been present—perhaps as a courtier or lady-in-waiting—when the new King addressed his court at Elsinore; describe the scene in a letter to your wife/husband. What impression did Claudius's first speech make on you? Did you think his nephew was rather odd?

B8   'O woe is me T'have seen what I have seen, see what I see' (3, 1, 162–3). In the character of Ophelia, write a confidential diary describing Hamlet as he used to be, and as he now appears. Try to describe your own feelings.

B9   As one of the Players, now returned to London, give an account of your reception and performance at Elsinore.

B10   Imagine you are Gertrude. What are your thoughts as you wait for Hamlet to come to your closet?

B11   As Gertrude, confide your thoughts to your diary after Hamlet has left your room.

B12   Tell 'Ophelia's story' in letters to her girl-friend.

B13   At the end of the play, Fortinbras says that Hamlet—had he lived—'was likely . . . to have prov'd most royal'. In the character of Fortinbras, describe your real feelings about the Prince of Denmark.

B14   What version of the whole affair—or of any part of it—would Gertrude have given to a confidante (in letters discovered after her death)?

B15   If Claudius had been writing his autobiography, how might he have described the events that followed his marriage to Queen Gertrude.

C   Activities   These can involve two or more students, preferably working *away from* the desk or study-table and using gesture and position ('body-language') as well as speech. They can help students to develop a sense of drama and the dramatic aspects of Shakespeare's play—which was written to be *performed*, not studied in a classroom.

C1   Act the play, or at least part of it. You don't need scenery or costumes—just space and people.

C2   Devise a scene in which Marcellus tries to persuade the reluctant Horatio (who does not believe in ghosts) to accompany the Guards on their midnight watch.

C3   'Never make known what you have seen tonight' (*1*, 5, 149). Hamlet swears his companions to secrecy—but suppose that Marcellus cannot keep a secret. How would he tell Barnardo (who witnessed the Ghost's first appearance) about this latest manifestation? Improvise such a scene.

C4   *Hamlet* is famous for the Prince's soliloquies. Speak any one of these aloud, using *your own words*.

C5   Arrange the seating of the royal party at *The Murder of Gonzago*—so that the audience for *Hamlet* can see and hear everything that is happening.

C6 Imagine you are a television reporter covering the fencing match between Hamlet and Laertes. Give a running commentary on the fight, and its unexpected outcome.

D Context Questions In written examinations, these questions present you with short passages from the play, and ask you to explain them. They are intended to test your knowledge of the play and your understanding of its words. Usually you have to make a choice of passages: there may be five on the paper, and you are asked to choose three. Be very sure that you know exactly how many passages you must choose. Study the ones offered to you, and select those you feel most certain of. Make your answers accurate and concise—don't waste time writing more than the examiner is asking for.

D1 Moreover that we much did long to see you,
The need we have to use you did provoke
Our hasty sending. Something have you heard
Of Hamlet's transformation . . .

(i) Who is speaking, and who is addressed?
(ii) Why does the speaker say 'we'?
(iii) What is 'Hamlet's transformation'?

D2 And I, of ladies most deject and wretched,
That suck'd the honey of his music vows,
Now see that noble and most sovereign reason
Like sweet bells jangled out of tune and harsh,
That unmatch'd form and feature of blown youth
Blasted with ecstasy.

(i) Who is the speaker, and to whom does she refer?
(ii) What has she just seen?
(iii) Who else witnessed the scene?

D3 See what a grace was seated on this brow,
Hyperion's curls, the front of Jove himself,
An eye like Mars to threaten and command,
A station like the herald Mercury
New-lighted on a heaven-kissing hill,
A combination and a form indeed
Where every god did seem to set his seal
To give the world assurance of a man.

(i) Who speaks these lines, and who hears them? What is their relationship?

(ii) Who is being described, and how is he related to the speaker?
(iii) What has the speaker just done?

D4 And then it started like a guilty thing
Upon a fearful summons. I have heard
The cock, that is the trumpet to the morn,
Doth with his lofty and shrill-sounding throat
Awake the god of day, and at his warning,
Whether in sea or fire, in earth or air,
Th'extravagant and erring spirit hies
To his confine; and of the truth herein
This present object made probation.

(i) Who is speaking, and to whom does he speak?
(ii) What has just happened?
(iii) What does the speaker decide to do next?

D5 My liege and madam, to expostulate
What majesty should be, what duty is,
Why day is day, night night, and time is time,
Were nothing but to waste night, day, and time.
Therefore, since brevity is the soul of wit,
And tediousness the limbs and outward flourishes,
I will be brief.

(i) Who is the speaker?
(ii) Who does he call 'My liege and madam'?
(iii) What has he really come to say?

**E Comprehension
Questions**
These also present passages from the play and ask questions about them, and again you often have a choice of passages. But the extracts are much longer than those presented as context questions. A detailed knowledge of the language of the play is asked for here, and you must be able to express unusual or archaic phrases in your own words; you may also be asked to comment critically on the effectiveness of Shakespeare's language.

E1 *Hamlet*

How all occasions do inform against me,
And spur my dull revenge. What is a man
If his chief good and market of his time
Be but to sleep and feed? A beast, no more.
Sure he that hath made us with such large discourse,   5

Looking before and after, gave us not
That capability and god-like reason
To fust in us unus'd. Now whether it be
Bestial oblivion, or some craven scruple
Of thinking too precisely on th'event—   10
A thought which, quarter'd, hath but one part wisdom
And ever three parts coward—I do not know
Why yet I live to say this thing's to do,
Sith I have cause, and will, and strength, and means
To do't. Examples gross as earth exhort me,   15
Witness this army of such mass and charge,
Led by a delicate and tender prince,
Whose spirit, with divine ambition puff'd,
Makes mouths at the invisible event,
Exposing what is mortal and unsure   20
To all that fortune, death, and danger dare,
Even for an eggshell.

  (i) What has prompted this outburst? Exactly where in the play
     does it come? What happens next?
 (ii) Give the meaning of 'discourse' (line 5), 'fust' (line 8),
     'Bestial oblivion' (line 9), 'charge' (line 16), 'puff'd' (line 18).
(iii) What does Hamlet mean in the first two lines of this extract
     ('how . . . revenge')? What other 'occasions' might he be
     thinking of?
(iv) Who is the 'delicate and tender prince' referred to in line 17?
 (v) What does this speech show of Hamlet's character?

E2 *Hamlet*

I have of late, but wherefore I know not, lost all my
mirth, forgone all custom of exercises; and indeed it
goes so heavily with my disposition that this goodly
frame the earth seems to me a sterile promontory, this
most excellent canopy the air, look you, this brave   5
o'erhanging firmament, this majestical roof fretted
with golden fire, why, it appeareth nothing to me but
a foul and pestilent congregation of vapours. What piece
of work is a man, how noble in reason, how infinite
in faculties, in form and moving how express and   10
admirable, in action how like an angel, in apprehension
how like a god: the beauty of the world, the paragon

of animals—and yet, to me, what is this quintessence
of dust? Man delights not me—nor woman neither, though
by your smiling you seem to say so.   15

(i)   Who is Hamlet speaking to, and at what point in the play?
(ii) Give the meaning of 'frame' (line 4), 'roof' (line 6),
      'congregation of vapours' (line 8), 'apprehension' (line 11),
      'quintessence' (line 13).
(iii) What is the cause of Hamlet's depression? Why does he
      pretend not to know the reason?
(iv) Express in your own words the thought of lines 8–13 ('What
      piece of work . . . animals').

E3   *Hamlet*

Being thus benetted round with villainies—
Or I could make a prologue to my brains,
They had begun the play—I sat me down,
Devis'd a new commission, wrote it fair—
I once did hold it, as our statists do   5
A baseness to write fair, and labour'd much
How to forget that learning, but, sir, now
It did me yeoman's service. Wilt thou know
Th'effect of what I wrote?

Horatio   Ay, good my lord.

Hamlet

An earnest conjuration from the King,   10
As England was his faithful tributary,
As love between them like the palm might flourish,
As peace should still her wheaten garland wear
And stand a comma 'tween their amities,
And many such-like 'as'es of great charge,   15
That on the view and knowing of these contents,
Without debatement further more or less,
He should those bearers put to sudden death,
Not shriving-time allow'd.   20

(i)   Where was Hamlet when he wrote the letter he is describing to
      Horatio? To whom was the letter addressed, and who were the
      'bearers' referred to in line 19?

(ii) Give the meaning of 'benetted' (line 1), 'prologue' (line 2), 'statists' (line 5), 'tributary' (line 11), 'palm' (line 12), 'stand a comma' (line 14), 'shriving-time' (line 20).

(iii) Comment on the style of lines 11–14 ('As England . . . amities'). Whose style is Hamlet imitating, and why?

(iv) What do the last two lines ('He should . . . allow'd') reveal about the change in Hamlet's character?

F Essays These will usually give you a specific topic to discuss, or perhaps a question that must be answered, in writing, *with a reasoned argument*. They *never* want you to tell the story of the play—so don't. Your examiner—or teacher—has read the play, and does not need to be reminded of it. Relevant quotations will always help you to make your points more strongly.

F1 'Horatio has no personality of his own; he is merely a device for imparting information.' Do you agree?

F2 Show how the two kings—Hamlet's dead father and Claudius, his brother—are contrasted with each other throughout the play.

F3 Hamlet accuses himself for failing to act (see *2, 2, 544–570*). What do *you* think is the main cause of his delay?

F4 Compare Laertes and Hamlet as revengers.

F5 Hamlet calls Denmark 'an unweeded garden' (*1, 2, 135*). Where do *you* see signs of rottenness?

F6 Polonius thinks it is necessary that someone should 'o'erhear' Hamlet's conversation with his mother (*3, 3, 32*). Describe other scenes in the play where characters spy—or plan to spy—on other characters.

F7 Describe the character of Polonius, remembering that we see him both as a father and a politician.

F8 Can you distinguish between Hamlet's madness and that of Ophelia?

F9 'Behind the mask of madness, both Hamlet and Ophelia can speak freely.' To what extent is this true?

F10 At the graveside Hamlet declares, 'I lov'd Ophelia' (*5, 1, 265*). Considering the way he has behaved to her, do you believe him now?

F11 How would you describe the character of Gertrude? Do you detect any change in her as the truth of the situation is gradually revealed to her?

F12 Hamlet is sure that 'There's a divinity that shapes our ends' (5, 2, 9). What events in the play have given him this impression?

F13 Will Horatio's description of events ('so shall you hear . . . inventors' heads' 5, 2, 385–390) be a satisfactory account of what has happened in Denmark?

G Projects   In some schools, students are asked to do more 'free-ranging' work, which takes them outside the text—but which should always be relevant to the play. Such projects may demand skills other than reading and writing: design and artwork, for instance, may be involved. Sometimes a 'portfolio' of work is assembled over a considerable period of time; and this can be presented to the examiners as part of the student's work for assessment.

The availability of resources will, obviously, do much to determine the nature of the projects; but this is something that only the local teachers will understand. However, there is always help to be found in libraries, museums, and art galleries.

G1 'Hamlet through the ages': make a study of famous actors who have played the part of Hamlet.

G2 Prepare one scene of the play for performance, and produce a director's script with details of staging, lighting, costume and movement etc.

G3 Explore Shakespeare's sources.

G4 Shakespeare's Theatre.

G5 Actors on Tour.

G6 Revenge in Life and Art.

G7 *Hamlet* as inspiration.

Background

England 1602

When Shakespeare was writing *Hamlet*, most people believed that the sun went round the earth. They were taught that this was a divinely ordered scheme of things, and that—for England—God had instituted a Church and ordained a Monarchy for the right government of the land and the populace.

'The past is a foreign country; they do things differently there.'

L.P. Hartley

Government

For most of Shakespeare's life, the reigning monarch was Elizabeth I. With her counsellors and ministers she governed the nation (population five million) from London, although fewer than half a million people inhabited the capital city. In the rest of the country, law and order was maintained by the land-owners and enforced by their deputies. The average man had no vote — and his wife had no rights at all.

Religion

At this time, England was a Christian country. All children were baptized, soon after they were born, into the Church of England; they were taught the essentials of the Christian faith, and instructed in their duty to God and to humankind. Marriages were performed, and funerals conducted, only by the licensed clergy and in accordance with the Church's rites and ceremonies. Attendance at divine service was compulsory; absences (without good—medical—reason) could be punished by fines.

By such means, the authorities were able to keep some check on the populace—recording births, marriages, and deaths; being alert to any religious nonconformity, which could be politically dangerous; and ensuring a minimum of orthodox instruction through the official 'Homilies' which were regularly preached from the pulpits of all parish churches throughout the realm.

Following Henry VIII's break away from the Church of Rome, all people in England were able to hear the church services *in their own language*. The Book of Common Prayer was used in every church, and an English translation of the Bible was read aloud in public. The Christian religion had never been so well taught before.

Education

School education reinforced the Church's teaching. From the age of four, boys might attend the 'petty school' (French *petite école*) to learn the rudiments of reading and writing along with a few prayers; some schools also included work with numbers.

At the age of seven, the boy was ready for the grammar school (if his father was willing and able to pay the fees). A thorough grounding in Latin grammar was followed by translation work and the study of Roman authors, paying attention as much to style as to matter. The arts of fine writing were thus instilled from early youth.

A very few students proceeded to university; these were either clever scholarship boys, or else the sons of noblemen. Girls stayed at home, and acquired domestic and social skills—cooking, sewing, perhaps even music. The lucky ones might learn to read and write.

Language

At the start of the sixteenth century the English had a very poor opinion of their language: there was little serious writing in English, and hardly any literature. Latin was the language of international scholarship, and Englishmen admired the eloquence of the Romans. They made many translations, and in this way they extended the resources of their own language, increasing its vocabulary and stretching its grammatical structures. French, Italian, and Spanish works were also translated and, for the first time, there were English versions of the Bible.

By the end of the century, English was a language to be proud of: it was rich in synonyms, capable of infinite variety and subtlety, and ready for all kinds of word-play—especially the *puns*, for which Elizabethan English is renowned.

Drama

The great art-form of the Elizabethans was their drama. They inherited a tradition of play-acting from the Middle Ages, and this was reinforced in the sixteenth century by the reading and translating of the Roman playwrights. At the beginning of the century, plays were performed by groups of actors, all-male companies (boys acted the female roles) who travelled from town to town, setting up their stages in open places (such as inn-yards) or, with the permission of the owner, in the hall of a noble house.

The touring companies continued, in the provinces, into the seventeenth century; but in London, in 1576, a new building was erected for the performance of plays. This was the Theatre, the first purpose-built playhouse in England. Other playhouses followed (including Shakespeare's own theatre, the Globe); and the English drama reached new heights of eloquence.

There were those who disapproved, of course. The theatres, which brought large crowds together, could encourage the spread of disease—and dangerous ideas. During the summer, when the plague was at its worst, the playhouses were closed. A constant censorship was imposed, more or less severe at different times. The Puritan faction tried to close down the theatres, but—partly because there was royal favour for the drama, and partly because the buildings were outside the city limits—they did not succeed until 1642.

The Theatre

From contemporary comments and sketches—most particularly a drawing by a Dutch visitor, Johannes de Witt—it is possible to form some idea of the typical Elizabethan playhouse for which most of Shakespeare's plays were written.

Hexagonal in shape, it had three roofed galleries encircling an open courtyard. The plain, high stage projected into the yard, where it was surrounded by the standing 'groundlings'. At the back were two doors for the actors' entrances and exits; and above these doors was a balcony—useful for a musicians' gallery or for the acting of scenes 'above'.

Over the stage was a thatched roof, supported on two pillars, forming a canopy—which seems to have been painted with the sun and stars for the 'heavens'. Underneath was space (concealed by curtaining) which could be used by characters ascending and descending through a trap-door in the stage.

Costumes and properties were kept backstage, in the 'tiring house'. The actors dressed lavishly, often wearing secondhand clothes bestowed by rich patrons. Stage properties were important for defining a location, but the dramatist's own words were needed to explain the time of day, since all performances took place in the early afternoon.

Criticism

Shakespeare has been well served by critics of *Hamlet* and interpreters of the character of the Prince. This is a selection of their comments.

The play is 'almost one continued *Moral*; a series of deep Reflections, drawn from *one* Mouth'.

Earl of Shaftesbury, 1710

'Who can read the Speech with which young *Hamlet* accosts him [the Ghost] without trembling?'

Joseph Addison, 1711

'The pretended madness of *Hamlet* causes much mirth, the mournful distraction of *Ophelia* fills the heart with tenderness.'

Samuel Johnson, 1765

'We do not like to see our Author's plays acted, and least of all *Hamlet*. There is no play that suffers so much in being transferred to the stage.'

William Hazlitt, 1817

'A Maxim is a conclusion upon observation of matters of fact, and is merely retrospective: an Idea, or, if you like, a Principle, carries knowledge within itself, and is prospective. Polonius is a man of maxims. While he is descanting on matters of past experience, as in that excellent speech to Laertes before he sets out on his travels, he is admirable; but when he comes to advise or project, he is a mere dotard. You see, Hamlet, as the man of ideas, despises him.'

S.T. Coleridge, 1827

'*Hamlet* . . . is the most popular play in our language. It *amuses* thousands annually, and it stimulates the minds of millions . . . The lowest and most ignorant audiences delight in it. The source of the delight is twofold: First, its reach of thought on topics the most profound; for the dullest soul can *feel* a grandeur which it cannot *understand*, and will listen with hushed awe to the outpourings of a great meditative mind obstinately questioning fate; Secondly, its wondrous dramatic variety.'

G.H.Lewes, 1855

Selected Further Reading

Sources
Muir, Kenneth, *The Sources of Shakespeare's Plays*, (London, 1977).

Date and Text
Honigmann, E.A.J., 'The Date of *Hamlet*', *Shakespeare Survey* 9, (Cambridge, 1956).
Jenkins, Harold, Introduction to the Arden edition of *Hamlet*, (Methuen, 1982).
Walker, Alice, 'The Textual Problem of *Hamlet*: A Reconsideration' (*Review of English Studies*, 1951).

Criticism
a) *Books*
Alexander, Nigel, *Poison, Play, and Duel*, (London, 1971).
Alexander, Peter, *Hamlet, Father and Son*, (London, 1955).
Granville-Barker, Harley, *Preface to 'Hamlet'*, (London, 1937).
Knights, L.C., *An Approach to 'Hamlet'*, (London, 1960).
Prosser, Eleanor, *Hamlet and Revenge*, (Stanford, Calif., 1967).
Wilson, J. Dover, *What Happens in 'Hamlet'?*, (Cambridge, 1935).

b) *Essays*: Valuable essays on *Hamlet* are included in:
Barton, Anne, Introduction to the Penguin edition of *Hamlet*, (Penguin Books, 1980).
Bayley, John, *Shakespeare and Tragedy*, (Routledge, 1981).
Eliot, T.S., *Selected Essays*, (London, 1932).
Gardner, Helen, *The Business of Criticism*, (Oxford, 1959).
Honigmann, E.A.J., *Shakespeare: Seven Tragedies*, (London, 1976).
Knight, G. Wilson, *The Wheel of Fire*, (Methuen, 1930).

c) *Essay Collections*
Jump, J.D. (ed.), *'Hamlet': A Casebook*, (London, 1968).
Muir, Kenneth, and Wells, Stanley (eds), *Aspects of 'Hamlet'*, (Cambridge, 1979).
Parker, Patricia, and Hartman, Geoffrey (eds), *Shakespeare and the Question of Theory*, (Routledge, Chapman & Hall, 1985).
Patterson, Annabel (ed), *Shakespeare and the Popular Voice*, (Basil Blackwell, 1989).

d) *Background Reading*

Blake, N.F., *Shakespeare's Language: an Introduction*, (Methuen, 1983).

Muir, K., and Schoenbaum, S., *A New Companion to Shakespeare Studies*, (Cambridge, 1971).

Schoenbaum, S., *William Shakespeare: A Documentary Life*, (Oxford, 1975).

Thomson, Peter, *Shakespeare's Theatre*, (Routledge and Kegan Paul, 1983).

William Shakespeare, 1564–1616

Shakespeare lived a very *ordinary* life. He was born in a small Midlands market-town (Stratford-upon-Avon in Warwickshire), where his father was a glove-maker. He probably attended the local grammar school; and when he left school, he probably worked in his father's business, making and selling gloves. When he was eighteen he married a local girl, Anne Hathaway (who was already pregnant with Shakespeare's child). The baby—a daughter, Susanna—was born in 1583; and in 1585 Shakespeare became the father of twins, Judith and Hamnet.

Births, marriages, and deaths are the stuff of local records. But William left his family in Stratford, and went to make his fortune in London. He attached himself to a company of players under the patronage of the Lord Chamberlain, and followed their success: they later became the King's Men, and the leading London company. Shakespeare acted some small parts—and he took a large share in theatrical management. His financial activities extended beyond the limits of the playhouse and, in the course of time, Shakespeare became a gentleman—and a rich one too.

With a lot of money and his own coat-of-arms, Shakespeare retired from London and went back to Stratford, where he bought the finest house in the town and lived there until his death in 1616. He was buried in the church of the Holy Trinity, where he had been baptized in 1564.

Today pilgrims come to Stratford from all over the world to visit the grave in Holy Trinity Church; the birthplace in Henley Street; New Place, the house which Shakespeare bought in Chapel Street; and, above all, the Memorial Theatre on the banks of the river Avon. The man who lived such an *ordinary* life wrote the most *extraordinary* plays, creating a drama which is the glory of the English language.

Shakespeare lived in exciting, and dangerous, times. He was still a boy when the Pope declared that the Queen of England was a bastard and absolved all Roman Catholics from their allegiance to her. There were plots to overthrow the monarchy and conquer the kingdom: Elizabeth was assailed by the Spanish Armada in 1588, and her successor, James I, was threatened by the Gunpowder Plot in 1605. The first London theatre was built in Elizabeth's reign, and the Authorized Version of the Bible was published for King James. Moralists, as always, worried about the state of the world—and scientists argued about its position: was the earth the centre of the universe, as they had always been told, or was it only another of the sun's satellites?

All these things—and not these alone—had their influence on Shakespeare's writing. His earliest dramatic efforts took English history for their subject: very patriotic audiences enjoyed watching the great moments of their own past, and Shakespeare was an intensely patriotic writer (who also had a shrewd sense of business). He went on to write clever, romantic comedies, imitating (and excelling) the manner of his university-trained contemporaries.

Towards the end of the sixteenth century the mood darkened. It was a time of personal distress—one of Shakespeare's twins had died—and public anxiety. Earlier in her reign Elizabeth I had been honoured as the virgin Queen, but it later became a matter of concern that she would die and leave no heir to the throne. The theatre of this period favoured plays that were melancholic, bitter, and satiric. Shakespeare confronted social, especially sexual, problems in his plays; he raised awkward questions, and offered no easy answers. These 'Problem Plays' were followed by the great tragedies, and then the 'romances'—plays with a happiness which is lost, and a greater joy which is found.

A few of Shakespeare's plays had been published before the dramatist died, but most of them were not available to readers until 1623, when two fellow-actors published all thirty-six plays (*Pericles* was omitted) in a massive folio volume. Some poems were printed during the author's lifetime. There were two long narrative poems on classical themes, and some sonnets which seem to tell of two love-affairs, but without giving away any secrets. The details of Shakespeare's personal life are hidden from us. Matthew Arnold uttered the frustration of all biographers when he wrote, in a sonnet 'To Shakespeare': 'We ask and ask—Thou smilest, and art still.'

There is not even a trustworthy portrait of the world's greatest dramatist.

Approximate order of composition of Shakespeare's works

Period	Comedies	History plays	Tragedies	Poems
I	Comedy of Errors Taming of the Shrew	Henry VI, part 1 Henry VI, part 2	Titus Andronicus	
1594	Two Gentlemen of Verona Love's Labour's Lost	Henry VI, part 3 Richard III King John		Venus and Adonis Rape of Lucrece
II	Midsummer Night's Dream Merchant of Venice	Richard II Henry IV, part 1	Romeo and Juliet	Sonnets
1599	Merry Wives of Windsor Much Ado About Nothing As You Like It	Henry IV, part 2 Henry V		
III	Twelfth Night Troilus and Cressida		Julius Caesar Hamlet Othello	
1608	Measure for Measure All's Well That Ends Well		Timon of Athens King Lear Macbeth Antony and Cleopatra Coriolanus	
IV	Pericles Cymbeline			
1613	The Winter's Tale The Tempest	Henry VIII		

- Did they use Dry Ice?
- How did the make the fog for Scene 5 Act 1 back then?